THE MAD COURTESAN

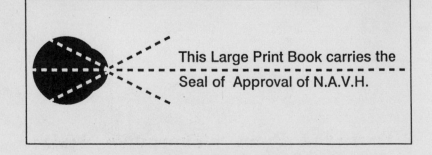

This Large Print Book carries the
Seal of Approval of N.A.V.H.

THE MAD COURTESAN

Edward Marston

Thorndike Press • Thorndike, Maine

Library of Congress Cataloging in Publication Data:

Marston, Edward.
  The mad courtesan / Edward Marston.
      p. cm.
    ISBN 1-56054-673-5 (alk. paper : lg. print)
    1. Large type books.   I. Title.
[PR6063.A695M3   1993]   92-46347
823'.914—dc20   CIP

Thorndike Large Print® General Series edition published
in 1993 by arrangement with St. Martin's Press Inc.

Cover design by Victor Cormier.

The tree indicium is a trademark of Thorndike Press.

This book is printed on acid-free, high opacity paper. ∞

To the Right Honourable and Truly Noble

BARBARA

Countess of Scottsdale

I here offer your Ladyship the ripest of my studies, which, though it carry vice in its title, seeks out your gracious shelter on account of its virtues. Accept these writings from a questing quill in the Old World and place them beside a poisoned pen in the New. And so, till some more worthy work flow from my hand, that may better express me, and more fit the gravity of your maturest inclination, I rest,

Yours at all parts most truly affected,

EDW. MARSTON

I am a profest Courtezane
That lives by people's Sinne.
With half-a-dozen Punckes I keepe
I have greate coming-in

Samuel Rowlands: *The Courtezan* (1590)

If, as their ends, their fruits were so the
    same,
Bawdry and usury were one kind of game.

Ben Jonson: *On Bawds and Usurers*

Chapter One

Nicholas Bracewell ducked in the nick of time and the rapier whistled above his head to describe a vicious semi-circle of thwarted rage. Backing away and drawing his own weapon, he had to repulse a violent attack as his adversary closed on him at once and scythed away with murder in his heart. Here was no occasion for the finer points of swordplay. It was a wild, undisciplined tavern brawl that called for strength of arm and speed of brain. Nicholas demonstrated both in equal measure as he parried further blows, flicked his wrist to expose his target then went down on one knee as he thrust his blade straight and true into his enemy's side. There was a howl of fury mingled with disbelief as the man staggered backwards, then, dropping his sword, clasping his fatal wound with both hands and emitting one last roar of anger, he fell to the ground in a writhing heap.

The applause was paltry but well-earned and Nicholas acknowledged it with a modest smile. Though he was only the book holder with Westfield's Men, he was an expert in the mounting of stage fights and he had proved that expertise once again. The watching actors and apprentices gave him due reward with their eager palms while Nicholas helped up the now grinning corpse of Sebastian Carrick and dusted him off with a few considerate smacks. The two men were standing on the makeshift stage in the yard of the Queen's Head in Gracechurch Street, the inn where the company performed most of its work and attested its claim to be considered the leading theatrical troupe in London. One of the main reasons for its pre-eminence was the crucial influence of Nicholas Bracewell behind the scenes. He was the sheet anchor to a vessel that sailed through an almost permanent tempest and he had saved untold mariners from a gruesome death below the mountainous waves.

Sebastian Carrick was the first to offer compliments.

'You excel yourself, Nick,' he said.

'It is easy when you have the trick of it.'

'But a devilish task to learn that trick. You can instruct us all in the art of fencing, seasoned though we be. I have never before encountered such a shrewd teacher as Master Nicholas Bracewell.'

'You are an apt pupil, Sebastian.'

'Aye,' said the actor with a grin. 'A grateful

one, too. I had rather be killed by you than by any man in London!'

General laughter broke out among the spectators. Sword fights were an integral part of theatre and they had to be choreographed with sufficient verve and realism to convince an audience that would press very close to the stage. The death of Sebastian Carrick had been so well-rehearsed that even those who had witnessed the sequence many times were momentarily fearful that they had indeed lost a friend and colleague. When Nicholas thrust home his blade, however, it simply passed between the side and the arm of his quarry but with a timing and accuracy born of years of experience.

Carrick gave the book holder a confiding nudge.

'I doubt that Owen will fight as fairly as you, Nick.'

'He is an able swordsman.'

'Able enough to cut me down for good and all.'

'You do him wrong, Sebastian.'

'Marry, that's *his* complaint.'

'Then must you settle your account with him.'

'I would be rid of this turbulent Welshman.'

'Soothe his turbulence.'

9

Owen Elias, the subject of their exchange, stood no more than a dozen yards away and glowered at his fellow-actor. He was a stocky man in his thirties with broad shoulders above a barrel chest. His face was striking rather than handsome with smouldering eyes that were ignited by some dark, Celtic passion. He had good reason to resent Sebastian Carrick. Not only had the latter borrowed money from him which he was refusing to repay, he had committed what was, in the Welshman's view, the cardinal sin. He was preferred as an actor. By virtue of his grace, charm and poise, Carrick was repeatedly cast in better roles than those offered to Elias and it rankled. Turbulence ensued.

It was time for the rehearsal to begin properly and Nicholas Bracewell took control with accustomed firmness. The stage was set for the first scene, the actors withdrew to the tiring-house, the musicians took up their positions in the gallery above. Westfield's Men steadied themselves for yet another performance of *Vincentio's Revenge,* one of the stock plays in their extensive repertoire, a brooding tragedy that was shot through with violence. Early in Act Three, the lascivious courtier, Lodovico — as played by Sebastian Carrick — would be killed in a tavern brawl by Owen Elias in a role that was not even dignified by a name. Lodovico might appear to die but it was The Stranger who suffered the more serious professional wound.

Even amid the happy turmoil of preparation, Nicholas spared a thought for the tribulations of Owen Elias. As an actor, the Welshman was incomparably better than Sebastian Carrick but the latter had physical attributes which made him more appealing and personal qualities that made him more acceptable. Tall, slim and dashing, he had the lazy confidence of a philanderer allied to an air of almost aristocratic refinement. Owen Elias was too ebullient and wilful. He was altogether too combative in urging his right to promotion within the company and he thus reviled the easy tact and plausibility which gained advantage for his rival. Nor could he forget or forgive the effortless skill with which Carrick had persuaded him to open his purse and part with money that he could ill afford to lose. *Vincentio's Revenge* was nothing beside the dire retribution that Owen Elias contemplated.

'Stand by!'

The command from Nicholas Bracewell stilled the murmur and put every man on the alert. On a signal from the book holder, Peter Digby and his musicians coaxed solemn sounds from their instruments as The Pro-

11

logue entered in a black cloak to introduce the play. For the next two hours, the company reacquainted themselves with *Vincentio's Revenge* and — even though their audience consisted of no more than some curious horses and some gaping ostlers — they gave the work their full concentration. No matter how many times they had performed a piece, they never took it for granted. A play was like a sword. It needed to be polished and sharpened each time before use. Audiences detested the sight of rust and the feel of a blunt edge. Westfield's Men always kept their weaponry in good order.

When the rehearsal was over, the actors drifted off into the inn itself to take refreshment before the paying public began to arrive. Nicholas had much to do before he could join them, supervising the stagekeepers as they struck the set for Act Five prior to sweeping the boards and strewing them with rushes, making sure that costumes and properties were in their appointed places, chiding the musicians for being noticeably late with their dirge in Act Four and attending to the ever-widening responsibilities of his job. Because it had been, for the most part, a good rehearsal, he went about his work with the quiet satisfaction of one who had made a substantial contribution to the successes of the morning. He was especially pleased with the tavern brawl. Owen Elias and Sebastian Carrick had never fought with such controlled venom. It had been a highlight of the drama.

Ensconced in the taproom, The Stranger was keen to re-enact the scene with his smiling Lodovico.

'Give me the money, you viper!'

'Would that I could, dear friend!' sighed Carrick.

'Friend, am I not: dear was I never!'

'I count you among my closest fellows.'

'Count out some coins instead, Sebastian.'

'You will be paid in good time.'

'I urge the reckoning now.'

'You do so in vain, Owen,' said the other with a shrug. 'Truly, I have no money, sir. I have borrowed afresh to buy myself food and drink.'

'To borrow and not repay is to steal.'

'Be patient but a little longer.'

'Give me my money, Sebastian.'

'As soon as I may.'

'Now!' yelled the fiery Welshman, grabbing him with both hands. 'Pay me forthwith or — by St David! — I'll tear you limb from limb and feed you to the innyard dogs.'

Sebastian Carrick tried to defuse the situation with an amiable laugh but it only enraged his attacker even more. Rising to his feet, Owen Elias hauled him up from his bench and flung him across the room with sudden power. Fury and envy surged up and conjoined in the Welshman's breast to send him hurtling after his honey-tongued colleague in order to belabour him unmercifully. Before he could even land the first punch, however, he was drenched from head to toe by a few gallons of cold, brackish water from one of the wooden fire buckets. Nicholas Bracewell had arrived in time to see the quarrel and to dampen it down before it got out of hand. Sebastian Carrick grinned with relief but Owen Elias only glowered as the whole taproom filled with derisive laughter. Chafed but chastened, he did not resist when the book holder hurried both him and his fellow out into the yard. Nicholas did not mince his words and his soft West Country vowels were hardened into a curt threat.

'Do you seek dismissal from the company, sirs?'

'Indeed not,' said Elias.

'Nothing would grieve us more,' said Carrick.

'Brawling will not be tolerated,' emphasized Nicholas with a warning finger. 'We are only here at the Queen's Head on sufferance and we must give our nagging landlord no more excuse to send us hence.

Save your argument for some private place or, better still, resolve it here and part as friends. Would you have Westfield's Men evicted over some petty difference between you?'

'It is not petty,' said Elias, still dripping wet. 'It is a very serious matter and I will be answered.'

Carrick smirked. 'That bucket was an eloquent reply.'

'You owe me six shillings, sir!'

'First, do but loan me a further five.'

'Scurvy rogue!'

'Peace, peace!' ordered Nicholas. 'Raised voices solve nothing. Let's hear this out calmly.' He turned to Carrick. 'Tell your tale first, Sebastian.'

'But *I* am the injured party!' wailed Elias.

'Your turn will come,' said Nicholas, quelling him with a glance. 'Your temper needs more time to cool.'

The Welshman knew better than to argue with the book holder. A big, broad-shouldered man with a muscular strength beneath his affable manner, Nicholas could assert himself if the need arose. His fair hair and full beard danced gently in the wind but his stern eyes kept Owen Elias subdued as the facts of the case were laid out. Sebastian Carrick made light of the whole business, promising that the debt would soon be paid and apologizing for any harm he had unwittingly inflicted on his fellow. Elias took several deep breaths before he trusted himself to words again but they came out in a remarkably measured and reasonable way. When both pleas had been voiced, the actors waited on Nicholas Bracewell to pronounce judgement.

'You are both in the wrong,' he said. 'Sebastian, you should have repaid this money long since. Owen, you should not have provoked a brawl to gain your purpose. Is that much agreed between us?' The actors nodded. 'Then let us find a way out of this dilemma. A creditor wants something that a debtor does not possess.'

'You have hit on the problem, Nick,' said Carrick with a nonchalant shrug. 'My purse is quite empty.'

'It is *always* empty!' challenged Elias.

'A man must live, sweet sir.'

'Live, yes, but not prey upon his fellows!'

'Pleasure comes at a price.'

'Then have it at your own expense and not mine.'

Nicholas interceded. 'Hear my device. It may suit the both of you in equal part. Sebastian has no money until I pay his wage at the end of the week. Master your pain

16

and indignation until then, Owen, and I will save one shilling of that wage for you.'

'It is not enough,' said Elias.

'It is far too much!' exclaimed Carrick.

But Nicholas stuck by his decision and — though neither man was pleased — both came to accept the compromise. Owen Elias realized that payment by instalments was better than nothing at all and he took comfort from the fact that it was Sebastian Carrick who had protested most. Evasion of his creditors was an article of faith with the latter. The only thing he ever willingly repaid was a debt of honour incurred at the gaming table. Money that was charmed from the purses of colleagues was his to keep. Friends were fair game.

He sighed. 'It is a grisly resolution, Nick, but I will abide by it. Here is my hand on it.' Owen Elias shook the proferred hand. 'Well, now that matter is done, I must away to borrow afresh or I will dwindle into complete poverty!'

Sebastian Carrick gave a mock bow then sauntered back into the taproom with an amused resignation. His attitude produced more sparks from Owen Elias.

'Look at him, Nick! Do but look at the saucy knave!'

'The dispute is settled, Owen. Be content.'

'He is a vile robber!'

'Your money will be restored.'

'It is my reputation that he is stealing,' protested the other. '*I* am the finer actor yet *he* filches the finer parts. *I* have laboured to establish myself with Westfield's Men yet this upstart displaces me within a few months. It is not just, it is not kind, it is not bearable.' He extended his arms wide in supplication. 'What am I to do, Nick?'

'Endure these slights with dignity.'

'Never!'

'Make friends with Sebastian. It is the only way.'

'I would sooner consort with a leper.'

'Do not come to blows with him again,' warned Nicholas.

'I dare not,' said Elias with lilting menace. 'For next time, nobody would be able to stop me. I would kill him.'

Cornelius Gant pointed the musket at the horse's head and callously pulled the trigger. There was a loud report and a cloud of smoke went up from the weapon. The animal staggered bravely for a few seconds then sank to the ground in a sorry heap and began to twitch violently as the last ounces of life poured out of its noble carcass. It was a grotesque and sickening sight. When its death throes were finally over and its frenzy mercifully abated, it lay cold and silent on the cobblestones, its black coat gilded by the sun and its body twisted into such an unnatural shape that it drew groans of horror from all who had witnessed the summary slaughter. A happy crowd became hostile in a flash. They cursed the cruel owner and formed a ring of gathering fury around him. Cornelius Gant was defiant. As they closed in, baying for retribution, he held the musket like a club and threatened to strike. The tension was heightened until it was on the verge of an explosion.

Then the horse neighed. As if waking from an afternoon sleep in a verdant meadow, it sat up, whinnied mischievously and gazed around its dumbstruck audience. Gant's ugly old face was split by a toothless grin as he saw the incredulity on every side. After entertaining the throng with all manner of clever tricks, horse and man had reached the climax of their act in the most dramatic way. Cornelius Gant had shot Nimbus dead and the animal had expired to such convincing effect that all present were completely taken in. Many were so relieved to see the horse alive again that they burst into tears. Relief gave way to joy and expressed itself in a riot of applause. Gant chose his moment well. He clicked his fingers and Nimbus got up from the ground to shake itself all over before knocking its owner playfully sideways with its rump. As fresh mirth greeted this latest trick, the horse rounded on Gant, took the brim of his hat in its teeth then lifted it off with another whinny. The hat was dropped into the middle of the yard and the crowd responded generously. A waterfall of coins gushed into the receptacle. Horse and owner took a bow in unison.

Cornelius Gant was a wiry man of middle height, shrunk by age and battered by experience. His apparel was that of a discharged soldier but his piggy eyes and distorted features suggested less honourable employment. Only when he grinned did he look even remotely personable. In gratitude for his handsome performance, however, the crowd ignored his defects of nature and showered him with congratulation. The whole inn buzzed with excited comment. Gant was glad that they had stopped at Coventry. Its welcoming hostelries had given him rich pickings for three days but it was now time to take his horse and its wondrous feats on the next stage of their journey to the capital. It was there in London, in the finest city in Europe, that true fame and fortune lay and nothing less would suffice his vaulting ambition.

Well-wishers sent them off with ringing cheers.

'Nimbus is the greatest horse alive!'

'And even greater when he is dead!'

'It is the most amazing sight that ever I saw.'

'No heart can resist them.'

'They will spread merriment wherever they go.'

'That animal is a gift from God.'

It was left to the waddling publican of the Shepherd and Shepherdess to sum up the feelings of his customers. Gant and Nimbus had not only astounded the onlookers, they had been good for business. Wiping podgy hands on his beer-stained apron, the publican beamed gratefully after the departing guests and gave a knowing chuckle.

'They will conquer London within a week!'

Lawrence Firethorn was in excellent spirits as he sat back in his chair and savoured the last of the Canary wine in his goblet. Flushed with success after another performance in the title role of *Vincentio's Revenge*, he was celebrating his triumph in a private room at the Queen's Head with Barnaby Gill and Edmund Hoode. All three of them were sharers with the company, ranked players who

21

were named in the royal patent for Westfield's Men and who were thus entitled to a portion of any income. Apprentices were given their keep and a valuable training, hired men — like Sebastian Carrick and Owen Elias — earned a weekly wage but it was the sharers who were the real beneficiaries. Not only did they get their slice of any profits, they also had first claim on the leading parts in any play. Their status was paramount. In the eyes of the law and the regulatory agencies, they *were* the company and other members of the troupe were merely their employees. Westfield's Men had ten sharers but its operational decisions were invariably taken by its three senior figures. Lawrence Firethorn dominated that trio.

'I was in good voice this afternoon,' he boasted.

'Too good a voice,' said Gill testily. 'You roared the lines like a wounded lion. Speak the speeches as they are written, Lawrence. Do not deafen your fellows with ranting.'

'The audience worshipped my Vincentio.'

'So might the rest of London for they must all have heard it. Why must you bellow so much? Even your silence is beset by too much noise.'

'Tragedy calls for sound!'

'Your sound was certainly tragic, sir.'

Firethorn bristled. 'At least I did not whisper my words like an old man muttering into his beard.'

'I conveyed meaning with every subtle gesture.'

'It is as well you did not rely on your voice, Barnaby. You sounded like a male varlet plying his foul trade in the stews of Southwark!'

'I'll brook no more of this!' exclaimed Gill, using a quivering fist to pound the table around which they sat. 'I demand an abject apology.'

'Demand what you wish. You will get nothing.'

'Gentlemen, gentlemen,' said Edmund Hoode wearily as he interrupted yet another of the all-to-frequent arguments between the two men. 'Both of you gave of your best in *Vincentio's Revenge*. I could not fault either performance. Each was soft enough, each was loud enough. Enough of this vain disputation. We have business in hand.'

Gill stood on his dignity. 'I have been insulted.'

'And so you will be again, sir,' said Firethorn. 'You invite ridicule. If you will hiss like a serpent on stage, we will find you a place in the menagerie at the Tower.'

'They will lock *you* in the neighbouring

cage for they surely have need of a trumpeting elephant!'

'Desist, sirs!' said Hoode, throwing himself between them once again to prevent the elephant from trampling on the serpent and to stop the serpent from wriggling its way up the elephant's trunk to spit its venom into the brain. 'This will not serve our cause at all.'

He poured more wine for both of them then gave them even more liberal doses of flattery. They slowly allowed themselves to be soothed and to forget their latest verbal duel. Lawrence Firethorn was the acknowledged leader of the company, a striking man in every way, hugely talented and hugely ambitious, blessed with genius but cursed with the vanity of his profession. Alert, handsome and muscular, he dressed like a gallant in the latest fashion. Barnaby Gill was shorter, older and less well-favoured. The established clown, he had an uncanny ability to reduce any audience to hysterical laughter with his comic songs, gestures, dances and facial expressions. Offstage, he was a lurking melancholic with a weakness for the society of pretty boys that had made the gibe about a male varlet particularly painful. He chose his apparel with great care but erred on the side of ostentation. Firethorn and Gill might wrestle incessantly in private but they worked in perfect harmony on stage.

One of Edmund Hoode's primary duties was to sustain that harmony by writing parts in which each man could display his undoubted brilliance. As an actor-playwright, he was required to produce a regular stream of new plays for Westfield's Men as well as to polish and adapt his earlier work for revival. Unlike the others, Hoode was not ensnared by pride or obsessed with the need to impress. Tall, slim and clean-shaven, he was a gentler soul, a dreamer and a romantic. His pale, round, wide-eyed moon of a face had been shaped to hang in the sky of unrequited love and he had no taste for the strident confrontations beloved by his companions.

Lawrence Firethorn addressed the issue before them.

'Gentlemen, we seek another sharer,' he said solemnly. 'Old Cuthbert is to retire and he must be replaced.'

'I do not agree,' said Gill.

'Wisdom never commended itself to you.'

'If we lose one of our number, we have a larger slice of the receipts. Old Cuthbert served the company well but he serves it better still by letting us divide up his share.'

'Put need before greed, Barnaby,' said Firethorn. 'Ten is a good, round number and we will hold fast to it. So, sirs. Who is to be brought into the fold?'

Hoode was unequivocal. 'If it were left to me, I would choose Nick Bracewell without a qualm. He is the rock on which Westfield's Men build their entertainments. Take but him away and we would all be sucked into the quagmire.'

'Master Bracewell is a mere book holder,' said Gill petulantly. 'We must not even consider bestowing such an honour upon him.'

'If worth held any sway, the honour is his already.'

'Indeed, Edmund,' said Firethorn. 'Nick is pure gold and nobody loves him more or values him higher than I. But he is not, alas, our new sharer. We must look elsewhere.'

'Outside the company?' said Gill.

'Inside,' said Hoode. 'It rewards loyalty.'

Firethorn nodded. 'We promote from within. It breeds goodwill and ensures us a known friend. I think there are but two men in the company whom we should weigh in the balance here. Sebastian Carrick and Owen Elias.'

'Then it must be Sebastian,' decided Hoode.

'The Welshman for me,' said Gill, puffing

at his pipe. 'He has been with us longer and learned more eagerly. Owen has a temper, I know, but this elevation might curtail it and turn him into a gentlemen.'

'Sebastian already *is* a gentleman,' said Hoode. 'He can grace the stage where Owen can only occupy it. I do not deny that Wales has given us the finer actor here. Owen Elias has qualities that Sebastian could never match. He has a voice and presence to rival Lawrence himself but he also has a wayward streak that goes ill with responsibility. As a hired man, he is an asset to the company: as a sharer, he might turn out to be a liability.'

'I side with you, Edmund,' said Firethorn. 'Sebastian has the better disposition. Sebastian Carrick it is.'

'Owen Elias,' insisted Gill.

'Carrick.'

'He gets my vote, too,' said Hoode. 'He is our sharer.'

'Then where will he find his proportion?' Gill puffed hard then exhaled a cloud of smoke. 'Sebastian has to *buy* his share. He is reckless with his own money and even more reckless with borrowed coin. Owen Elias is conscientious and frugal. Sebastian is too fond of his pleasures.'

'No man can be blamed for that,' said Firethorn easily, 'or none of us would escape whipping. But you raise a fair question, Barnaby, and it must be answered. How will Sebastian furnish us with his investment?'

'He has many rich friends,' said Hoode.

Gill grimaced. 'They are poorer for his acquaintance.'

'He will find the money somehow. He longs to be a true member of the company. Stay with him, Lawrence.'

'A doubt begins to form,' admitted Firethorn.

'We have the means to still it,' said Hoode. 'Let us not commit ourselves too soon. We will put Sebastian to the test by offering him a half-share in the company. Should he come through that trial, he takes up Old Cuthbert's place. Is this not the best way?'

Lawrence Firethorn stroked his dark, pointed beard as he pondered. Barnaby Gill tapped out his pipe on the edge of the table and sniffed noisily. After long consideration, both men nodded their agreement. Sebastian Carrick would be put on probation. It remained only to determine the length of that probation and the scale of his financial contribution.

Gill foresaw a possible difficulty.

'How can we persuade him that a half-share is a form of distinction rather than a humiliation?'

28

'I'll make light of that task,' said Firethorn airily.

'Sebastian will see it as one step towards full glory,' said Hoode. 'He will understand our caution.'

Gill snorted. 'It is more than caution in my case.'

'Throw aside all objection,' urged the playwright.

'Yes,' reinforced Firethorn. 'To win his confidence, we must show him ours. Have no fears about Sebastian Carrick. He will prove a fortunate choice. I'd stake my life on it.'

Turnmill Street was the most notorious thoroughfare in the whole of Clerkenwell, a long, dark, dangerous, disease-ridden strip of sin that ran parallel with the River Fleet before bending round to thrust itself into Cow Cross with bestial familiarity. In its fetid lanes and alleys, in its narrow courts and yards, in its filthy taverns and tenements, all manner of lewd delight was bought and sold. Turnmill punks were the wildest and most willing in London and they made nightly assignations with courtiers and commoners, soldiers and sailors, merchants and men of law, gapers from the country and gallants from the town. At the sign of the Cock, the Fleur de Lys, the Blue Axe, the Red Lattice, the Rose and other bold outrages against decency, a lustful client could send his soul to eternal damnation and purchase the pox in exchange. Turnmill Street was a warren of infamy. Stews and gambling dens, inns and ordinaries, courtesans and catamites knew but one landlord. He dwelt in Hell itself.

Of all the houses of resort, none was more popular than the Pickt-hatch, so-called because its upper half-door was surrounded with spikes for security. The pickt-hatch was a common name and sign for brothels but the establishment in Turnmill Street outstretched its rivals in venery. It was run by a wobbling mound of flesh named Bess Bidgood and its reputation brought in ample custom for the large stable of whores whom the motherly hostess kept beneath her wicked roof. Quality and quantity were on tap at the Pickt-hatch.

The young man who lay naked on the bed in a state of joyous near-exhaustion had opted for quality and he had not been disappointed. When Bess Bidgood had lined up her ladies for him to choose at his own discretion, his practised eye had picked out the leanest of them. Frances was not the plump and eager wench in red taffeta that most men coveted but a thin, watchful, feline creature with a carnal charm that was all her own. He wanted an angry lover and none could have been more feral than this wildcat. She bit and fought him every inch of the way and left her own special trademark on his back as she raked it from shoulder to buttock with searing fingernails, pain and pleasure intermingling so closely that they became one. He was in ecstasy.

Frances was content. Here was no sweating husband who talked of his wife, no crude swaggerer who pumped mindlessly into her, no drunken fool whose manhood failed them both and who snored on top of her. She had found a real lover for once, a handsome swain who sensed her needs and matched them with his own. As she ran a hand down the vivid red furrows on his back, she admired the sleek muscularity of his body and relished the feel of his soft beard between her breasts. In a squalid room whose dank walls were covered in painted cloth, they shared a mild sensation of love. It was soon over, however. He rose and dressed while she waited for payment, combing her long black hair with languid movements and resigning herself to more brutish passion from her next client.

His smile was warm and grateful. Dropping some crowns into the goblet on the floor, he slipped an arm around her to give her one last, long kiss then he opened the door and went swiftly out. Frances reached instinctively for the goblet and found it empty. His farewell embrace had been a cruel trick to recover his money and she was left with nothing but a sour memory. Grabbing the knife beneath her pillow, she raced out into the murky passageway but he was already vanishing down the steps. She went quickly back to her bedroom window and flung it open, waiting until her deceitful lover came out into the street before giving a signal with the knife. She then turned back into the room and flung the weapon with such force at the door that it sunk two inches into the wood and vibrated almost as angrily as she did.

The young man, meanwhile, ambled happily along and told himself that the gift of his body was reward enough for any woman and that — by rights — Frances should have paid him. He laughed aloud as he imagined her horror at finding the goblet raided by his sly hand and congratulated himself on getting so much out of the Pickt-hatch for so little. It had been a most pleasant night.

'Stay, sir!' called a voice behind him.

'Why so?'

He turned to ask the last question of his life and got the answer in the shape of a hand-axe that came out of the darkness with vengeful power to cleave his head open and put an extra inch between his staring eyes. Blood drenched him in an instant and the open mouth filled with gore. Before he hit the ground and lay in the offal, he was dead.

Sebastian Carrick had paid for his pleasure after all.

Chapter Two

Theatre companies were like families, haphazard groups of people who were bonded temporarily together by a shared home and a common objective. Filial affection was spontaneous and intimacies flourished. Loyalty was deep. Idiosyncrasies were tolerated in the capacious bosom of the family. Blood was thicker than water. If actors fell idle, they were friendless vagabonds cast out into the wilderness: hired again, they got instant access to the comforts of hearth and home. The lonely exile became the prodigal son.

Nicholas Bracewell did much to foster the spirit of kinship among Westfield's Men so that each time it changed its face, the smile remained the same. Continuity of style and purpose was essential. Nobody was more attuned to the different moods and personalities of the company members and he helped to blend them into a single clan. While Lawrence Firethorn was the stern father of the family — and Barnaby Gill the clucking mother-hen — Nicholas brought an avuncular concern to his role and cared profoundly for all his nephews. It did not take him long to learn their habits.

'Good morning, Master Bracewell.'

'Good morning, Thomas.'

'What do we play today?'

'*Marriage and Mischief.*'

'Bushes and benches.'

'As you say, Thomas. Bushes and benches.'

It was early morning and Nicholas had, as usual, arrived first at the Queen's Head. He knew the precise order in which his colleagues would make their appearance. Leading the procession was Thomas Skillen, the ancient stagekeeper, a man whose forty years in the theatre enabled him to reduce all plays to one telling phrase. *Marriage and Mischief* was a lively comedy of misunderstanding which made great use of eavesdropping in a garden. It was a glorious romp with colourful characters and a complicated plot but the old man had summed it up perfectly. Something to hide behind and something to sit on. Bushes and benches.

A youth raced up to them. 'Good morning, masters.'

'You are late, George,' grumbled the stagekeeper.

'You are in good time, lad,' said Nicholas warmly. 'Now stand still and catch your breath.'

'I have been running.'

'Rise earlier and walk to your employment,' said Skillen. 'You are sweating like a pig on a spit.'

George Dart was the smallest, youngest and most-abused member of the company. He was a convenient whipping-boy and not even the friendship of the book holder could protect him from the lash. As an assistant stagekeeper, he was always given the most menial chores and he had already resigned himself to a day of moving the prickliest bushes and the heaviest benches on and off-stage. Thomas Skillen might be gnarled with age but he could still clip an ear of his underlings with effect. *Marriage and Mischief* would bring the customary round of prods and pushes for George Dart who would find an odd kind of reassurance in them. They proved that he was accepted by the company. Pain was home.

Nathan Curtis was the next to stride into the yard at the Queen's Head. As the company's master carpenter, he was always in demand, making new properties and scenery or restoring old ones. Hard on his heels came Peter Digby, the leader of the musicians, a thin, ascetic man of nervous disposition, who liked to be there well before he was needed. When the first of the actors

36

joined them, Nicholas did not even need to turn around to see who it was. As soon as he heard the approach of footsteps behind him, he believed that he could identify the newcomer.

'Good morrow, Sebastian.'

'You insult me,' said a Welsh voice.

Nicholas swung round in surprise. 'Owen!'

'Even he.'

'I had expected . . .'

'For once, I am first in line.'

The book holder gave him a proper welcome and talked about Owen Elias's role in the forthcoming drama, showing a genuine interest in his colleague's performance and making some useful suggestions. As they conversed, however, he kept one eye on the main entrance to the yard as he awaited the imminent arrival of Sebastian Carrick. The latter might have the inclinations of a dissolute but he was also a committed professional who put his acting before anything else. Even after a long night of indulgence, he would be the first of the hired actors to report to the Queen's Head, indeed, it was this unquenchable enthusiasm for his work — carefully hidden beneath an easygoing disdain — which made him a potential sharer with Westfield's Men. Lateness was almost unknown to Carrick so his continued absence was worrying.

Nicholas kept watch but there was no sign of him. Hugh Wegges, the tireman, was the next to show up, followed by the skipping eagerness of Richard Honeydew, the youngest and most talented of the boy apprentices. New faces came in twos and threes until the majority of the company was assembled in the yard but Sebastian Carrick still refused to come. As the stragglers drifted in, Nicholas's anxiety was fringed with alarm. Only the most serious mishap could detain the actor from a rehearsal, especially one of a play in which he had an important supporting role.

Lawrence Firethorn, predictably, was the last to turn up so that he could make a dramatic entry on his horse. As he rode into a yard that was now humming with activity, he surveyed his fellows with a lordly air then raised his hat in acknowledgement of the greetings he attracted. When an ostler came to take his horse, the actor-manager dismounted and summoned his book holder.

'Nick, dear heart! A word, sir.'

'As many as you wish,' said the other.

'Let's stand aside.' Firethorn whisked him into a quiet corner. 'We had private conference yesterday to settle on the choice of a new sharer. Sebastian Carrick was preferred to Owen Elias. Does that win your good opinion?'

'Not entirely,' said Nicholas. 'Both men are worthy, in their several ways, but Owen Elias has the greater ability and range of experience.'

'Other reasons spoke against him.'

'Sebastian has defects, too.'

'We have decided to overlook them and offer advancement to him. I want you to impart the glad tidings.'

'He is not here to receive them.'

'Not here? Our early bird still abed for once?'

'I hope that is the case.'

'What else?' said Firethorn. 'He will be here anon. I will warm his ears for being laggard then you can soothe them with this timely news.' He saw the disquiet on the other's brow and clapped him familiarly on the shoulder. 'Do not fret, Nick. No harm has befallen him. Sebastian can walk the darkest streets of the city with safety. Be assured of it. He will not fall among thieves.'

When the rider appeared on the horizon, the two men could not believe their luck. Travel through open country was always a hazardous business. Rogues, vagabonds, outlaws, robbers, beggars and masterless men were a constant threat to the unwary and the unguarded. Occasional bands of gypsies posed a further threat to the solitary traveller. Most people sought company when they moved between towns and long journeys were rarely undertaken without adequate convoy. Yet here was a man completely on his own, well-dressed, as far as they could judge at that distance, and mounted on a sturdy black stallion that moved along the rough track at a steady canter. The closer the rider came, the more convinced were the two men that Fortune was indeed favouring them. Sitting astride their own horses, they lurked in the shelter of a copse as their prey descended the hill towards them with an obliging readiness. A glance between them sealed his fate and they drew their swords for the ambush.

But the attack was not even necessary. When the man was no more than forty yards away, he suddenly reined in his mount beside some gorse bushes and slipped from the saddle. Fiddling with his breeches, he went behind the bushes with the obvious purpose of relieving himself and his spectators grinned. They would not even need their weapons for this work. The horse was their target, as fine an animal as they had seen in a long time with good conformation, a sleek coat and a touch of real breeding that made their own flea-bitten nags look like the tired jades they were. Black all over, it had a white blaze that ran from ear to nostril like a flash of lightning exploding from a mass of black cloud. Horse and saddle were rich enough bounty in themselves but the pouches that were slung across its loins — embroidered leather that bulged with promise — could bring greater reward yet. During those two fateful minutes behind a gorse bush, the rider would be relieved of more than his discomfort.

The highwaymen did not delay any longer. Spurring their horses into action, they closed on the stallion and one of them gathered up its reins as they passed. As three sets of hooves clacked on the hard surface of the track, a yell of utter horror went up from behind the bushes. The robbers laughed aloud at what they took to be the bare-arsed abuse that pursued them until they were out of earshot but the hapless wayfarer was now letting his own mirth show. With breeches now up again, he sat in the shade of an elm and pulled out an apple from inside his doublet. He took a first bite and chewed away happily in the confident knowledge that he would not have long to wait.

When they had put a mile or more between themselves and their victim, the two men paused in a clearing in the wood to assess their takings. The stolen horse was even more of a prize than they had imagined and its saddle was a work of art. They dismounted at speed and ran to clutch at the leather pouches but it was a mistake that they would rue for a long while because the stallion reared up on its hind legs and kicked out savagely. Taken completely by surprise, they fell to the ground in mortal terror. Instead of trampling them while it could, however, the animal emitted a high neigh that produced an answering call from the other horses. Before the men could do anything to stop them, all three went galloping off in the direction from which they had come.

Cornelius Gant had almost finished his apple by the time that Nimbus brought its two companions up to him. The old man gave him a slap of thanks then fed him the core as a further sign of congratulation. It was the work of minutes to search the other two horses for booty. Small sacks that hung from pommels yielded up food, money and other stolen items. When he had transferred the provender to Nimbus, he gave each of the other beasts a slap on the rump that sent it careering wildly off into the undergrowth. Cornelius Gant and Nimbus continued briskly on their way towards Banbury.

It was proving to be an eventful journey.

Marriage and Mischief was a perennial favourite which brought a large and vocal
audience to the yard of the Queen's Head
and they were not disappointed by the latest
rendering of the piece. The comedy was
driven along at a cracking pace with a control
that never faltered. As the spectators howled
with glee or shook with mirth, they never
suspected for a moment that the real drama
had occurred backstage and jeopardized their
entertainment completely. Sebastian Carrick's
failure to appear had forced eleventh hour
changes on the company which had sapped
its morale and sent it out on the stage with
some trepidation, but it found itself both
equal to the emergency and able to disguise
it from the onlookers. Owen Elias was given
instant promotion and he seized his opportunity with a relish, playing his rival's part
as if he had been rehearsing it all his life.
He fumed and foamed as a jealous husband
who wrongly suspects his wife of infidelity,
giving a performance that was at once more
comic and incisive than that of the actor he
had replaced. Elias's freewheeling confidence
was a tonic to his fellows and they responded
accordingly. As Lawrence Firethorn led his
troupe out to acknowledge the ovation at

the end of the play, he knew that they had given as good an account of *Marriage and Mischief* as they had ever done.

Standing in his accustomed place, Nicholas Bracewell gave his full concentration to the task of prompting, giving cues, issuing advice and generally controlling the swirling chaos behind the scenes. He was able to relax slightly now and to address the problem of Sebastian Carrick's absence. It was as distressing as it was untypical. An actor who prided himself on his work and his punctuality had committed the unforgivable sin of leaving the company in the lurch. He had not even sent a word of warning that he was indisposed. Was he ill? Had he been deliberately led astray? Could he *still* be sleeping off a night of debauchery? Nicholas had grave doubts on all three accounts. A more grim explanation suggested itself and the book holder felt a sharp pang of apprehension.

It was not eased when he looked across at Owen Elias who was now bowing low and drinking in the applause as if he had played the leading part. When asked to step into the breach at such short notice, the Welshman showed neither surprise nor alarm but simply grabbed the book to study the new part. While the actor conned his lines, Hugh Wegges helped him into his costume and used a deft needle to make the adjustments that were necessary. Owen Elias was supremely relaxed. It was almost as if he *knew* that he would be required to cover for an erring colleague and he did so with impressive skill. Much as he liked his friend, Nicholas was bound to wonder if he was in some way connected with the convenient disappearance of Sebastian Carrick.

As the applause began to fade, Lawrence Firethorn took one last flamboyant bow before bringing the cast back into the tiring-house. Beaming actor became outraged employer.

'Where the devil *is* he, Nick?' snarled Firethorn.

'I wish I knew,' said Nicholas.

'He will be dismissed from the company!'

'Do not be too hasty, master. Sebastian may not at fault here. Something must have prevented him. He is too loyal an actor to betray us deliberately.'

'We faced disaster on that stage!'

'Yet you created a triumph.'

Firethorn preened himself. 'I thrive on adversity.'

'Owen Elias was our hero this afternoon,' said Barnaby Gill, seeing the chance to needle the actor-manager. 'I hope you will now see how foolish it would be to elect Sebastian

Carrick as our new sharer. His conduct is unforgivable. The Welshman is made of truer steel. His performance today had something of your genius, Lawrence.'

'It sufficed,' said Firethorn.

'It saved us, man.'

Barnaby Gill praised every aspect of a portrayal which he knew could pose a distant threat to the actor-manager. Firethorn's main objection to Owen Elias was the latter's weird similarity to him in appearance and technique. Elias might never have the towering capacities of his employer but he could handle a speech with something of the same attack and make a profound impact when given the chance. Lawrence Firethorn was less threatened when the Welshman was kept languishing down among the small parts. Gill — whose lustre and position were not touched by Elias — could acclaim him freely and cause maximum discomfort to his colleague.

'Where is your precious Sebastian?' he teased.

'Would that I knew, sir!'

Gill gave a brittle laugh. 'This is the man you staked your life upon, Lawrence. Prepare yourself for death.'

He laughed again and sauntered off. Firethorn wheeled round to confront Nicholas and bark an order at him.

'Find Sebastian!'

'I will go as soon as I am finished here.'

'Find him at once!'

'It may not be an easy task.'

'Find him and bring him to me.'

'I fear for his safety.'

'You have good cause, sir,' said Firethorn with feeling. 'When I see the villain, I'll break his traitorous head open for him!'

Thick bandages had been wrapped around the skull to restore some semblance of normality but they were quite inadequate. Instead of binding the wound up, they simply made it look even more grotesque with its blood-soaked dressing and its awesome finality. The body was naked on its slab beneath a dirty white shroud. Sightless eyes stared upward and the mouth was still wide open. Caked blood disfigured the sad face below the red bandaging. Other corpses lay at peace all around, accepting their fate and awaiting burial in a spirit of Christian resignation. But Sebastian Carrick was still troubled. During his last, cruel, fleeting moment on earth, he had asked a question that pursued him into the mortuary and continued to exercise his vacant mind. In the cold silence of death, his hideous visage was a bellowing enquiry.

Who *did* it?

Giles Randolph was not as yet the most outstanding actor in London but he intended to win that accolade at all costs. As the resident star of Banbury's Men, he chose his parts with the utmost care and played them with great panache. Large audiences flocked to see him and his company was feted but Randolph was not satisfied. Amid the loudest cheers, he could still hear whispers of doubt about his art. He had yet to prove and sustain his superiority over Lawrence Firethorn, a man for whom he reserved a grudging respect that was all but smothered beneath an implacable hatred. Since Banbury's Men had found a permanent home at The Curtain — one of the few custom-built theatres in London — they held the whiphand over their rivals at the Queen's Head but they could not always make that advantage tell. Whenever the ambitious Giles Randolph created a new role with which to dazzle his public, Lawrence Firethorn somehow found a means to outshine him once more. That state of affairs could not be allowed to continue. The company's illustrious patron was disturbed.

'The rogue does have a modicum of talent,' said the earl with casual disgust. 'But not enough to account for their success.

Wherein lies their secret?'

'Outrageous good fortune, my lord.'

'There is more behind it than that.'

'Edmund Hoode is a tolerable playwright.'

'His work holds the stage better than our dramas.'

'Barnaby Gill can always scrape a few laughs.'

'He is as popular a clown as any in London,' said the earl contemptuously. 'But these explanations still fall short of the full truth. Firethorn, Hoode and Gill are not in themselves sufficient cause for the damnable fame of Lord Westfield's damnable company.'

They were in a private room at the Bull and Butcher, the sprawling inn that stood near The Curtain in Shoreditch. It was early evening and they had repaired to the hostelry after yet another stirring performance by Banbury's Men at their theatre. Giles Randolph was a tall, thin, stately man with an Italianate cast of feature that gave him a faintly sinister air. His voice was a superb instrument for poetry but he was too aware of this fact. Even in conversation he tended to pose and project. In the company of his patron, he knew how to fawn and flatter. The Earl of Banbury was a lascivious old man with a goatee beard that he continually scratched with ring-laden fingers. Though he had a sincere and long-standing interest in the promotion of the arts, he wanted more than his due reward of gratitude. His theatre company was there to advance his own interests and to help him eclipse the rising sun of Westfield's Men.

A venal, corseted dandy untouched by finer feeling, the Earl of Banbury detested Lord Westfield as much as Giles Randolph detested Lawrence Firethorn. With the two contending patrons, however, there was a political dimension. In a court that was rife with intrigue and aspiration, the two men wore their companies around their necks like chains of office. What happened on a stage at the Curtain or the Queen's Head thus had a bearing on an aristocratic duel which had been fought out for many years now.

The earl drained his silver goblet of wine.

'Banbury's Men must take first place forthwith.'

'They shall, my lord,' said Randolph deferentially. 'We will blaze across the heavens like a comet.'

'I would have you wipe the name of Westfield from the sky. It offends my sight.'

'Plans have been already set in motion.'

'Show no mercy to the wretches.'

Giles Randolph sat back and gave a thin smile.

'They will be wounded where they hurt most.'

By the time he inspected the corpse, the caked blood had been washed off the face but it was still impossible to recognize the man. The axe which split open his skull had rearranged his features into a gruesome mockery of their former good looks. Nicholas Bracewell identified his friend more by instinct than by any facial characteristics. The apparel and effects of the deceased served to confirm beyond reasonable doubt that it was indeed Sebastian Carrick. A proud actor had made an ignoble exit but there was faint consolation for Nicholas in his grief. Carrick's death had been instantaneous. The crude butchery of his murder left no room for prolonged pain or suffering. Final agonies had been spared.

As Nicholas gazed down at the slaughtered figure on its cold stone slab, his grief soon gave way to a surge of anger. A dear colleague had been cruelly cut down in his prime. On the verge of promotion from the ranks of hired men, Sebastian Carrick had been separated for ever from the world of theatre that he loved and adorned. The sense of waste and injustice made Nicholas seethe with indignation. He turned away from the body, fighting hard to contain his impotent rage and direct it to more useful purpose. Westfield's Men forged a brotherly concord between the two friends. Nicholas wanted vengeance on behalf of the whole family.

The keeper of the mortuary was a wraithlike individual with a voice like rustling leaves. He nudged his visitor.

'There was good sport in his last hour,' he said.

'What say you?'

'Look, sir.' The keeper pulled the body over on to its side to reveal the red channels down its back. 'Behold the work of a woman! That's the sign of a leaping house.'

He let out a harsh cackle. Nicholas studied the long parallel scratches on the white flesh, then gently lay the body on its back before covering it with the shroud. Though the mortuary was perfumed with herbs, the prevailing stink of death could still attack the nostrils and throat. When Nicholas began to cough and retch, he knew it was time to leave. He offered up a silent prayer, then went swiftly after the salvation of fresh air. A grim duty had become an excruciating ordeal.

His worst fears were now realized. The mortuary had been his first port of call. Convinced that only death could make Sebastian Carrick miss an entrance onstage, he went to review the latest crop of cadavers to be harvested from the dark suburbs. The actor was amongst them, his face tormented by the manner of his death and his eyes still glassy with appalled surprise. Others had met violent ends that night but none could match him for stark horror.

Nicholas hurried immediately to the coroner to make formal identification of the deceased but he was embarrassed to find that that was virtually all the information he could supply. The coroner pressed him for details that he simply did not have. Beyond the man's name and employment, Nicholas knew almost nothing of Sebastian Carrick, taking him on trust in a profession where talent was the only real currency and where the life of the company was all. Actors talked mainly about acting. Carrick seemed to spend most of his spare time drinking, gambling, wenching and borrowing money to support these interests.

'What of his family?' said the coroner.

'He never spoke of it,' replied Nicholas.

'Was the deceased born and raised in London?'

'No mention was made.'

'Can you tell me *nothing* of his circumstances?'

'I fear not, sir.'

'But he was your fellow.'

'And fondly remembered.'

'Master Bracewell,' said the coroner, a plump old man with heavy jowls and drooping eyelids, 'you have harboured a stranger in your midst. Can you call a man a friend when he is so secretive about his condition?'

'Doubtless he had good reason.'

'We shall never divine its nature. My verdict is a stale one. Murder by person or persons unknown.'

'Who found the body?' asked Nicholas.

'Two officers of the Watch. Josiah Taplow and William Merryweather. Sound fellows both who know their duty.'

'Where may I find them?'

'About their business even now, sir.'

Nicholas thanked him and took his leave. Deeply shocked by the murder and its implications for the company, he was also disturbed by his ignorance of the dead man's private life. There might be a family somewhere with a right to know of his demise. There might be dependants for whom the tragic turn of events would be a catastrophe. The sooner Nicholas identified and contacted these people, the more considerate it would be. Instead of touring Clerkenwell in search of the two watchmen, therefore, he hastened across to the Shoreditch lodging of Sebastian Carrick. It was a small, sagging, ugly dwelling in a narrow lane but the landlady was a tidy housewife. She heard his tale with motherly concern, and then she ushered him upstairs to a cramped but exceptionally clean room whose oak beams and floorboards gave off a cosy sheen. Carrick's possessions extended largely to items of clothing and to a few tattered playbills advertising past performances by Westfield's Men. As he perused everything with care, Nicholas questioned the landlady about her lodger but she could furnish little beyond the confidence that he had been a charming guest whom she would miss greatly. When she began to sob, her visitor was glad that he had suppressed the grisly details of the murder. In the short time he had been there, the actor had clearly gained the affections of his stout hostess.

'Is this all you can tell me?' said Nicholas.

'Except that he was tardy with his rent,' she said with mock scolding. 'But he always gave such a pretty excuse that I did not truly mind.'

'Did he have many callers?'

'None, sir, to my knowledge.'

'Can you name his tailor? His barber? His friends?'

'We saw but little of him.' A memory

surfaced. 'His chest may give some answers, sir. I forgot his chest.'

Nicholas rallied. 'Where did he keep it?'

'Even here, sir. I will find it this instant.'

She flung herself on to her knees and groped beneath the bed to pull out an empty chamber pot. Behind it she found a small wooden chest with iron bands around it. When she handed it to Nicholas, he saw there was a key in the lock and rightly gauged that it contained nothing of value. He opened the lid and examined the contents, his hopes all but shattered when he discovered only trinkets and unpaid bills. Then his interest quickened again. At the bottom of the chest was a letter that had been delivered only days before and it provided invaluable clues about its recipient. It was a missive from his father, one Andrew Carrick, whose elegant hand and stylish turn of phrase proclaimed a gentleman.

The father patently disapproved of his son's choice of profession but he nevertheless made solicitous inquiries about the latter's progress. But it was the buoyant tone of the letter which astonished Nicholas. Given the situation, the father was entitled to complaint if not to self-pity yet there was no hint of it. Optimism somehow shone through. It was quite remarkable, for Andrew Carrick was not writing from the comfort and freedom of his own home in Suffolk.

He was imprisoned in the Tower of London.

Chapter Three

Lawrence Firethorn rode slowly home to Shoreditch in an uncharacteristically jaded mood. Performances in front of an adoring public usually increased his normal ebullience and turned him into a gushing fountain of affability and good will. He would then conduct a post mortem on the play with Barnaby Gill and Edmund Hoode, striving always to improve and refine each offering so that it would be even better the next time around. Firethorn also took care to seek the opinion of Nicholas Bracewell which was invariably sound, objective, honest and completely free from the tiresome prejudices of the fellow-sharers. Business done, the actor-manager could turn to pleasure. Applause still rang in his ears to keep him happy and exhilarated. Firethorn would therefore take the edge off his excitement by dining in style with friends or pursuing his latest dalliance with a female admirer. Life was seductively rich and bountiful.

Tonight, however, it seemed poor and niggardly. As he let his horse trot homeward, Firethorn heaved a sigh of deep desolation.

Marriage and Mischief had been as well-received as ever but its leading man had not been allowed to enjoy the occasion. Shaken by the apparent desertion of Sebastian Carrick, he was in two minds about the latter's untried deputy, hoping that Owen Elias would somehow come through unscathed and yet fearing that the Welshman might steal some of his personal thunder. The post mortem had been deadly. In place of the customary praise and self-congratulation, he had to endure the bitter mockery of Barnaby Gill who kept asking Firethorn why he had nominated as their new sharer a man who had committed the ultimate sin against the company. Edmund Hoode rubbed salt into professional wounds by suggesting that Owen Elias should retain his new role in the play and that it should be enlarged to give his talents more scope.

There was no evening feast to soften the impact of all these blows, no indulgence from Lord Westfield himself, no fair lady waiting for him at an appointed place. Firethorn was despondent. When he reached home, there would be the torments of a scolding wife to greet him. He had to steel himself before crossing his own hearth.

'Welcome home, my prince!'

'Margery . . .'

'Your honour was but lately on my tongue.'

'I am pleased to hear it.'

'Then come from tongue to lips.'

The kiss was as enjoyable as it was unexpected. Margery Firethorn enfolded her husband in her arms, plucked him to her capacious bosom and bussed away a day's absence. His spirits were rekindled at once.

'What means this salutation?' he said when he had enough breath back to get the question out. 'What does it betoken, my angel?'

'Is your memory so short, sir?'

'Jog it a little, Margery.'

'Cambridge.'

'A pretty town. I played Pompey the Great there once.'

'Does it hold no other meaning for you?'

'Why, yes,' he said with a roguish smile that was suppressed instantly as wifely suspicion stirred. Firethorn continued quickly. 'Cambridge is dear to me because of your dear sister. Mistress Agnes Jarrold. The very copy of your portrait, yet neither so comely nor so enchanting.'

'I travel to Cambridge in the morning.'

'Your husband had not forget,' he lied. 'Why else would I have returned so early to your warm greeting?'

'Come on in and take your ease, sir,' she said as she conducted him to a chair. 'I have wine ready for you and supper stays in the kitchen. Tell me your news before I stop your mouth with more kisses. How did Westfield's Men fare?'

'Do not ask, sweet wife. Do not ask.'

'Why so?'

Margery Firethorn was the only woman who could have survived domestic life with the wayward genius she had married. Handsome, well-proportioned and outspoken, she had a bellicose charm which could still ensnare him. A proud housewife and a caring mother, she was also — even after all these years — his true love and that fact impressed itself upon him now. Instead of bustling about the place in her usual working attire, Margery was wearing her best dress and her most appealing expression. Whenever they were to part for a while, the couple always took a fond farewell of each other the night before. Firethorn was the more regular traveller but it was his wife's turn to ride off now. Her younger sister, Agnes, married to a Cambridge bookseller, was due to have a baby in the near future. Since she had lost her two previous children within hours of their birth, she had requested Margery's help and support during the third ordeal. It was an entreaty that could not be denied.

Firethorn was keen for his wife to stand

by the bedside of his sister-in-law and quick to appreciate the advantages to himself. The most immediate ones now became clear. He was given a cordial welcome, a cheering stoup of wine, a delicious supper and a sympathetic ear. As soon as he retailed the miseries of his day, they were soothed by her attentive concern and lost all power to hurt him. Relieved of his worries, he was taken upstairs to his bedchamber and reminded just how voluptuous Margery could be when not encumbered by children or chores. It was like their marriage night all over again. Pounding the mattress with their shared ecstasy, they endorsed their union in the most strenuous way and were quite unaware of the vicarious pleasure they gave to the servants and apprentices who were listening through the floor of the room above. Theirs was a love that truly enclosed the whole household.

As they lay panting in each other's arms, Margery spoke fondly of their marriage and its undying bliss. Firethorn was doubly delighted, savouring the wonder of what he had just experienced while looking forward to blessings of like nature in other bedchambers. His wife was going to Cambridge for a couple of weeks. He would be free from all restraint. This thought was uppermost in his mind when he mounted her for a second time and let out a whoop of joy that woke up half of Shoreditch. Marriage blended with mischief.

It was late when he finally tracked them down in the upper reaches of Clerkenwell. They were plodding along together like two old oxen pulling a heavy cart that taxed their combined strength. Josiah Taplow and William Merryweather were typical watchmen, public-spirited individuals who did an unpopular job to the best of their mean abilities. Attired in long, dark robes that were belted at the waist, they had large caps shaped like helmets. Josiah Taplow carried a staff and a lantern while William Merryweather bore a bell along with his lantern and halberd. Their weapons were more for show than use. Like most watchmen, they were more adept at warning people of their presence than of apprehending any malefactors. Indeed, it would be difficult to find officers who would be less use in a fracas than Josiah Taplow, a retired plasterer and William Merryweather, an unemployed poulterer. Worthy and well-intentioned they might be but they had little practical effect on the crime-infested area that they were doomed to patrol like lost souls in the outer darkness. It was unlovely work.

Nicholas Bracewell stepped out to accost them.

'Hold, sirs!' he said politely.

'We are watchmen both,' said Taplow defensively. 'Stand off a little further. We are armed.'

'I intend you no injury,' said Nicholas. 'It was the coroner himself who sent me in search of you. Master Taplow and Master Merryweather, is it not?'

The two men exchanged a bovine glance of bewilderment then held up their lanterns to illumine the newcomer's face. Josiah Taplow was a wrinkled old man with a hook nose and a tufted beard. William Merryweather was bigger, sturdier but altogether more somnolent. He used a series of nudges to communicate with his colleague and left all the talking to him. Taplow took stock of the book holder.

'Who are you, good sir?' he asked.

'My name is Nicholas Bracewell.'

'What business have you with us?'

'You found a dead body but yesternight, I believe.'

'That we did.'

'The gentleman was my friend.'

'I am sorry to hear that, Master Bracewell,' said Taplow with a wheezing note of apology, 'for that gentleman did not die as a gen-

64

tleman rightly should.'

'I have seen him and know the worst.'

'Words could not describe the horror of it, sir. We have seen many foul sights in this occupation but none so foul as this. Is it not so, William?'

Merryweather grunted and nudged his corroboration.

'Where did you find him?' said Nicholas.

'On the corner of Turnmill Street and Cow Cross.'

'Could you take me to the place?'

'It is a tidy walk from here.'

'I think I can keep pace.'

Reassured that Nicholas posed no threat to them, they ambled along the murky lane with the book holder in tow. It took them fifteen minutes to reach Cow Cross and another five to decide on the spot where the corpse had lain. There was a lot of chuntering from Taplow and nudging from Merryweather before agreement was reached. When they held their lanterns low, Nicholas could see the blood of Sebastian Carrick still staining the ground. The sight touched off his vengeful feelings once more and he had to master them before he spoke again.

'At what hour did you find him?' he said.

'Not long after midnight,' recalled Taplow.

'How was he lying?'

'Dead, sir. Stone dead.'

'On his front? On his back? Curled up on his side?'

'On his back,' said Taplow. 'As if knocked down by a single blow that split his poor brains in two.'

'Which way was he facing?'

'Up toward Heaven, sir.'

'I talk of his feet, Master Taplow.'

'They pointed toward Turnmill Street.' The watchman had a tentative stab at detection. 'We believe he was about to enter that sinful place when he was cut down.'

Nicholas doubted this judgement. Sebastian Carrick was a denizen of dark areas and knew how to protect himself. He would not easily have fallen to a frontal attack. It was more likely that he had been trailed by his killer who spun him round in order to strike the fateful blow. That meant that Carrick was leaving Turnmill Street rather than entering it. Somewhere in the festering warren lay the clue to his barbaric demise.

'Was anyone else hereby?' asked Nicholas.

'None save me and William, sir.'

'What did you do?'

'All that we could, master. We fetched a cart and took the body to the coroner. It was a dolorous journey.'

'You did well, sirs, and I thank you both.'

'We did our duty.'

'Indeed. Is there anything else you can tell me?'

'You know it all, Master Bracewell. Bleak as it is.'

Nicholas was about to take his leave when he noticed the vigorous nudging from William Merryweather. The elbow drummed out a message on his colleague's ribs and Josiah Taplow remembered a significant detail.

'He was not the first, sir,' he said.

'First?'

'With that wound upon his head. We found another poor wretch with just such a gash as that.'

'Who was the fellow?' said Nicholas.

'A discharged sailor bent upon pleasure.'

'When was this earlier murder?'

'Some four or five weeks past.'

'And where did you find him?'

'Not far from this very spot, sir. Hercules Yard.'

'With a like wound from a like weapon?'

'Yes, Master Bracewell.' Taplow responded to another flurry of nudges. 'And one thing more besides. He had the same marks upon him.'

'Marks?'

'Ten long scratches right down his back. The gentleman and the sailor together. A most peculiar sight, sir. They were like the stripes on a wild animal.'

William Merryweather leaned in close to make his one contribution to the discussion.

'Aye, Josiah,' he said righteously, 'and it was a wild animal who put them on those two bodies.'

It was his first visit to the Pickt-hatch and he found it quite overwhelming. Too callow to take on someone like Frances and too drunk to do himself justice with any of the other whores, he was relentlessly urged on by his friends until he gave in. The couple were sent off upstairs with a rousing cheer that gave the young man a momentary boldness. He put an arm around her but it was out of desperation rather than affection and Frances practically carried him along the passageway to her room. Helping him inside, she closed the door and propped him up against it, standing back to appraise him with hands on her hips. He was no more than sixteen and barely able to stand on his long, spindly legs. Frances had taken dozens like him to her lair and she had never needed more than five minutes to bring their ardour to sticky fruition.

In this case, she doubted whether his arousal would last even that long and so it proved. Pulling down the top of her dress to expose small but shapely breasts, she lay back on the mattress and lifted her skirt invitingly. She gave him an open-mouthed grin that allowed her tongue to stick out provocatively between her teeth. A gorgeous serpent was enticing with her fangs. He needed no more encouragement. Gathering his strength, he stared at her through blurred eyes then made a beery lunge. As he hit the mattress beside her, she turned him over and gave him a kiss that drained every last ounce of energy out of him and left him snoring noisily. Frances wasted scant time on him. She emptied his purse, grabbed him by the feet and dragged him out into the passageway. Leaving him in his stupor, she adjusted her dress and tidied her hair before going back downstairs in search of the next client. It was a profitable night in Turnmill Street.

Alone in his lodging, shut away from the world, Edmund Hoode sat at his table and worked by the light of a tallow candle. He was a nocturnal creature, a gifted poet whose Muse visited in the silence of the night and kept him from his slumbers. All of his best plays and most of his best sonnets had been written in the hours of darkness when his creative juices were in full flow and he could apply himself without distraction. It was at once gruelling and inspiring. Quill pen, inkhorn and parchment became closely acquainted and formed a willing partnership right up until dawn. It was only when the first rays of light tapped softly at his window that Hoode paused to read and reflect.

As the resident playwright with Westfield's Men, he was required to provide a number of new plays each year. *Love's Sacrifice* was his latest composition, a moving tragedy that was shot through with irony and pathos. It was the tale of a mighty king who bravely extended his empire into unconquered and hitherto unconquerable territory. Though he won a famous battle, however, he lost his heart to the queen of the subject nation and remained in thrall to her. The fiery passion which drew them together burned its remorseless way through all that he held most dear. Crackling flames consumed his wife, his children, his friends, his honour, his reputation, his sanity and his imperial crown. Love then exacted the final sacrifice from him by taking his life.

Though set in Ancient Britain, the play owed much to the story of Antony and Cleopatra but even more to the doomed romance in the author's own life. He reached the end of Act Five with the mangled bodies of King Gondar and Queen Elsin entwined together in their tomb before the warring parties from their respective countries. Death ennobles them both. As Edmund Hoode stood among the soldiers and gazed down sadly at the tragic scene, he was reminded of the most recent calamity in his severely charred private life. Queen Elsin was his own lost love, forbidden yet irresistible, forever out of his reach, one more corpse for the over-stocked mausoleum of his despair. He used the quill to brush away a tear.

It was in this mood of suffering, with his sensibilities tingling and his faculties heightened, with his pain and his poetry fusing in perfect harmony, that he penned a long valedictory speech to king, queen and every woman he had ever worshipped. Words came easily but beautifully and the result was a minor miracle. Reading the verse quietly to himself, he knew that he had brought *Love's Sacrifice* to a most poignant and affecting conclusion. What he did not realize was that a speech of twenty lines would have a significance that went far beyond the boundaries of his play to put the whole company in mortal danger.

★ ★ ★

'And has Master Firethorn been informed of this horror?'

'I will speak to him within the hour.'

'It is a grievous blow to Westfield's Men.'

'Sebastian was well-respected and well-liked, Anne. We will all feel his loss keenly.'

She gave a shudder. 'To die in such a fashion!'

'His murder will be revenged,' vowed Nicholas.

'You must first find the murderer.'

'It will be done.'

'How?'

'By patience and persistence.'

She smiled. 'You have both in large supply.'

'Sebastian Carrick was a friend of mine.'

'And of everyone he met,' she said wistfully. 'I never encountered a more engaging young man. He was joyful company indeed. Who could have hated him enough to kill him?'

It was early morning and Anne Hendrik was seated in the living room of her house in Southwark. She was a tall, well-groomed woman with easy charm and a natural grace. The English widow of a Dutch hatmaker, she had spurned the many offers of marriage that came her way in order to retain her independence and run her husband's business in the adjoining premises. Under her shrewd eye, it flourished. Since she had no children with whom to share the house, she elected to take in a lodger. Nicholas Bracewell had lived at the Southwark abode for some time now and his landlady had become a good friend and — when need arose and occasion served — a lover. A secretive man found someone in whom he could confide.

Anne Hendrik saw the practical consequences.

'This will affect the new play at The Rose,' she said.

'Sebastian was to have taken an important role.'

'To whom will it now fall?'

'My choice would be Owen Elias.'

'What of Master Firethorn?'

'He will resist the idea strongly at first.'

'Can you win him around?'

'Edmund Hoode and Barnaby Gill are of my persuasion. And there is no other actor in the company who could carry the part as well as Owen.' Nicholas grew serious. 'We need the best man we have, Anne. *Love's Sacrifice* brings us here to Southwark. Much rides upon the event. We must give off our true fragrance at The Rose.'

'I will be there to inhale it,' she promised.

Over a light breakfast of bread and meat, he had told her the full details of Sebastian

Carrick's death. She was frankly appalled. Anne Hendrik was well aware of the multiple burdens under which Westfield's Men laboured to make their precarious living. This new crisis would only make matters worse. Though she had great sympathy for the company itself, her main object of concern was Nicholas Bracewell. She became fearful.

'Take care, sir,' she said anxiously.

'The murderer must be brought to justice, Anne.'

'But you will need to search the stews of Turnmill Street to find him. There are many perils there. I would not have you meet the same end as Sebastian himself.'

'I will show all due caution.'

'Go armed, Nick. Take friends.'

'More may be achieved alone.'

'Add discretion to your valour.'

He grinned fondly. 'That is why I live in your house.'

'I'd have you continue here,' she said softly. 'For my sake, therefore, tread warily in Clerkenwell.'

'My search begins elsewhere.'

'With whom?'

'A father has the right to know of his son's death.'

'Master Andrew Carrick?'

'I must find a way to reach him.'

★ ★ ★

The Tower of London was the oldest and most secure building in the city. Founded by William the Conqueror on the site of a Roman fortification, it still dominated with its awesome combination of elegance and strength. It was set between neat gabled houses and lawns sloping down to the glittering havoc of the Thames. The Norman citadel had been constructed of white stone from Caen and its enormously thick walls rose to a height of ninety feet. Successive kings enlarged and reinforced the edifice until it became a huge complex of towers, baileys, domestic buildings and outworks. By the time Elizabeth came to the throne, the Tower had fulfilled its usefulness as a royal residence but her family left vivid mementoes in the crypt of the Chapel Royal of St Peter's ad Vincula where the vast majority of decayed bodies lacked heads. The obvious headquarters for the Mint, the building also housed the Crown jewels, the royal armoury and the national archives. In addition, it was the most feared prison in England. Above all else, however, the Tower remained what it had always been — the focal point of a burgeoning city that was planned around a main river and encircled by fields, forests, marshes and hills.

Andrew Carrick had admired its imposing exterior for many years until he was invited to sample its accommodation. His view of the Tower of London was more jaundiced now. It had robbed him of his freedom and kept him away from his family and his friends. In its cold and comfortless way, it had shut him out of life itself and forced him into an idleness that was a kind of death to him. Carrick was an able lawyer with eager clients awaiting his services. But the slim, poised, well-dressed man with an incisive mind was now a rather plump and indolent creature with a shabbiness to him that he detested. Imprisonment was irksome. There were, however, compensations.

'Good morrow, sir.'

'Good day, Master Carrick.'

'How does the world find you?'

'In excellent heart. And you, sir?'

'I survive, I survive.'

'Have faith, my friend.'

'It goes hard with me, Master Fellowes.'

'We pray for your release.'

'You are most kind.' Andrew Carrick made an effort to shake off his melancholy. 'But what of life beyond these walls? Tell me all the news, sir. It is a week and more since we spoke last and I am starved of intelligence. Who rises? Who has fallen? What are the rumours? Give me some interest. Unlock my mind at least.'

'I'll try what keys I may . . .'

Harry Fellowes offered all the news he could and each morsel was snapped up greedily by the prisoner. Fellowes was a short, round, self-satisfied man whose inclination towards pomposity was held in check by his genuine sympathy for Andrew Carrick. Enemies of state deserved to be incarcerated in the Tower before their execution but the lawyer was no traitor. He was an honest, patriotic, God-fearing Englishman whose offence was slight if ill-judged. Because he was so harmless a guest, Carrick was given licence to leave his cell and roam his tower for exercise. On one such walk he had been fortunate enough to meet and befriend Harry Fellowes. It was a relationship that kept the prisoner's hope alive and sustained him through the long reaches of boredom. The Tower of London was a place of work to Fellowes. As Clerk of Ordnance, he was a regular visitor to the armoury and he always came equipped with a fund of stories about court and city. Carrick was sincerely grateful and his lone friend warmed to him.

'That is all I have to tell you, sir.'

'I cannot thank you enough, Master Fellowes.'

'Does it bring relief to your plight?'

'It does, sir,' said Carrick with tattered dignity. 'It does. Would that I could repay you in some way.'

Harry Fellowes appraised him shrewdly for a long time.

'Haply, you may,' he said. 'Haply, you may.'

Nimbus spent the night in the largest stable and on the deepest bed of straw. As shafts of sunlight penetrated the cracks in the timber to fill the place with endless golden dots, the horse woke, raised itself up and looked around. It yawned a welcome to a new day then got to its feet in a gentle rustle. A flick of the head opened the top half of the stable door, a dextrous mouth pulled back the wooden bolt. Kicking the lower half of the door open, Nimbus went off in search of service and he soon found it. He was back less than a minute later with his teeth clamped on the collar of a terrified ostler who was virtually carried along by the horse. The dishevelled young man was thrown into what he thought was an empty stable. As he stumbled over a pile of blankets, however, he had his second shock of the morning. A human voice roared abusively. The blankets then opened like giant petals to allow a bleary-eyed Cornelius Gant to emerge. He glared at the ostler and broke wind.

'Fetch our breakfast, boy!' he ordered.

'Yes, sir.'

'Hay for Nimbus. Ale and bread for me.'

'Yes, sir.'

'Do not stand there shivering like that. About it.'

'Yes, sir.' The ostler moved away then turned to look back in wonderment at Gant. 'You spent the night here, sir?'

'Nimbus and I are never parted.'

'But you kept the whole inn amazed with your tricks. I have handled many horses in my time but none like this of yours. He is without compare. You were showered with coins for your performance and rightly so. Why sleep in a stable when you could afford the finest room at the inn?'

Gant chuckled. 'The bed was too small, boy.'

'Too small?'

'It would not hold me *and* Nimbus.'

The horse raised its head and gave a manic laugh.

Lawrence Firethorn played the farewell scene with his wife as if it were the climax of a drama. His arms flapped in protest, his lips kissed at random, his tongue poured out a stream of pious nonsense about how he would pine and wilt in her absence. Onlookers were convinced that the couple would be parted for ever instead of simply endure with a mere fortnight's separation. Margery shifted between romance and reality with practised smoothness, basking in the effusive compliments while at the same time issuing orders about the running of the house. The beautiful damsel torn away from her handsome prince wanted to make sure that her children were properly looked after and her servants kept in line. When it was time for the travellers to depart, Firethorn embraced her once then helped her into the saddle of her horse. Believing there was safety in numbers, she set off on the road to Cambridge with a sizeable company.

Her husband waved his hat after her until she was out of sight then his expression changed completely. A sense of liberation coursed through him and he gave a ripe chuckle. Fame brought him a large following. Lovely ladies threw themselves at his feet all over London. For the first time in years, he would be able to bend down and pick them up at will without having to look over his shoulder. Marriage brought many blessings but none, he now decided, as sweet as the occasional release from its chafing yoke.

Pulling on his hat and slapping his thigh with joy, he strode back towards his own horse but his euphoria was short-lived. Nicholas Bracewell came hurrying towards him.

'Nick, dear heart!'

'Good day, sir.'

'What brings you to Shoreditch this early, man?'

'Heavy news.'

'I'll hear none today. I feel as light as a feather.'

'It concerns Sebastian.'

'You found the rogue?'

'Alas, I did.'

'Bring him to me. I'll roast the rascal alive!'

'Sebastian is beyond recall.'

They were standing in the street so Nicholas moved him into the doorway of a shop to gain some privacy. He then told his tale briefly and calmly. Stunned at first, Firethorn shaded quickly into irritation and then into a black rage. He wanted the murderer brought to justice so that he could take revenge on him with his own hands but these feelings did not arise out of any sense of loss at the death of a loved one. What Firethorn could not forgive was the damage which had been done to his company. The killer of Sebastian Carrick would be called to account for the cruel injury he had inflicted

81

on Westfield's Men.

'What am I to do, Nick?' he said with both arms flailing away. 'This heavy news of yours flattens me to a wafer. I named Sebastian Carrick as our new sharer and the fool gets himself axed to death in a squalid brawl.'

'That is not what happened,' said Nicholas firmly.

'No matter for the details, man. I have to live with the consequences. At one fell stroke, I have lost my sharer, my reputation for good judgement and my hopes of happiness. I have also lost a fine actor who was about to shine in a new play. Who is *doing* all this to me?'

Nicholas kept a tactful silence while his employer vented his self-pity. They then strolled back together along Bishopsgate Street towards the city walls. Firethorn had been sobered. Instead of cantering in through Bishopsgate itself in search of his first conquest, he was leading his horse somnolently along and wondering how he would face the barbed gibes of Barnaby Gill. When his fury had blown itself out, he turned as ever to Nicholas for counsel. The latter argued that their first priority was to contact Andrew Carrick to inform him of the death of his son. Firethorn agreed at once and undertook to solicit the help of their patron, Lord West-field, to gain admittance to the Tower. He offered to visit the prisoner with Nicholas but the book holder insisted on going alone. Out of consideration to the bereaved father, he would keep a vain actor away from him and save an already painful situation from becoming an agony.

As they merged with the jostling crowd which pressed in through the gate, an immediate problem exercised Firethorn.

'What of *Love's Sacrifice?*' he asked.

'It will have its hour at the Rose.'

'Sebastian was to have played Benvolio.'

'Assign the role to someone else.'

'Edmund has written the part with him in mind.'

'A good actor will trim the role to suit himself,' said Nicholas, 'and we have the ideal substitute in Owen Elias.'

Firethorn was dismissive. 'He is not competent.'

'He proved his mettle in *Marriage and Mischief.*'

'A harmless romp of no consequence. *Love's Sacrifice* is richer material. It is drama in a tragic vein.'

'Then Owen elects himself. Tragedy is his strength.'

'I beg leave to doubt that.'

'Put him to the test, sir.'

'We will look elsewhere for our Benvolio.'

'Against the wishes of the author?' said Nicholas. 'I have it from Edmund Hoode himself. He told me that Owen would be a wiser choice for Benvolio than Sebastian. Your worthy poet will confirm that opinion and Master Gill will lend his authority to it as well.'

'Ha!' snarled Firethorn with a contemptuous snap of his fingers. 'What do playwrights know of true players? What do mincing comedians know of real men? Edmund and Barnaby may say what they wish. I am proof against their folly.'

'But I share it, Master Bracewell.'

'You side with them against *me!*' accused the other.

'I support Owen Elias to the hilt.'

'Treachery!'

'No, sir. Fair dealing.'

Firethorn turned an apoplectic stare on him but Nicholas met it without flinching. A silent battle of wills took place. Without his book holder's support, Firethorn would have enormous difficulty in getting his way against the combined determination of Hoode and Gill. He tried to cow Nicholas with a growl of disapproval but the latter stuck bravely to his guns. Few people dared to obstruct the freewheeling tyranny of Lawrence Firethorn. Fewer still could do so with such audacity and composure.

Nicholas was adamant. 'Owen Elias is your man.'

The actor-manager put all his anger into another long stare but it lacked the power to frighten or subdue. He was up against the one person in the company whom he could not bully into submission, the one person who was a match for him. He eventually accepted it. Stamping his foot hard on the cobbles, he capitulated in a pained gurgle.

'So be it.'

The decision would have dire repercussions.

Chapter Four

Whitehall was the biggest palace in Christendom. Covering some twenty-four acres, it incorporated all the grandiose extensions and refinements that Henry VIII had bestowed upon it with such kingly zeal. Like Hampton Court, it was one of the rich spoils of Wolsey's fall, but every sign of the Archbishop's occupation was ruthlessly swept away to be replaced by the distinctive symbols of the Tudor dynasty. In its decorative solidity and its sprawling wonder, it embodied the pomp and circumstance of the new monarchy. By the time that Queen Elizabeth came to the throne, Whitehall was firmly established as the seat of government and it was here that she so often presided over her court.

Attendance at court was the social obligation of the aristocracy and the distant hope of lesser mortals. It was the setting in which the Virgin Queen lived out her public and private lives. The court was the centre of affairs, the source of patronage, and the regular avenue to profit and promotion. Those who wished to rise in the world or simply maintain the eminence they had already achieved were duty bound to make regular appearances at court and participate in its sophisticated games and rituals. It was an expensive commitment since courtiers were expected to dress finely at all times and to spend long hours gambling and gossiping in the corridors of power but it was a charge that could not be shirked. To be out of court was to be out of favour and so the nobility flocked to Whitehall to show due respect, to mingle with their peers and to gain advancement.

The Queen set high standards for her courtiers. She valued intelligence in a man, ability to sing songs to a lute, skill in the composition of lyric poetry and prowess in the tiltyard. Her favourites tended to be those of all-round excellence. Like her father, she wanted her court to be a cultural centre where music, drama, poetry and the dance could flourish. To this end, she allowed the Great Hall to be used on many occasions for music recitals and the performance of plays. Those few enlightened souls who retained their own theatrical companies were thus looked upon with special favour. It made Lord Westfield's visits to court a source of continual pleasure.

'What is the new piece called, my lord?'
'*Love's Sacrifice.*'

'We have all made that in our time.'

'And will hope to do so again.'

Polite outrage. 'My lord!'

'I will never be too old to admire a trim shape and a fair countenance, nor yet too wasted to desire a closer acquaintance with such an angel.'

Lord Westfield's entourage laughed obediently. He was a portly man of cheerful disposition who devoted himself to the promotion of the arts and the pursuit of pleasure. Excess intruded upon his style of life and choice of apparel. As he led his little group of sycophants towards the Presence Chamber at Whitehall, he was wearing a slashed doublet of aquamarine hue above bombasted trunk hose in a lighter shade. A white ruff supported the amiable, bearded face and the long grey hair was hidden beneath a dark-blue hat that was a forest of light-blue feathers. Rings, jewels and a gleaming sword added to the ostentation. A golden chain that let its medallion rest on his sternum completed the dazzling effect. Lord Westfield liked to catch the eye. It was one of the ways he tried to assert his superiority over the loathed Earl of Banbury.

'Who comes here?' he said. 'Stand aside, friends.'

'The Earl is much moved.'

'I did not think his legs could scurry so fast.'

'What can this mean, my lord?'

'My prayers would have him expelled from court but this sudden departure may betoken something else.'

'Will you speak to him?'

'Only with a naked blade.'

Muted sniggers from the entourage before they offered perfunctory bows to the approaching Earl of Banbury. With his own cronies in attendance, the latter was making a hasty and not altogether dignified exit from Whitehall. He threw a glance of hostility at his rival as they passed, then curled a lip in amusement. Lord Westfield's ire was aroused at once. The Earl knew something that he did not and he was rushing off to act upon his intelligence in order to seize the advantage. Only a matter of the gravest significance could send the noble gentleman away from Whitehall at such a canter and Lord Westfield was desperate to know what it was. He did not have long to wait. Other figures came streaming down the corridor in busy conference and he pounced on one of them without ceremony.

'What is the news, sir?' he demanded.

'The Queen will not hold court today.'

'How so?'

'Her Majesty is indisposed.'

'What is the nature of her illness?'

'Physicians are in constant attendance.'

Lord Westfield stood back to let the man beat his own retreat from Whitehall. The general exodus could now be explained. Queen Elizabeth was unwell. A monarch who prided herself on her health, who was abstemious with her food and drink, who exercised regularly and who paced her life with extreme care, had actually taken to her bed. It was no minor indisposition. The Queen knew the importance of being seen by her subjects and it was not only her courtiers who viewed her on a daily basis. The main road from Westminster to Charing Cross ran straight through Whitehall so ordinary citizens could express their affection for their sovereign by bringing small gifts for her or simply by waiting for hours to be rewarded by the glimpses of her person that she would considerately afford them. Elizabeth was a visible Queen who revelled in her visibility. But she was also on the verge of her sixtieth year and the burdens of her long reign must have taken their toll. If her physicians had been called then a crisis was in the offing.

Lord Westfield turned on his heel and led the way back to his coach. The news was alarming enough in itself but its implications were even more disturbing. A wave of general sympathy would wash over the ailing queen but her courtiers looked beyond it to a contingency that had to be faced.

If Elizabeth died, who would succeed her?

It was a question that was fraught with all kinds of possibilities and it transformed the stately waddle of Lord Westfield. For the first time in a decade, he broke into a breathless run, fervently wishing that his steps would take him in the right direction.

Giles Randolph expired with a vulpine screech that echoed around the hushed auditorium. As he sank slowly from sight through the trap door in the stage at The Curtain, the spectators genuinely believed that he was being lowered into a vat of boiling oil. Steam rose up from below to reinforce the illusion and Randolph's screech hit a new note of horror before vanishing with gurgling suddenness. *The Spanish Jew* was the lurid tale of a villainous money-lender who rose to power through unscrupulous means then held the whole country to ransom before overreaching himself. There was a comic relish in his devilment that somehow endeared him to the onlookers and gave his fall a sad dimension. A man who had consistently lied, cheated, stolen, poisoned and stabbed his way to the top was now claiming frank sympathy. It was an astonishing achievement and a tribute to the skill with which Giles Randolph had played the title role.

The piece itself was a somewhat ramshackle affair but his performance had given it a drive and a unity that it did not really deserve. *The Spanish Jew* was blatant in its prejudices, attacking Spaniards, Jews, usury and other things with a coarse brutality which Randolph softened to some extent but which nevertheless produced a deal of derisive laughter at its intended victims. There was an abundance of action and comedy to delight the groundlings but those who looked beneath the surface of the play could see a real figure lurking there and this gave the drama its extra bite and relevance. Giles Randolph had been handed the sort of part in which he could exhibit the full range of his genius and he held nothing back for two wonderful hours.

Banbury's Men came out to take their bow in the firm knowledge that they had at last found a winning play. With their actor-manager in the lead, *The Spanish Jew* would go on to thrill and move many an audience. Word of mouth was the best possible advertisement and the shouts of praise that now deafened their ears told them that their triumph would be voiced abroad in no time. Giles Randolph would die his terrible death many times at The Curtain and elevate their custom-built amphitheatre above all other venues.

Randolph was not troubled by even a hint of modesty. He took his ovation like a conquering hero on a procession through the streets of a grateful capital. Even his bow had a lordly condescension to it. The sustained clapping was not seen by him as pure gratitude. It was an act of homage to a superior being and he replied with an arrogant smile. Heady compliments fell from the galleries like warm snowflakes and he stretched both arms wide to catch them. Giles Randolph was still luxuriating in the prolonged adoration when a loud voice speared its way through to him.

'Sublime, sir! Almost the equal of Master Firethorn!'

He stalked off the stage with high indignation.

The insult was far worse than the boiling oil.

Preoccupied as he was with the dramatic turn of events, Lord Westfield responded promptly to the request that was made of him. He always showed a proprietary affection towards his theatrical company and was stunned to learn of the murder of one of its number. He was anxious to do all that he could to further any inquires into the crime. Word was duly passed along the line and a fulsome letter was written. Nicholas Bracewell was given right of access to the Tower of London.

'These are mean quarters in which to receive visitors.'

'No matter, sir.'

'Yet the straw is fresh. I can vouch for that.'

'Do not trouble yourself.'

'And the casement catches the sun at noon.'

'I did not come to mock your lodging, Master Carrick.'

'Nobler guests than I have sheltered here.'

'I do believe it.'

'Finer souls have breathed this noisome air.'

Nicholas let him ramble on. They were in the lawyer's room in the massive Beauchamp Tower, a cold, bare, featureless apartment that looked down on Tower Green to give its tenant a privileged view of any executions that took place there. Andrew Carrick sensed the bad tidings as soon as his visitor introduced himself and he tried to keep them at bay with an inconsequential stream of chatter. Nicholas could see the family likeness at once. Carrick had his son's cast of feature and his proud bearing. Imprisonment had bowed his shoulders slightly and lined his face with disillusion but it had not taxed his essential goodness. The book holder knew he was in the presence of a man of integrity.

Andrew Carrick eventually worked up enough courage to face the grim news that he feared. He sat on a stool and gestured towards Nicholas with a graceful hand.

'Speak, sir. You have been very patient.'

'I bring word of your son, Master Carrick.'

'Do not hedge it about with consideration,' said the other. 'Tell me straight. Is Sebastian ill?'

'Dead, sir.'

'Dead?'

'Murdered.'

The lawyer winced at the blow. It was minutes before he was able to resume. Fatherly love was tempered by a note of weary resignation. His sigh carried its own history.

'I feared that it might come to this,' he said. 'My son had many virtues but his vices were too profuse.'

'Sebastian was a fine man and a fine actor, sir.'

'You speak like a friend, Master Bracewell.'

'His death is a loss we must all bear.'

'Present me with the details.' He saw the hesitation. 'Hold nothing back, sir. I doted on Sebastian but he brought me much pain while he was alive. I am prepared for the worst account. Your face tells me it was a heinous crime. Remember that I am a lawyer who would weigh the full facts of the case before I make a judgement. Speak on.'

Nicholas recited the tale without embellishment and the older man listened intently. A long silence ensued. It was broken by the hoarse voice of a distraught father.

'The murderer must be brought to justice.'

'He will be,' said Nicholas. 'The law must exact full payment.'

Andrew Carrick rose to his feet and paced the room with restless anxiety. At a time when he wanted to devote himself to the pursuit and attest of his son's killer, he was himself in custody. He paused to lean against a wall and to slap its cold stone with an open palm. Nicholas sympathized with his obvious frustration. Carrick gave an apologetic shrug.

'Forgive me, sir,' he said. 'Your news has made this prison like the pit of hell. I would

96

give anything to be out of its confines and free to avenge my son.'

'Is there any prospect of *that?*'

'In time, Master Bracewell. In time.'

'May I ask why you are detained?'

'By special order of Her Majesty.'

'Indeed?'

Carrick bristled. 'You would think there were traitors enough to fill these dungeons. You would imagine that London had no shortage of foul criminals and hired assassins to occupy this Tower. Felons abound yet I — an upholder of the law — am put under lock and key. It is barbarous, sir.'

'What is your offence?'

'Attendance at a wedding.'

'You lose your liberty for *that?*'

'The bride was a gentlewoman of the Privy Chamber.'

'This was a secret marriage?'

'Yes,' said Carrick. 'I took charge of arrangements. The Queen's anger turned upon the noble groom and upon myself. We are held here at her pleasure while the bride weeps nightly in an empty bed. It is a poor wedding present.'

Andrew Carrick was not the first man to feel the weight of his sovereign's outrage in the matter of an unlicensed wedding. Queen Elizabeth demanded total obedience and unswerving loyalty from those chosen to attend upon her. In this respect, Blanche Parry was the archetype, a studious woman who had served with tireless devotion for over thirty years and who had a clear-sighted view of her duties even though she was now blind. The example of Blanche Parry was held up to all. She was a first gentlewoman of irreproachable virtue. Others fell short of her high standards and allowed themselves to be led astray by covert passion. More than one attendant had requested the Queen's permission to marry only to be summarily rejected. Those who dared to put love before royal service were given stern rebuke. When a secret wedding came to light, Elizabeth always found just cause and impediment why those two persons should not be joined together.

Six weeks of incarceration had given Andrew Carrick ample time in which to meditate upon the patent injustice of it all. In witnessing the happiness of one noble lady, he had provoked the ire of another. In helping a friend, he had made the worst possible enemy. A law-abiding lawyer, he was being treated like the vilest outlaw.

Nicholas probed gently for more information.

'Sebastian never talked of his family, sir.'

'No, sir,' said Carrick sadly. 'We were a hindrance to him. He was bound to outgrow his family and his career.'

'Career?'

'Sebastian was a lawyer of some promise, sir. He studied at Oxford before coming to London to join the Middle Temple. It was there that he first encountered temptation.'

'In what disguise?'

'Your own, sir.'

'He was distracted by the theatre?'

'Intoxicated with it,' said the other harshly. 'When he saw plays performed at the Middle Temple, they were not just idle amusement for a working lawyer. They offered another way of life that was palpably free from the restraints of his father's calling. In short, sir, he turned his back on an honourable profession to embrace the tawdry delights of the theatre.' He grew conciliatory. 'I do not mean to impugn your choice of occupation, Master Bracewell, but it lacks the security of the law. And it has led my son to his death.'

'I dispute that,' said Nicholas. 'Had he still been at the Middle Temple, he might have met the same fate. Lawyers seek pleasure in the stews as well as actors. It is unfair to lay the blame squarely on the theatre.'

Andrew Carrick accepted the point with

a nod but he was still troubled by a residual resentment against the theatre. He studied his visitor closely.

'What drew you into the profession?' he asked.

'A deep interest.'

'So it was with Sebastian.'

'He was a natural actor. I am not.'

'Did your father approve, Master Bracewell?'

'No, sir. He wished me to be a merchant like himself.'

'You have no regrets in the matter?'

'None, Master Carrick. And I am bound to observe . . .'

'Go on. I value your opinion.'

'Sebastian himself had no regrets.'

The grieving father accepted the judgement and thanked his visitor profusely for conveying the bad news with such tact and promptness. He talked fondly of his son, recalling childhood incidents that were early signs of the wildness and impetuosity that made him abandon a career in the law for the ambiguous freedom of an actor's life. Nicholas learned a great deal about his erstwhile friend and he was interested to hear that Sebastian had a younger sister. His compassion reached out to her. With a mother long dead and a father imprisoned in the

Tower, she was unfortunate enough without having to bear this additional horror. Nicholas wished that there was some way to minimize the distress that now stalked Mistress Marion Carrick.

'What of the funeral?' said the lawyer.

'It will be delayed now that we have traced Sebastian's family. You have the right to make all decisions here.'

'Not while I am a common prisoner.'

'Her Majesty must take account of your predicament.'

'She has placed me in it.'

'We will see what Lord Westfield may do to help.'

'You earn my gratitude once more.'

Andrew Carrick shook him warmly by the hand. There were tears of remorse in his eyes now and his sense of loss drew an odd confession out of him.

'I wish I had seen Sebastian upon the stage.'

'He adorned it even in the smallest part.'

'My anger got the better of my curiosity. I should have relented. Now, alas, it is too late.'

'He will be well-remembered by his fellows.'

The lawyer pondered briefly then gave a wistful smile.

'That thought brings me some comfort.'

★ ★ ★

Comfort was singularly lacking at the Queen's Head where the company met for its first rehearsal of the new play. Before they could even begin, there was a sudden cloudburst and the inn yard was awash within minutes. Soaked by the rain and saddened by the news about their colleague, Westfield's Men retreated into the room that they used as their tiring-house and continued their work in a dispirited mood. It was an inauspicious start for *Love's Sacrifice* and its author was plunged into the kind of despair that he usually reserved for failed romances. Edmund Hoode lounged somnolently in a corner, dividing himself between anguish at the death of a friend and morbid predictions about the future of his new work. Lines which had sprung joyously from his brain to dance on the page now seemed dull and lifeless. Characters whom he had fleshed out with care now appeared skeletal. A plot which drove forward in a rising trajectory now limped along without purpose.

Lawrence Firethorn tried to lift the general gloom with a booming attack on the leading role but he made no headway. Even in the hands of such a gifted clown as Barnaby Gill, the comic moments sounded tedious. The only performance which cut through the torpor to excite and uplift was that given by Owen Elias in the inherited role of Benvolio. He did not so much play the part as ambush it with greedy enthusiasm, so much so that it might have been written purely as a vehicle for his talents. It was an altogether exuberant reading that brought Sebastian Carrick to mind only to dismiss his claim to this particular role. Owen Elias proved beyond doubt what many had argued for some time. He was the better actor. When he declaimed his final speech over the entwined bodies of the dead lovers, he was deeply moving.

Moistened eyes and dry throats broke out in all parts of the room. Edmund Hoode was coaxed back from dejection to the belief that his latest play might — against all the odds — be redeemed.

Lawrence Firethorn tampered with that belief.

'I require a few changes, Edmund,' he said.

'You were always a man of habit.'

'Give me a longer speech at the end of Act Two and a shorter one at the start of Act Four. Let me dally less, let me suffer more. I would have a song to lighten my final hour on earth. Make it play upon the heart-strings.'

'All this will be done, Lawrence.'

The two men had repaired to the tap room with Barnaby Gill to lubricate their sorrow and to analyse the morning's work. No play was ever accepted without reservation by the actor-manager and Hoode was braced to add refinements to order. Gill, too, invariably suggested improvements in his own role and an extra dance was conceded to him yet again so that he could offset a dark tragedy with his comic antics. Firethorn was not yet finished.

'There is one more amendment . . .'

'I await your command,' said Hoode.

'That closing epitaph . . .'

'The music of truth,' complimented Gill with unwonted gravity. 'You have never brought a piece to such a beautiful conclusion, Edmund.'

'I thank you for that, Barnaby.'

'It has a quiet magnificence to it, sir.'

'As did the man who delivered the speech.'

'Owen Elias surpassed himself.'

'I could not wish for a finer Benvolio.'

'That speech alone will seal his fame.'

The remark served to reinforce Firethorn's decision.

'Cut the lines, Edmund.'

'Cut them!'

'Completely, sir.'

'It is the most affecting speech in the play.'

'I care not for that,' said Firethorn airily. 'It is a distraction from the death of two tragic figures. We need no words to carry us to the grave.'

Gill disagreed vehemently. 'Cut those lines and you geld the whole play, Lawrence.'

'*I* am the stallion in this drama, Barnaby.'

'But *I* am the author,' said Hoode.

'Commissioned by me. Do you flout my authority, sir?'

'Be reasonable, Lawrence.'

'Trim your play, sir.'

'This is the greatest sacrifice yet!'

'Put your company first for once.'

'I say the same to you!' shouted the playwright. 'Think what harm you do to Owen Elias if you remove that speech.'

'That is Lawrence's earnest intention,' said Gill.

'I will resist him on this!'

'I will support you, Edmund.'

'My words are sacred!'

'Indeed, they are,' said Firethorn softly, 'and I would fight to retain each one. But the piece is over-long, Edmund. We can spare twenty meagre lines spoken by a rogue who has words enough in the rest of the play. Do as I bid, sir. It will give a rounder ending to your drama. Believe it well.'

Argument ceased. The speech was cut.

The offer was far too good to refuse. They were in a small village to the south of Oxford when they were accosted by the farmer. Cornelius Gant was reclining against the trunk of a chestnut tree and counting his booty from a full day in the university town. Nimbus cropped the grass nearby then ambled across to the pond to stare at its own reflection for a few moments before dipping its muzzle into the cool water. The heavy wagon came to a creaking halt and the farmer got down to the ground. He was a big, broad, red-faced man in his forties whose manner and clothing suggested moderate wealth. He came straight to the point.

'That is a fine animal you have, my friend,' he noted. 'I would like to buy him from you.'

'Oh, sir, I could not sell him,' said Gant.

'Is there no price that would tempt you?'

'He is worth more than you could possibly offer.'

'Do not doubt the strength of my purse,' said the farmer, walking over to Nimbus to appraise him at close quarters. 'I am as good a judge of horse-flesh as any in Oxfordshire. When I watched the blacksmith shoe this sturdy fellow, I could see the horse's mettle. Come, sir. I have great need of such a beast.

Let us talk terms.'

Gant pulled himself lazily to his feet and glanced at the dappled carthorse between the shafts. The dark stripes along its back and loins showed that the farmer was fond of his whip. Gant strolled over to Nimbus and stroked the sleek coat with calculating affection.

'He is no jade, sir. I would not have him beaten.'

'Nor shall he be,' assured the other. 'I have beasts enough in my stable for the drudgery. This fellow here would be kept in style for my personal use.'

'Where is your land, sir?'

'Some five miles hence.'

'And you would care for him?'

'Like a father with a child.'

Gant knew that the farmer was lying but went along with the deceit to drive a hard bargain. When a bag of crowns was tipped into his hands, he reluctantly agreed to the sale. He gave Nimbus a farewell pat on the neck.

'Goodbye, old friend,' he said with evident sadness. 'I am sorry to part with you but you go to a good master. Spare me further suffering and leave quickly. I will turn my back and rest beside this tree.'

Nimbus gave a forlorn neigh then turned

obediently to the farmer who instantly hitched his reins to the back of the waggon and drove off. Cornelius Gant waited until they were out of earshot before he cackled with delight. It was the second time in a week that he had sold Nimbus for such a handsome profit. He sauntered across to the inn and ordered the best meal that they could provide. By the time he had washed it down with ale, some two hours had passed. Gant paid the reckoning and went back to the chestnut tree near the pond to find Nimbus contentedly grazing once more. Five miles away, an irate farmer was examining his bruises and cursing the horse which had so unexpectedly thrown him from the saddle. He vowed revenge but it was a vain boast.

Nimbus was already galloping out of his reach.

'On, on!' urged Gant happily. 'We go to see the Queen!'

London buzzed with rumour and speculation. The enforced absence from court of an ageing sovereign put a new zest into a languid nobility. Royal physicians and ladies-in-waiting were offered large bribes to reveal the true facts of the situation but they were proof against all inquiry. Queen Elizabeth was wrapped in a blanket of silence that only seemed to confirm the worst diagnoses. Since there was no official denial that she was fading away, it came to be generally accepted by those who stood to gain or lose most by a change of monarch. No heir existed, no successor had been named. Factions hardened. Solemn conclaves were held to discuss the various claimants to the throne.

One such gathering could be found at Croxley Hall in the Strand, the palatial London home of Roger Godolphin, Earl of Chichester. This distinguished old soldier with silver hair and beard encroaching upon a face of wrinkled parchment still retained the habit of command. As one name came firmly into favour, his fist pounded the table and his voice rose above the babble with peremptory authority.

'It is decided,' he announced. 'About it, sirs.'

His confederates streamed from the room to implement their scheme in a dozen different ways and places. The political dice had been cast and they had to move fast to ensure that they would pick up the winnings from the game. Two senior men in the enterprise were left alone together. The Earl of Banbury was at the other end of the long table.

'Well, Roger?'

'Our plan of campaign is sound,' said his host.

'It will mean a heavy investment.'

'Handsome rewards await us.'

'We must spend money in order to make it,' reminded the other. 'Do you have funds at your disposal?'

'None!' said the old soldier with a shrug. 'You?'

'Not a penny.'

'Then must we find some capital.'

'Where?'

The Earl of Chichester considered the matter with a furrowed brow then he gave a brittle laugh. As Master of the Ordnance, he was supremely aware of the importance of having plenty of ammunition in store for an encounter. His coach was soon carrying him towards the Tower of London.

A long and tiring day became even longer and more tiring in its closing hours. Nicholas Bracewell had hardly stopped since dawn. After the visit to Andrew Carrick, he had set the funeral arrangements in motion, returned to Southwark to see the manager of The Rose about the forthcoming presentation of *Love's Sacrifice*, reported back to Lawrence Firethorn at the Queen's Head, discussed the play's requirements with its jaundiced author, placated the ever-grumbling landlord of the inn and tried to reconcile Owen Elias to the loss of the finest verse ever written for him. A further session with Firethorn had been followed by long debates with two crucial members of the company, Hugh Wegges, the tireman, and Nathan Curtis, the master carpenter. Both were being called upon to make a major contribution to a new play that was being staged at London's newest theatre.

It was late evening before Nicholas could even begin the task of searching the stews of Clerkenwell. Turnmill Street was seething with custom. Easy lust and ready money were all that gained respect there. Nobody welcomed awkward questions about a murder victim. At most of the places he visited, Nicholas found himself ignored, spurned, threatened or even buffeted. Haunts which had been familiar to Sebastian Carrick were full of danger to his friend. Nicholas was a patent outsider. Much against his will, therefore, he had to pose as a client to gain acceptance.

'What would you have, sir?' she said.

'The wildest creature in the house.'

'We have punks of all ages, all sizes, all colours.' The old woman gave a toothless grin. 'Name your pleasure.'

'I would like to choose my company.'

'What price did you set on it, kind sir?'

Nicholas slipped a few coins into her grubby palm and was rewarded with a foul-breathed kiss. She conducted him along a passage and into a low room that was filled with the stench of sin and tobacco smoke. Noisy men lolled at tables with their whores. By the light of a candle, others played cards in a corner. The old woman waved a hand and Nicholas was confronted by a semi-circle of trulls, each one of them showing off her body and shooting him bold glances.

'Take one or take all,' said the old woman.

'I like true madness,' he explained.

'You heard the gentleman,' continued the hostess. 'He wants some lunacy in his loving. Which of you will serve him best?' She grinned a challenge. 'Who is the mad courtesan?'

He was gentle and compliant when she took him up to her room but he proved a savage lover. Once inside her, he punished her with cruel bites and hard blows until he reached the height of his passion. Frances was bleeding from the nose and the mouth by the time that he drifted off to sleep. She rolled him over on to his back and reached under the pillow for her knife. One deep thrust into his fat throat was all that it needed. Frances watched him grunt his last then she went to the window to give a signal. One more dead body was soon being lugged away from her murderous embrace.

Chapter Five

The Rose was an aptly-named symbol of the flowering of the London theatre under Queen Elizabeth. It was not simply a source of entertainment for idle pleasure-seekers but one of the results of that great upsurge of creative energy which had established the Tudor dynasty as a major force in world politics. Like the two outdoor playhouses in Shoreditch — The Theatre and The Curtain — it helped to meet the rising demand for new plays of all kinds. The stage was a truthful mirror of its time. It celebrated all that was best and castigated all that was worse. It provoked, it enchanted, it mocked, it inspired. On occasion, it even destroyed. With its bustling freedom and its dangerous spontaneity, it had an impact which was unique and which stretched far beyond the confines of the actual playhouses. Drama was beloved at court. It was an art that was practised with royal assent.

Floral tribute was inevitable because the capital's most recent theatre was built on the site of a rose garden to the east of Rose

Alley in the Liberty of the Clink. The choice of Southwark was deliberate. Like Shoreditch, it was conveniently outside the city boundaries and thus spared the civic hostility and narrow-mindedness that hindered work at the few remaining inn yard venues such as the Queen's Head. Material which would arouse moral outrage in Gracechurch Street could be presented with undiluted vigour at The Rose. It had given Edmund Hoode wider scope for his imagination and more leeway for his daring. *Love's Sacrifice* could never be staged at the Queen's Head in its original form. The irony was that Southwark permitted a freedom that was offset by an act of self-imposed censorship.

Owen Elias was outspoken in his wrath.

'It is treachery of the basest kind!' he exclaimed.

'You have lost but one speech,' said Nicholas.

'I have been stabbed in the back by my fellows.'

'That is not true, Owen.'

'Those twenty lines crown the whole play,' argued the Welshman with hopeless fury. 'They lift the drama and redeem the hero in his tragic fall.' Self-interest emerged. 'They give my Benvolio an opportunity for which

I have waited this long time. I am *betrayed*, Nick!'

'Do not be cast down.'

'I am mortally wounded,' said the other. 'Sebastian would not have suffered this slight. Had *he* played the part, it would have been seen without mutilation. Benvolio would have delivered his last oration.'

'That is something we will never know.'

'Fight for me here. Take up my cause.'

'I have done so many times.'

Nicholas Bracewell had profound sympathy for the actor. He yielded to none in his admiration of Lawrence Firethorn but he was not blind to the other's faults. Professional envy had dictated the omission of the final speech. The dead hero did not want to cede any of his glory to another. It was unjust but it was not altogether untypical and the book holder heard himself making the same soothing sounds he had made before to others in a similar predicament. Firethorn liked to occupy more than his place in the sun.

Owen Elias and his friend were standing on the stage of The Rose not long after the morning's rehearsal had ended. Because the theatre now had its own resident company — Lord Strange's Men — access to its boards was limited and the new play had to content itself with one full rehearsal before being

116

launched upon the public. Most of the work on *Love's Sacrifice* had thus been done at the Queen's Head and the preparation was thorough. Westfield's Men had no difficulty in adapting their performances to the special demands of The Rose.

Lawrence Firethorn berated his company with his usual gusto but they knew that his criticism was largely for show. He was clearly delighted with the rehearsal and confident that the afternoon would add yet another classic role to his gallery of triumphs. It gave his ebullience a slightly manic edge. As the actor-manager came strutting towards them, Owen Elias sidled off and watched mutinously from a corner. The beaming Firethorn closed on his book holder.

'Nick, dear heart!' he said jovially. 'What do you think of it, sir? Is not this place a marvel?'

'I like it well.'

'Master Henslowe has worked wonders and we must repay him with like amazement on the stage itself.'

'Indeed, sir.'

'How many souls will it now encompass?'

'Some four hundred more.'

Firethorn grinned. 'That takes the tally almost to two thousand and a half. Westfield's Men will pack them in to the full number.'

He paraded around. 'But this stage, Nick! This joyous scaffold! I feel as if I could reach out and touch every spectator. Truly a miracle of construction.'

Nicholas had already noted all the improvements. The Rose had been built a few years earlier on the initiative of Philip Henslowe, a former dyer and pawnbroker, and one John Cholmley, a grocer. Used at first for animal-baiting as well as for the performance of plays, the building had undergone extensive alteration during the previous winter. Henslowe had laid out the substantial sum of £105 to enlarge a structure that would henceforth operate exclusively as a theatre. By demolishing a wall at the rear, he was able to move the stage back and produce more standing space in the pit as well as additional seats in the galleries on both sides. The thrust of the acting area was consequently reduced and this made for the sense of intimacy which so impressed Firethorn. It was an architectural paradox. The audience expanded and yet somehow got closer to the performance.

The actor-manager had been quick to assess every last advantage that he could gain onstage but Nicholas was more interested in the improvements behind the scenes. An enlarged backstage area meant a more comfortable tiring-house for the actors and more generous storage space for properties and scenery. Henslowe had wisely created the preconditions for bigger and more ambitious productions. The Rose could compete more effectively with its rivals. After the privations of the Queen's Head, it was a privilege to work in a custom-built theatre and Westfield's Men responded eagerly. *Love's Sacrifice* would not lack spirit.

'Our dear patron graces the occasion,' said Firethorn.

'He will not be displeased.'

'I am in a mood for greatness.'

'Your fellows will not let you down.'

'I'll take them with me to the very heights!'

He declaimed a few lines from the play for effect then made an exit. Nicholas was still smiling as Owen Elias came back over to him. The latter's rage was now muffled beneath a vague sense of guilt.

'I did not mean to speak ill of him, Nick,' he said.

'Of whom?'

'Sebastian. I had reason to hate the man but none to want him cut down so callously. Had he been here, he would have given a good account of Benvolio.' Pride reasserted itself. 'But my performance will be better.'

'It will be different, Owen.'

'Very different, sir, and much better.' His face clouded. 'I must make confession to you. I miss him.'

'Sebastian?'

'Even though I profit from his death, I miss the rogue. Let them hang his murderer on the highest tree in the city.'

'We must catch him first.'

'Is there hope of that?'

'Not yet,' admitted Nicholas. 'But I will persist.'

'Call on me for help.'

It was a sincere offer and the book holder was touched. Sebastian Carrick had borrowed money from the Welshman which he had no intention of repaying. Owen Elias had many reasons to despise an actor who had always been preferred to him yet he was prepared to join in the hunt for the killer. Nicholas was grateful. It made him consider his friend's plight anew.

'Have you conned the lines?' he asked.

'I know that speech by heart.'

'Could you deliver it this afternoon?'

'Master Firethorn has expressly forbidden it.'

'Master Firethorn will be dead.'

'What say you?'

'Benvolio will have no interruption.'

Owen Elias let out a wicked chuckle. He

knew the risk he would be running if he disobeyed Lawrence Firethorn but that did not frighten him in the least. An actor who had been kept back time and again was not going to squander a heaven-sent chance to make his mark. *Love's Sacrifice* might yet enhance his career. He thought of the prostrate figure of Lawrence Firethorn, lying at his feet and powerless to control him. It was a moment that had to be seized and then savoured to the full.

Wild laughter reverberated around The Rose.

Money could purchase most things at the Tower of London. A small bribe to his gaolers had already gained Andrew Carrick relative freedom within the Beauchamp Tower and a slightly larger outlay of coin bought him an occasional release from his prison. The lawyer posed no threat. He was not held for any real crime and would never even try to escape. It was safe to let him wander at will, to visit the chapel for his spiritual needs, to watch the guard being drilled, to climb the south ramparts and gaze down at the busy Thames. It helped to relieve his enforced idleness and gave him a keen insight into the administration of the citadel. A casual stroll always furnished him with valuable information.

Carrick was coming around the angle of the White Tower when he saw them standing outside the main door. They were deep in animated conversation. The portly frame of Harry Fellowes was bent forward in an attitude of deference. The fluttering hands of Roger Godolphin, Earl of Chichester, were expressing an authority that was mixed with gratitude. They formed an interesting double portrait and Carrick studied it with growing curiosity. From random chats with the affable Fellowes, he had gleaned a number of facts about the inner workings of the Ordnance Office. He knew, for instance, that its operations had enlarged dramatically in recent times. During the decade that led up to the Armada year of 1588, the Office had handled, on average, £9,000 per annum. According to Harry Fellowes, that amount had now almost doubled and it was still rising fast. Supplying the army and navy was a vast undertaking. War turned the Ordnance into one of the major spending departments.

Expenditure of another kind was under discussion.

'When will I receive it?' said the Earl. 'There is need for quick dispatch here.'

'I will bring it to Croxley Hall in person, my lord.'

'This afternoon?'

'This evening at the latest,' promised Fellowes.

'You oblige me in this, Harry.'

'I am always your humble servant, my lord.'

'Do not delay in this matter.'

Harry Fellowes bowed his acquiescence then walked with the Earl towards the Tower gate. Their earnest discussion continued. Andrew Carrick had got close enough only to hear faint snatches of what passed between them but the language of body and gesture had been very clear. What surprised him was that the venerable Earl of Chichester had deigned to visit his military depot at all. In his sinewy and grasping old hands, the Mastership of Ordnance had been largely a titular appointment and he was only shaken into action at moments of national emergency. The real work of the Office was done by the Clerk, Surveyor and Lieutenant of Ordnance. Though last in line, Harry Fellowes had boasted more than once that he was, in some sense, first in importance. It made his lively exchange with the Earl of Chichester all the more intriguing. Carrick soon got more elucidation.

'I see the very man!'

'Good day, Master Fellowes.'

'I have need of that favour, sir.'

'Ask it,' said Carrick. 'It shall be granted.'

Having seen the Earl off the premises, Harry Fellowes was retracing his steps towards the White Tower. The sight of the lawyer brought a flabby smile to his face and he reached for a paper that was concealed inside his cloak.

'I require the signature of an attorney at law.'

'Even when he is a prisoner?'

'A legal quibble, sir.' They traded a laugh. 'Will you aid me in this business, Master Carrick?'

'Gladly, sir. What document must I witness?'

'One that may presently liberate you from your cell.'

'I will sign it at once.'

'This paper contains the terms of a loan.'

'Between yourself and the Earl of Chichester?'

'You are very observant,' said Fellowes with a smirk. 'The details need not concern you but this you may be told. My loan and your signature may bring us both advantage.'

Andrew Carrick followed him with willing steps.

★ ★ ★

A fine day, a fanfare of playbills and the ever-increasing fame of Lawrence Firethorn brought a large audience hurrying to The Rose. Gatherers collected the money at the doors then ushered the spectators through into the theatre. Standees soon crowded the pit and the benches in the galleries were filled with equal enthusiasm. The whole theatre buzzed with a hum of expectation. Westfield's Men were held in high regard and there was no better place to display their wares than at this inspiring playhouse in Southwark.

Lord Westfield timed his own arrival to gain maximum effect, sweeping into his cushioned chair in the upper gallery amid his usual entourage and acknowledging the sporadic applause that broke out by waving a gloved hand. A new play by his beloved company was not to be missed but the sybaritic patron was not there simply to lend tacit support. He expected to reap his share of the harvest of praise. Lord Westfield was not a man to hide his light under a bushel. He was more inclined to let it blaze in the afternoon sun. It was the one certain way to annoy and frustrate the Earl of Banbury.

Anne Hendrik also took her place on the benches. Since the theatre was virtually on her doorstep, she had willingly accepted her

125

lodger's invitation to come along and she had brought Preben van Loew with her. The Dutchman, an impassive character of middle years, was her most skilful hat-maker and he affected an almost puritanical distaste for the theatre but his presence lent her respectability and guaranteed her safety. As on previous occasions — Anne felt sure — her employee would end up enjoying the play hugely while doing his best to disguise the fact. She herself had been given a specific task by Nicholas Bracewell. He had contrived a series of special effects for *Love's Sacrifice* and needed a pair of eyes in the auditorium. Anne Hendrik was there to be entertained and to sit in judgement. Handsomely dressed for the event, she looked incongruous beside the dark apparel of her laconic companion but she was used to this situation.

A new play imposed additional responsibilities on the company. It was like fighting a battle with untried weapons. They might taste glorious victory or ignominious defeat. Only when they set their verse on its first cavalry charge into the ears of its spectators could they gauge the possible success of the encounter. In a world of swirling fashion, nothing was certain. Plots and themes which had held sway one month could become tedious the next. Characters who impressed

126

in one piece could find they had no life outside it. Novelty was in request but its precise nature shifted all the time. Westfield's Men hoped that *Love's Sacrifice* would come through unscathed but they could not predict it with any confidence. In the heat of war, strange things could happen. For this reason, the tiring-house was pervaded by an even greater degree of nervous excitement than usual. Players and playwright alike were fearful lest there should be heavy casualties.

It was at times like this that Nicholas Bracewell and Lawrence Firethorn came into their own. The book holder was a calming presence with a comforting smile while the actor-manager was an impatient general who was eager to lead the first attack. They put heart into the entire company and even Edmund Hoode's faith in the play was restored. He had followed his usual practice of writing a cameo for himself that showed off his not inconsiderable talent as an actor. Barnaby Gill lapsed into his customary testiness and made useless last-minute complaints about the size and scope of his role. Collectively and individually, the company was going down some well-trodden paths.

Lawrence Firethorn then diverged from them. As the moment of truth drew near and the excitement spiralled even higher, he twitched the curtain to get a brief glimpse of his latest audience. It was a fateful action. A sea of faces came into view but he saw only one of them. She was seated in the middle of the lower gallery with a poise that set her completely apart from the jostling bodies all around her. A heart-shaped face of inexpressible beauty was framed by black hair that swept upwards and vanished into a most enchanting feathered hat. The dark velvet dress and the white ruff only served to highlight the marmoreal loveliness of an exceptional young woman but the most arresting feature of all was her eyes. Dark and proud, they invested her whole being with a fiery disdain that made Lawrence Firethorn grin inanely. He had an even greater incentive to lead his troops into battle now.

True love beckoned. Conquest was imperative.

Owen Elias was as taut as a lute-string but nowhere near as melodious. Sitting in a corner of the tiring-house, he tried to work up his concentration for the important task in hand and he brooked no interruption. An apprentice who nudged him by mistake and an assistant stagekeeper who brushed past him by accident both felt the sting of his tongue. The irascible Welshman was feeling

128

the strain. Nicholas Bracewell took note of this and drifted across to him for a quiet word.

'Have no fears, Owen,' he said. 'You will excel.'

'There is no doubting that,' said the other with a touch of his old bravado. 'Benvolio will rescue me from this oblivion in which they keep me. I will prove myself as fit a man as any in the company.'

'Then why the long face?'

'Because of Sebastian.'

'You feel guilt?'

'And sadness, Nick. When all my hatred of the man is put aside, I must acknowledge that this was his part. Benvolio was written with Sebastian in mind.'

'Serve his memory by playing the part well.'

'I will, sir.'

'He would expect no less of you, Owen.'

'Indeed.' He resorted to a whisper. 'As to the last speech in the play . . .'

Nicholas winked. 'That must be your decision.'

Owen Elias grinned and felt more confident about what lay ahead. There was no more time to deliberate because a dozen bells were chiming out the hour in the vicinity of the theatre. It was two o'clock and Nicholas

Bracewell was in position. With the chimes still echoing, he gave the signal and the performance started. Music was played from above and the Prologue stepped out in a black cloak to acquaint the audience with the mood and matter of the play.

Love oftentimes exacts too high a price,
For no man loves without some sacrifice.
Dan Cupid may be Venus's only joy
But he can be a cruel and wanton boy
Who shoots his arrows far and wide at
  will.
Trying to wound, he oft contrives to kill.
Such is our case here . . .

Having relayed the plot in rhyming couplets, Edmund Hoode brought his protagonist bursting on to the stage in a torrent of blank verse. Gondar was angry and no actor could express royal ire like Lawrence Firethorn. With underlings trailing at his heels, he raged and ranted until the whole audience was cowed by his majesty. He wore only a saffron robe over a simple tunic but he was every inch a king as he berated his guards for the unkind treatment of the captured Queen Elsin. Magnanimous in victory and with his own strict code of honour, he sent for his beautiful prisoner to release her from the shackles that bound her and to offer his heart-felt apologies. It was the first meeting between them and it robbed them of all hostility towards each other. Courtship began from the second they laid eyes upon each other. The howling Gondar became a tender and considerate lover.

Never less than remarkable in any part, Firethorn had found one that drew a towering performance out of him. Long before the First Act came to a close, the spectators had surrendered to him with the same willingness as the queen and he wooed them with a range of voice and gesture that was irresistible. Richard Honeydew was a wholly convincing Elsin with a wan loveliness that was only increased by adversity. As the actor-manager soared, the young apprentice responded well and their love took flight.

Firethorn slowly pushed out the frontiers of his art. He was not just giving a superb account of himself in a fine play, he was dedicating his talents to a particular person. The fine phrases that he showered upon his queen were really aimed at the inscrutable beauty in the middle of the lower gallery, the eloquent movements were a dance of desire to ensnare her interest. But whenever he stole a glance at the object of his passion, she remained calm and uninvolved. This

131

drove him on to even more sublime heights but she still refused to show obeisance before her king. Black eyes hardly flickered in an impassive face. He was acting at someone who seemed to have a heart of stone.

And yet she was not indifferent. Her attention did not wander and her interest did not slacken. *Love's Sacrifice* got the same level gaze throughout. It held her without moving her. The Rose bestowed its wonder on Lawrence Firethorn. The intimacy on which he commented earlier allowed him — in his mind's eye — to reach out and touch her a hundred times. Indeed, his wooing of Queen Elsin became a gentle fondling of the mysterious creature in the audience. When he had done this with other female spectators, they had usually succumbed to his charms with gushing readiness but he had signally failed on this occasion. That failure only sharpened the edge of his desire and turned up the flame of his already crackling performance. When he and his star-crossed queen lay dead together at the end of the play, a communal groan of horror went up. Gondar had been the epitome of military honour and courtly love. His fall was the stuff of tragedy.

The play was not yet over. As the soldiers stood around the royal corpses, the actor who had been such a mesmerizing Benvolio held up his hands to command silence. When he had drawn out the pause to its full, agonizing length, he used sonorous tones to deliver a speech that had been cut during the rehearsal. Lawrence Firethorn stiffened and let out a growl of disapproval from beyond the grave but Benvolio would not be deflected. The still, sad music of his voice was a fitting epitaph for the doomed lovers.

Adieu, sweet friends, and take thy praise
  to heaven,
Embrace that joy for which you both have
  striven.

Benvolio shed a real tear then motioned in the soldiers to load the bodies on to their respective biers. As the pair were borne out with due solemnity, King Gondar half-opened an eye to catch a fleeting glimpse of the lower gallery. The exercise was a painful one. For the first time in the whole afternoon, his inamorata was visibly moved. Sadness crumpled her face and she brought a hand up to her mouth. In one brief and unscheduled elegy, Owen Elias had achieved what Firethorn — with a hundred speeches — had failed to do. It was galling. The actor-manager bristled posthumously.

Once offstage, he abdicated his kingship to direct a string of foul oaths at his colleague but his imprecations were muffled by the avalanche of applause that tumbled down on their ears. Postponing his fury, he put on his most imperious smile and led out his company to take their bow. *Love's Sacrifice* was an unqualified success, a superb account of a brilliant new play that was set to take pride of place in the company's repertoire. Though feeding greedily on the ovation, Lawrence Firethorn was interested in only two people in the auditorium. His most obsequious bow went to the delighted Lord Westfield and a more cavalier flourish was aimed at the lower gallery. While his patron responded with frantic clapping, however, the dark lady of his fantasies gave him no more than a level stare. It was enough. The desire which had steadily grown throughout the last two hours now blossomed into complete infatuation.

The spectators clapped, cheered and stamped their feet for minutes on end but one of them declined to join in. He was a tall, saturnine figure who had sat in discomfort all afternoon as the drama's excellence was unfolded and as Firethorn's primacy was reinforced yet again. His visit to The Rose had been redeemed in the closing speech.

Twenty lines of verse had made him look with intense curiosity at Owen Elias and bank down his envy. As an idea began to form in the recesses of his mind, the man even managed a smile. *Love's Sacrifice* had given him a potent weapon to use against his rival.

Giles Randolph was content.

Nicholas Bracewell was on hand to protect his friend from verbal abuse. Before Firethorn could even begin his attack on Owen Elias, the book holder stepped in to congratulate the actor-manager on his performance and to smother him with fulsome praise. It blunted the edge of Firethorn's rage somewhat but that was all it did.

'God's blood!' roared the actor. 'Are you mad, Owen?'

'Me, sir?' said the other.

'Are you blind? Are you deaf? Are you insensible?'

'No, Master Firethorn.'

'When I die, the play has ended.'

'Save for that last speech, sir.'

'It was cut, man!'

Mock innocence. 'Was it even so?'

'It was excised from the play. So should *you* be, you scurvy rogue, you canting villain, you Welsh dung-heap!'

'Take heed,' warned the other, smarting

at the insult. 'Do not insult my nation.'

'Wales is an insult in itself!' howled Firethorn. 'It breeds nothing but lechers and thieves. Show me a Welshman and you show me a foul, ugly, leek-faced barbarian. You stole my moment of supreme glory, you dog-breathed Judas!'

Owen Elias turned puce with anger and Nicholas had to jump in quickly to calm both men and to stop the argument from getting out of hand. He diverted the blame to himself by admitting that it was his suggestion to include the final speech but he insisted that it in no way infringed the greatness of Firethorn's performance. The crowded tiring-house was voluble in its agreement, as eager as the book holder to prevent a violent confrontation. It was Barnaby Gill who ended the row with a malicious whisper.

'Let *her* be the judge, Lawrence,' he said.

'Who?'

'Mistress Black Eyes. Ask her if she would cut those lines of Benvolio's. I fancy she would not.'

'The devil take you, sir!'

During this short exchange, Nicholas seized the chance to usher Owen Elias over to the far side of the tiring-house where he was hidden by a rack of costumes. When Firethorn turned back to them, they were gone.

With his mind now fixed on a higher priority, he glared around for assistance. It came in the shape of George Dart who was staggering past with an armful of props. Firethorn's hand gripped his collar like an eagle fastening its talons on its prey.

'George Dart!'

'Yes, master?' gibbered the other.

'Find out her name.'

'Whose name, sir?'

'*Her* name.'

Firethorn's strong hand lifted him from the ground and swung him round to face the drawn curtain. Twitching it back a few inches, he pointed to the goddess in the lower gallery.

'Do you see her now, George?'

'Yes, sir. No, sir.' He was baffled. 'Which is she, sir?'

'That creature without compare.'

'You lose me, sir.'

'*There,* imbecile!'

He boxed George Dart's ears so hard that the boy let go of his cargo and it fell to the boards with a clatter. The pointing finger of his employer, the hissed description and the threat of more pain combined to identify the lady in question for the squirming stagekeeper. As soon as he was released, he went scuttling off about his business.

Lawrence Firethorn wanted action.

It was a quiet funeral. No more than a dozen people were gathered together in the small churchyard in Islington to see the last remains of Sebastian Carrick laid to rest. Light drizzle made a sombre occasion even more depressing. The priest's incantations were a barely audible murmur. Grief was expressed in gentle sobbing. Nicholas Bracewell watched it all with a muted distress that was increased by an ironic observation. The stage management of the event was at fault. Sebastian Carrick deserved a more central role on a much larger stage. An actor whose life and work was a hymn to exuberance was now slipping out of the world in furtive silence. Damp soil waited to take him beyond applause.

The drizzle and the drone continued.

'Forasmuch as it hath pleased Almighty God of his great mercy to take unto himself the soul of our dear brother here departed, we therefore commit his body to the ground; earth to earth, ashes to ashes, dust to dust; in sure and certain hope of the Resurrection to eternal life, through our Lord Jesus Christ; who shall change our vile body, that it may be like unto his glorious body . . .'

The words floated into his ears to give

Nicholas a mild sting. He thought of the hideous corpse he had seen laid out on its cold slab. A vile body indeed. Its head was split asunder. Its limbs were bruised. Its back was a blood-red signature on a death warrant.

He glanced around the mourning family, relieved that none of them had been forced to see their beloved Sebastian in his final incarnation. Their memories of a handsome and dashing young man would be untarnished. No parents were present. The mother had long since died and the father was detained elsewhere. Not even the influence of Lord Westfield had been able to release Andrew Carrick from the Tower of London in order to attend the funeral of his only son. The lawyer was keeping a silent vigil in his cell. This meant that the principal mourner was Marion Carrick, younger sister of the deceased, supported by an uncle, an aunt, a few cousins and an old maidservant.

Edmund Hoode had come along with Nicholas to represent the company. They were pleasantly surprised when Owen Elias attached himself to the fringe of mourners. He had come to pay his respects to a man with whom he had many differences in life. It was a worthy gesture. When the coffin vanished beneath a thin layer of earth, the funeral party began to disperse in subdued bewilderment. Nicholas Bracewell was moving away with Edmund Hoode when there was a tug at his sleeve. He turned to view the pallid loveliness of Marion Carrick who was dressed in seemly black.

'I must thank you, Master Bracewell,' she said.

'We are sorry to intrude upon your grief.'

'Sebastian's friends are welcome, sir, and he counted you as one of his best friends. My father wrote to tell me of your consideration in this grim affair. We are indebted to you. It will not be forgotten.'

'Your brother was an excellent fellow,' said Nicholas. 'He will be fondly remembered by Westfield's Men.'

'Indeed, he will,' added Edmund Hoode.

'Thank you, sirs.'

Marion Carrick was a neat young woman of middle height with a restrained beauty that was not chased away by evident sorrow. She had none of her brother's extravagance and yet her charm was almost equal. Anguish lifted for a second to allow a flash of anger to show.

'This was a most heinous crime,' she snapped.

'It shall be answered,' said Nicholas.

'May we count on your help, Master Bracewell?'

'I will not rest until the matter is settled.'

'This wounds me to the quick. I loved Sebastian with all my heart. I could kill the murderer with my own hands.'

'He will be brought to justice, Mistress Carrick.'

'I trust you to fulfil that promise, sir.'

'It is a most solemn oath.'

Even before he attended the funeral, Nicholas Bracewell was pledged to hunt down the man who had wielded the fatal axe. That pledge now took on new force and urgency. The plea from Marion Carrick had given it a spiritual dimension. He stood beside the grave as a dear friend and colleague. When he walked away, he was a man with a mission.

Chapter Six

Cornelius Gant and his ever-obedient Nimbus were seasoned professionals who knew how to adjust their act to the needs of their spectators. The Falcon Inn at Uxbridge was a small and rather decrepit establishment which stood on the edge of the village and which was patronized by the lower sort. When Gant rode up on his horse, he saw that the company was too poor to offer much remuneration, too coarse to want subtlety and too drunk to cope with entertainment of any length. It was time for 'The Saga of the Six Buckets'.

'Place them here, friend,' said Gant, indicating the spot with a finger. 'Set them in a line, two paces apart.'

One of the drawers had come out to help him, putting the three full buckets of water in position first before adding the three empty wooden pails. Beer-sodden locals trailed out into the yard with noisy curiosity. The glowering landlord watched through a window. A couple of mangy dogs crept up. It was an uninspiring group but it was nevertheless an audience and the performers responded accordingly.

Gant began by doffing his hat while he made a bow then got his first laugh as Nimbus sent him flying by swinging a flank against his owner's exposed rump. The horse did a form of curtsey by way of apology and the spectators roared with appreciation. Gant and the animal went through some more by-play until the guffawing rustics were thoroughly warmed up. The next bow was in unison with the curtsey.

'Gentlemen,' announced Gant, 'we present a little drama entitled "The Saga of The Six Buckets". You see them before you and I now give each of them a number.' He started with the full pails and kicked each one as he walked past. 'One — two — three — four — five — six. Remember those numbers, I beseech you. Nimbus will remind you what they are.'

The horse did so with well-rehearsed aplomb, giving the first bucket one kick, the second bucket two and so on up to the sixth bucket which received six taps with the hoof. To prove that it was no accident, Nimbus then went through the buckets in reverse order to check off their numbers. The applause was mixed with cheers and whistles. Cornelius Gant used raised palms to quell the beery tumult.

'You have seen nothing yet, good sirs,' he warned with a roguish wink. 'We will now show you a feat of conjuration. Standing in front of you are three full buckets — one, two and three; with three empty buckets — four, five and six.'

'What's the trick?' called out one of the locals.

'To make water move by magic,' said Gant. 'Without stirring from this spot, I will empty the full buckets and I will fill the empty ones. Can such a thing be done?'

'Never!' came the first cry.

'Impossible!' yelled another.

'Only witchcraft could do that!' howled a third.

'No witchcraft,' promised Gant. 'Only the Eighth Wonder of the World — Nimbus. Mark, gentlemen. "The Saga of The Six Buckets" is about to begin.'

He was standing some ten feet away from the pails and remained motionless throughout the act. Nimbus waited for his cue, his eyes never leaving his master. Gant reminded the audience of the number that each bucket bore then he snapped his first command.

'One!'

Nimbus sunk its nose into the first bucket and began to slurp away. The water level

144

sank visibly. When a half had been drunk, Gant altered the command.

'Three!'

The same treatment was accorded to the third bucket. Gant then sent his horse back to the first, on to the second and on to the third once more. It slaked an almighty thirst at a quite alarming speed and the audience was enraptured. Awe soon turned to vulgar amusement.

'Four!'

Nimbus pulled its nose out of the water and straddled the bucket next in line before urinating straight into it with remarkable precision. It produced wild hilarity.

'Five!'

The animal seemed to have an endless supply that it could turn on and off like a tap. Steam rose from the fifth bucket and the hilarity shaded into hysteria.

'It is an old trick,' said Gant, 'but I'll venture to stale it once more.' They hooted at the pun. 'Six!'

Nimbus obliged once more then gave a ladylike curtsey. Three full buckets of water now stood empty and three empty buckets were now brimming. Gant held out his hat to collect the coins that were thrown then he snatched it away as Nimbus pretended to relieve himself into the haul. There was

145

free ale for the visitor that evening and free hay for his horse. Both slept soundly in the same stable.

As they left at dawn next morning, Cornelius Gant cursed the poor quality of the company and the even poorer quality of the ale. They deserved better. The journey to London was in the nature of a social ascent for them. They came from the most humble and degrading circumstances. By working so long and so hard together, they had fought their way out of their misery to create a promise of better things. Gant had come to despise his origins and did not care to be reminded of them in the way that he had been at the Falcon Inn. He owned a remarkable horse who could ensure their fame and fortune if handled properly. Nimbus would not have to debase his talents again in the way that the rustics had compelled and Gant gave him an apologetic slap to reinforce the point.

'One day we'll play before the Queen,' he said proudly. 'You'll not fill buckets for Her Majesty. But when we take London by storm, we'll be able to piss gold!'

Two more days of cancelled public appearances confirmed many suspicions and inflamed much debate. Queen Elizabeth was seriously ill. None of her physicians was ready to admit this openly but none could be found to deny it absolutely. Their silence was disturbing. Equally revealing was the brusque attitude of Burghley, the Lord Treasurer, a wise old statesman whose long partnership with his sovereign had been largely responsible for the stability of her government. A man of great judgement and with a rare ability to master the complex issues of the day, Lord Burghley was a person whose high sense of duty was tinged with real affection for his Queen. She, in turn, relied upon his acumen and his sagacity. It was no wonder that she called him "my Spirit" for his counsel informed nearly all that she said or did. When this paragon remained tight-lipped, therefore, trouble was very definitely in the wind. When a supreme politician like Burghley was for once bereft of words, then he sensed the death of his own career as well. Now over seventy, racked by gout, he was on the verge of extinction.

The woman at the centre of the crisis did nothing to dispel it. Locked in her private apartments and enclosed by a wall of secrecy, she dwindled towards a death that seemed more inevitable with each new day. The passing of any monarch was a cause for national mourning but the imminent demise of Queen

Elizabeth would be a tragedy of far greater moment. Her rule had produced one of the finest and most fruitful periods in her country's history, at once over-shadowing what came before and giving promise to what lay ahead. When she went, a potent symbol of England's glory would fade away. Nobody could replace her but the need to have a successor in readiness now became even more pressing.

The Earl of Banbury sought elucidation on the matter.

'How do we stand, sir?' he said.

'In good order. Negotiations have been started and they have already brought in good results.'

'Do we have firm promises?'

'Firm promises from stout fellows. Powerful names are supporting our cause. Others will follow in their wake.'

'Then money has been well-spent.'

'Favours of all kinds have been used to effect.'

Banbury was ruthless. 'We must stop at *nothing* here.'

'Nor shall we,' said his companion grimly.

They were standing in the dining room at Croxley Hall. Roger Godolphin, Earl of Chichester, was playing host to his inner circle of friends. First to arrive was the Earl of Banbury who was eager to know what progress their schemes had made. Some of the most influential members of the court had declared their support and he nodded with satisfaction as their names were listed. Others gave tacit approval to the machinations without committing themselves to the risk of direct involvement. It was the Earl of Chichester's last campaign and he was determined to be on the winning side. They had chosen the next sovereign and now faced the far more daunting task of securing the succession.

'Have letters been exchanged?' asked Banbury eagerly.

'You will see them all, sir.'

'The strength of our loyalty is fully understood?'

'Do not fear,' said the old soldier, tossing his silver mane. 'We will receive ample recompense from the throne.'

'You must speak in person to the heir.'

'I depart from London tomorrow.'

'Nothing should be left to chance, Roger.'

'That is why I will take you on the long journey.'

'My help is yours to call upon.'

'There is another reason why you must ride with me.'

'Well?'

'Your presence has been requested.'

The Earl of Banbury gave a smile of self-congratulation that graduated into a full-blown chuckle. Next day, on the vital embassy north, he would not simply be there to lend his weight to the Master of Ordnance. He would be answering a direct summons by the new monarch. It was a sign.

A restorative night in the arms of Anne Hendrik helped to sustain him throughout a long day. Nicholas Bracewell had no time to rest in the service of Westfield's Men. His work began early with the erection of the stage in the yard at the Queen's Head. The rehearsal of *Black Antonio* occupied him for most of the morning and it left him with a fund of problems to solve before the performance that afternoon. A letter then arrived for him by messenger and he took time off to unseal it. As he did so, a small silver object fell out and only the speed of his hand saved it from landing on the ground. It was a tiny picture of Sebastian Carrick in a silver frame and it touched off some more painful memories for him. The miniature was the work of a mediocre artist but it offered an acceptable likeness of its subject and caught something of his suave vitality. Nicholas saw that the letter was from Marion

Carrick who put practical help before a cloying bereavement. Hoping that the miniature might be of assistance to him, she enjoined the book holder to take especial care of something which was even more precious to her now that her brother was dead. He accepted the charge willingly and was grateful to her.

Lawrence Firethorn now became his major anxiety. After his triumph at The Rose, the actor had at least managed to learn the name of his new beloved — Beatrice Capaldi — and he had been repeating it to himself ever since in a variety of sweet tones. Unfortunately, her name was all that George Dart had been able to glean, except for the fact that she was a lady of some distinction with a coach in attendance. As was his wont in such matters, Firethorn brought Nicholas into action, urging him to mark and track the mystery figure on her next appearance in the audience. But that appearance had not as yet been made. Though Firethorn selected two plays which showed him off to best advantage — *The Loyal Subject* and *Pompey the Great* — she did not watch either and he was left in ruins. *Black Antonio* was a third offering aimed directly at her and he was confident that she would this time be drawn to view his genius. But the play waxed for two whole hours without eliciting one minute of interest from the Mistress Beatrice Capaldi.

Lawrence Firethorn was plunged into desolation.

'Where *is* she, Nick?' he implored.

'I wish I knew, sir.'

'Why must she punish me in this way?'

'Haply, she is detained elsewhere.'

'How much longer must I suffer?'

'Put her out of your mind,' said the book holder.

A gargantuan sigh. 'But she fills it so completely. I am half the man I was when she is not here.'

It was true. Roles in which Firethorn customarily shone had been played with little more than competence. Three times in a row he had disappointed a following which had come to expect Olympian standards from him. Nicholas was distinctly alarmed. The roving lust of Lawrence Firethorn always had an invigorating effect on his performances but this latest fancy was having a destructive impact. A hideous truth had to be faced. Firethorn was in love. Westfield's Men were bearing the brunt of this phenomenon.

'I want my Beatrice!' wailed the actor.

'We have no means of reaching her, sir.'

'Help me, Nick. Track this temptress down.'

'She may already have quit London.'

'Perish the thought!' cried Firethorn in anguish. 'If that be so then I am shipwrecked. There must be a way to bring her back to me. There has to be a key to unlock her ice-cold heart so that it will admit me. Be my saviour yet again, Nick. Where is that way? What is that key?'

'Play *Love's Sacrifice* once more.'

It was a random suggestion but it transformed Firethorn in a flash. His body stiffened, his chest swelled, his face coloured, his eyes sparkled, his hope was a tidal wave that washed all before it. The drama which had brought him and Beatrice Capaldi together would be the agency of their reunion. Though it was not due to be staged again for over a week, he would change the agreed programme in order to put *Love's Sacrifice* on as soon as possible. Nicholas proffered the advice in all innocence. He was not to know how much potential damage he had just done to Westfield's Men.

'I love you for this, Nick,' said Firethorn warmly.

'Thank you, sir.'

'Beatrice Capaldi! She has Italian blood, I warrant. Hot Italian blood that courses through her veins.'

'Do not build on vain fantasies.'

'Oh, I could kiss you for this, you lovely bawcock!'

'Forbear, Lawrence,' said the eavesdropping Barnaby Gill with a grimace. 'My lips are already spoken for, good sir!'

Nicholas left the two of them arguing in the taproom and stole quickly away. While his employer was desperate to trace one object of desire, the book holder went in search for another. His unknown woman was no Beatrice Capaldi, no lady of quality with a hard beauty that could enchant and ensnare. She was a common whore in the stews of Clerkenwell and she had given one of her clients a signature that he had taken to his grave. Nicholas saw those rivulets once more and was doubly grateful that the sight had been kept from the already distraught Marion Carrick.

Armed with the miniature of the victim, he went back into the lanes that he had already tramped on the previous nights. All the establishments drew him gladly in but his welcome evaporated when it was seen that he was no customer in search of a punk. He was reviled, he was threatened, he was forcibly ejected but he bore it all with equanimity, moving on to the next brothel to continue his investigation. None of the trulls recognized the portrait but a few of the more high-class courtesans claimed to have known him. When and where they had last seen him, however, they could not recall because their brains were too addled by drink and their apprehensions too dulled by the nature of their calling. Before Nicholas could coax out more detail, he was usually expelled by a brutish landlord or a watchful madame.

Another long, taxing and frustrating night finally took him into the Pickt-hatch. Bess Bidgood wobbled her charms at him and he put coin into her hand to buy himself drink and time. Nicholas was in a small, low, smoke-filled room with a dozen or more other men who lolled at tables as they were blandished by the resident whores. As soon as the newcomer sat down on a bench, two young women came to perch either side of him with grinning familiarity. He bought them a drink, pretended to respond to their attentions and worked slowly to win their confidence. One of them planted a kiss on his cheek and told him the Pickt-hatch was the most celebrated house of resort in the district.

'I come upon recommendation,' said Nick.

'Who sent you, sir?' asked one girl.

'Did he mention Peg?' said the other. ' 'Tis me.'

'My brother sent me here.'

Peg giggled. 'With two like you, we could both be well-satisfied. You are a pretty piece of flesh, sir.'

'Let me show you my brother . . .'

'He is here?'

'I have his likeness.'

Nicholas produced the miniature and held it up to the candle. The two women squinted at it before making ribald comments. One of them had never seen the face before and the other only had the dimmest recollection of the man but they were both keen to help. Before Nicholas could stop her, Peg snatched the portrait and lurched across to one of the tables to show it to her colleagues. There were more coarse remarks and a few vague memories but none could put a name to the face or locate it at the Pickt-hatch on the night in question. One girl — a sinuous creature in red — stared at the miniature for a long time before shaking her head and tossing it back to Nicholas. Denying all knowledge of one client, Frances was soon luring another up to her room.

Peg tried to entice Nicholas up to her own bed but he feigned a stupor and staggered out to continue his quest elsewhere. Retracing the steps of Sebastian Carrick was proving to be a demoralizing exercise and he knew that he could never divulge any of his nocturnal activities to the trusting sister. Marion had sent him a mission whose true nature would distress her beyond measure if she ever found out what it really was. For her sake, he must press on. For her sake — and that of her brother — he had to persevere in his grisly work in the hope that it would finally deliver up a vile murderer.

He was about to knock on the door of the neighbouring premises when he heard a stealthy tread behind him. Nicholas turned just in time. A sturdy figure came out of the dark with an arm raised to strike. His victim moved his head sharply but the club caught him a glancing blow on the temple that made his senses reel. Nicholas tottered a few steps then fell into a pool of liquid offal with a splash. He had enough presence of mind left to cover his head from further attack but it never came. Voices were raised nearby and all that he had to suffer was a vicious kick in the ribs before his assailant took to his heels. Nicholas rolled over in pain and shook his head to try to clear it. A lantern was held over him and four curious eyes surveyed the damage.

'Master Bracewell, is it not?' said a voice.

'Indeed, it is,' confirmed another. 'Bless my soul!'

'We came upon you just in time, sir.'

Nicholas had no breath left to thank the two watchmen but he recognized them both and was eternally thankful for their arrival. Josiah Taplow and William Merryweather had prevented another murder in Clerkenwell. As the old men helped him up from the ground, Nicholas felt an odd sense of elation. Someone had tried to kill him but the man had given himself away in doing so. The night had finally yielded its reward. Nicholas Bracewell was getting close.

In an Eastcheap tavern, Cornelius Gant was also learning about London after dark. It was his first visit to the capital and he was still trying to come to terms with the sheer size of the city. By comparison with the towns in his native Cumberland, it was overpowering in its vastness. Every stage of his journey had provided a new source of fascination. He had seen huntsmen in Hyde Park, dead bodies dangling from the gibbet at Tyburn, cows grazing contentedly in St Giles with the mansions of the mighty spearing the sky in the distance alongside the broad Thames, the rambling inns of Holborn and the massive city wall that rose to a height of eighteen feet and wrapped its brawny arms protectively around the capital. As Gant and Nimbus entered through Newgate, they found fresh wonders to transfix them at every turn. Houses, shops, taverns and ordinaries jostled for position beside imposing civic buildings. Street markets turned major thoroughfares into swirling maelstroms. Noise was deafening, smells were pungent. Churches abounded in every ward but all were dwarted by the majestic bulk of St Paul's Cathedral. The Tower was a spectacle in itself.

After spending the day absorbing it all, Cornelius Gant was passing the night at the Feathers. While Nimbus rested in his stable, his master joined the company in the taproom to sample the ale and sound out his chances. With money to spend, he soon bought himself voluble drinking companions.

'And what of entertainment, sirs?' asked Gant.

'London has all that a man could wish,' said one of his new-found friends. 'We've taverns to refresh him, executions to amuse him, stews to supply him with good sport.'

'What may this man see for further diversion?'

'Whipping, branding and vile treatment in the pillory.'

'I have heard tell of bear-baiting.'

'Southwark will bait you a bear or a bull,' said the other with an oily grin. 'And you may wager on the outcome if your purse is deep enough. There are also houses where dog will eat dog or where cocks will fight to the death.'

'Are there no animals that do tricks?' said Gant.

'Why, yes,' said his guide knowledgeably. 'There is no marvel that London has not seen. We have had a fish that talked, a cat that sang, an ape that did somersaults to order and a camel that danced a jig. One old sailor even taught a snake to play on a set of pipes. It is all here.'

'Do you have a horse that can fly?'

'There is no such animal.'

'London has never witnessed this miracle?'

'Never, sir.'

'It will,' said Gant with a smile. 'It will.'

'Hold still!' she chided softly. 'I must bathe the wound before I can bind it up for you. Do not shake your head so. Be patient for a while longer.'

'I want no bandage around my head,' said Nicholas.

'You will have what I decree,' decided Anne Hendrik with affectionate firmness. 'And you will take more care next time you walk through Clerkenwell.'

'But I found what I sought, Anne.'

'A broken crown and a bloody face?'

'That was a small price to pay.'

'You might have endured far worse if the watchmen had not disturbed your assailant.' She kissed him on the cheek. 'Take no chances, Nick. Think on those who care for you.'

'I do.'

He squeezed her hand then let her finish her work. The blow on his head had opened up a long cut on his temple and sent a dark bruise looping down the side of his face like a crescent. His wound looked far worse than it felt but he submitted to her tender ministrations and let her bandage away. He also let her put his soiled clothes into a washtub to soak. Anne was shocked when he first returned home in such a condition. That shock had now given way to an anxiety that was tinged with a faint jealousy.

'Who is this young lady with the miniature?'

'Marion Carrick is his sister.'

'I know that. But why do you jump to her command?'

'It was an entreaty,' he explained. 'Over the very grave of her brother, she asked me to find his killer. I could not refuse such an appeal.'

'That is clear, sir.'

'Why have you become so cold towards me?'

'I?' she said coldly. 'You are mistaken.'

'Not as mistaken as you, I think.'

Anne turned away. 'I am deeply sorry for what happened to her brother but that gives her no rights over you.' She let her irritation build before she blurted out her protest. 'I would not have you lose your life over a pretty face.'

'Nor shall I,' said Nicholas, taking her in his arms to pull her close. 'Not as long as I have a far prettier face waiting for me back at my lodging.'

He stilled her with a kiss and they were reconciled. Anne now voiced her real concern over the dangers that he faced but he calmed her. It was at moments like this — when he was injured or late home — that she realized just how much he had come to mean in her life. His was a warm and unobtrusive presence in the house but she never took him for granted. Much as she wanted a vicious murderer to be brought to justice, she did not want to risk the life of Nicholas Bracewell to achieve that end. It vexed her greatly.

'Come, Anne,' he consoled. 'Put away your fear. I have troubles enough without all this to tax me.'

'Troubles enough?'

'Master Firethorn is in love.'

'With his wife, it is to be hoped.'

'With the long-suffering Margery, to be sure,' he said. 'But she has travelled to Cambridge and left her husband unchecked. He is not a man who should have such freedom.'

'His wandering eye has wandered once more?'

'This lady could prove a most perilous adventure.'

'Who is the creature?'

'Mistress Beatrice Capaldi. All I know of her is her name and his extravagant report.' Nicholas clicked his tongue. 'If he would stay true to his acting, he could rule the world. But he falters. This new love of his could lead him ruinously astray.'

'Is she as beautiful as Mistress Carrick?'

'Why do you ask that?'

'Simple curiosity.'

'I hear an edge in your voice.'

'Is she or is she not?' pressed Anne.

Nicholas gave her a smile of tender sincerity.

'Both of them pale beside you . . ."

His head pounded away as she embraced him afresh but it was a pain he was happy to suffer in such a worthy cause.

Time which had already hung heavy now

163

pressed down upon him with cruel force. Andrew Carrick found life in the Tower of London even more oppressive. His cell seemed to shrink in size. Its atmosphere grew staler, its voice more hostile. During nights that stretched out to interminable lengths, he lay on his rough bed and reflected on the misery of his lot. Because he attended a wedding, he was unable to go to a funeral. Because he offended a dying queen, he could not pay his respects to a dead son. It was a running sore in his mind and it would not heal. The lawyer took every opportunity that he could to leave his cell and prowl the stairs. When he could bribe his way out into the fresh air, it was a merciful release for him.

Harry Fellowes knew something of his distress and went out of his way to offer sympathy. Carrick seized gratefully on the chance of conversation.

'How fares Her Majesty?' he said.

'The situation is bleak,' replied Fellowes.

'What do her physicians report?'

'They will not disclose the truth of her condition.'

'A bad sign indeed.'

'We must be prepared for the worst.'

Fellowes lightened the exchange by retailing bits of gossip about affairs of the day and he even coaxed a few smiles out of his friend. Carrick was quite intrigued by the plump and loquacious Clerk of Ordnance. The more he learned about the man, the more interesting he became. Harry Fellowes was no ordinary employee of the state. Previous holders of his position had a military background but he had distinct literary inclinations. Though he matriculated at St John's College, Cambridge, where he was a Beresford scholar, he took no degree. Instead, he became a gunner at the Tower, served as Clerk to the Armoury and translated an abstruse book about Turkey from the original Latin. The catholicity of his career was at variance with his waddling self-importance.

In the year that he moved to Ordnance, Fellowes was ordained deacon by the Bishop of London who was faced — as was the entire episcopate — with a gross deficiency of able clergy. Installed as Vicar of Grain in Kent, the new shepherd tended his flock with fluctuating enthusiasm. He also replaced his father as Master of Sevenoaks School where he continued his literary endeavours by publishing translations of Seneca as well as a book of his own poems in Latin. His income placed him in the ranks of the county squirearchy and he made wise use of his inheritance when his father died. Scholar, schoolmaster, cleric, civil servant and gunner, he took on a new role with astute buying and selling of property. Carrick surmised that it was this lucrative development of his friend's career that made possible his additional work as a money-lender.

When Harry Fellowes exhausted his chat, the lawyer took him back to the question of the succession.

'Where does the Earl of Chichester stand?'

'How would I know?' said the other evasively.

'Is he not your Master of Ordnance?'

'I am not privy to his thoughts, sir.'

'You must have a notion of whom he would prefer on the throne,' probed Carrick. 'Might it be James VI of Scotland?'

'That would be unthinkable!' snapped Fellowes.

'He can advance a strong claim.'

'It will not be supported by the Earl of Chichester. Let Scotland suffer the eccentricities of their king. We shall not, Master Carrick.' He adopted an ecclesiastical pose for once. 'King James is rumoured to have strange ways.'

'How so?'

'My choirboys would not be safe in his presence.'

'But the king is married.'

'His wife may be but a cloak to his true designs,' said Fellowes. 'But there are other obstacles which make him a fearful choice as our monarch. The Earl will look elsewhere. However . . .' He became more confidential. 'The Scottish king will have his party and I know who will help to lead it.'

'Who is that?'

'Lord Westfield.'

'Why?'

'King James likes the theatre.'

She was there. Long before he stepped out onstage to gain visible proof of the fact, he knew that Mistress Beatrice Capaldi had come to the performance of *Love's Sacrifice* at the Queen's Head that afternoon. Lawrence Firethorn felt her presence and purred with delight. His book holder's counsel had borne fruit. The latest play by Edmund Hoode was the love-knot that would bind actor and inamorata together. It was the answer to his prayer. Since the departure of his wife, Firethorn's bed had been intolerably empty and his heart gaped equally wide for a new tenant. Beatrice Capaldi would fill both venues with sublime ease. She had come. It was the proof for which he had longed.

Others were quick to perceive the change. Edmund Hoode was relieved that his play

167

would get a stirring performance out of its leading actor. When Lawrence Firethorn was below his best — as he had been for days — he dragged down the whole company and took the shine off even the finest drama. A toiling playwright like Hoode wanted due recognition of his talents and this could only come from a committed rendering of *Love's Sacrifice*. Barnaby Gill flitted between pleasure and disappointment. He was glad that the reputation of Westfield's Men would not suffer any more but peeved that he would no longer be able to gain at its expense. When Firethorn was subdued, it was the agile comedian who came to the fore to steal the plaudits. Gill also expressed rank disgust that a mere woman could have such an effect on the work of an actor and, by extension, a whole company.

The situation caused Nicholas Bracewell quiet alarm. He hoped that Beatrice Capaldi was a bird of passage who would not return to haunt them and he was confident that Firethorn would soon forget her when some other female sparked off his lechery. Nicholas foresaw grave difficulties and knew that he would be pressed into service.

'Nick, dear heart!'

'We begin in five minutes, sir . . .'

'I was never more ready. But first, a favour.'

'Ask it when I am less busy,' suggested Nicholas.

'It will not wait,' said Firethorn, thrusting a letter at him. 'When the performance is done, give this to her.'

'But I will be needed here, sir.'

'Do as I bid, man. Put it into her hand and wait for a reply. My happiness depends upon it.'

Nicholas sighed and slipped the missive inside his buff jerkin. It was not an assignment to relish. He turned his full attention to the play itself. Its success at The Rose had brought a full audience to the Queen's Head and, although the piece would be given in a slightly attenuated form, its merits were still plentiful. One of the omissions from the text, however, was causing deep resentment. Owen Elias had lost his funeral speech. Retained in the part of Benvolio at the insistence of Nicholas Bracewell, the actor had seen that part trimmed and weakened at the morning rehearsal. Elias brooded malevolently in a corner of the tiring-house. He would not be able to make the same impact again.

Firethorn came up with a growled reminder to him.

'We want no final speech from Benvolio,' he said.

'It suits the play best,' argued Elias.

'It does not suit me, Owen. Remember that.'

'You give me no choice.'

'Breathe one word of that funeral oration and I will rise from the dead to cut out your treacherous Welsh tongue! Do you understand, sir?'

Owen Elias crackled with an anger that found no outlet because Nicholas Bracewell took charge of affairs and *Love's Sacrifice* began. King Gondar now ruled supreme. Benvolio could only fume away in the background.

She was very definitely there. Beatrice Capaldi once again sat in a prominent position in the centre of the lower gallery with a poise that set her apart from all the other young ladies around her. The dark velvet of her earlier appearance had now given way to a brightly coloured dress in the Spanish fashion. She wore a pale-green corseted bodice with a deep point. The long, heavy stomacher front in a deeper hue dipped to a point over the stiff farthingale skirt. Full trunk-type sleeves of blue with large, laced wrist cuffs were revealed under the huge hanging sleeves. The royal-blue gown fitted the shoulders and the figure to the waist then blossomed out over the hips to fall stiffly to the ground. The wide lace ruff was starched and wired. A narrow jewelled sash encircled the waist with a pomander dangling from it. Black hair was drawn back from her exquisite face and set off by a few well-placed jewels. A folding fan was carried in a gloved hand.

Lawrence Firethorn took it all in at a glance and read the message in her apparel. Beatrice Capaldi had warmed towards him. Though she was as aloof as before, her vivid attire conveyed her true feelings. The actor responded by displaying the full rainbow of his talents. His performance was a tour-de-force which made a fine play seem brilliant and which drew his company up to the very summit. The momentum gathered until it became its own undoing. Benvolio was simply carried away by it.

Look down upon these star-crossed lovers
   here,
Two souls that soared above a common
   pitch
To reach the very height of earthly joy
Before their tragic fall to grievous
   death . . .

The funeral speech was laid over the sad carcasses like a soft and respectful shroud. Owen Elias had never been more moving

171

with his soft lilt. He tasted each line with care and let it roll around his mouth until he had exacted its full sweetness. Lawrence Firethorn hissed unregarded at his feet. The Welshman drew even more tears than at The Rose. It was not just an epitaph for a pair of fallen lovers. Owen Elias knew that he was delivering the funeral oration over his own career with Westfield's Men. His moment of supreme glory was also an act of suicide but it was worth it.

King Gondar was carried out once more to solemn music. He leapt off his untimely bier in the tiring-house to accost the traitor but the ovation drowned out his curses. With an audience to enjoy and a love to advance, he swept out onto the stage with his company and took his first bow. His eyes went straight to hers and a momentary flame was lit between them. Beatrice Capaldi showed no emotion but she applauded politely as she gazed down at him. Her presence was a signal to him, her bright attire an invitation, her restrained approval a firm promise.

Lawrence Firethorn capitulated before her.

Giles Randolph knew the importance of keeping a spy in the enemy camp. A sharp-eyed ostler at the Queen's Head reported all that was needful. Basking in his renewed success as *The Spanish Jew,* the leading light of Banbury's Men was annoyed to hear of another triumphant revival and of the scintillating performance by his rival as King Gondar. Lawrence Firethorn had once again eclipsed him but good news followed this all-too-familiar intelligence. Randolph took immediate action. After dining with friends that evening, he made his way from Shoreditch to Gracechurch Street. A large hat and a long cloak guaranteed him an anonymity which let him slip into the Queen's Head unobserved. It was very late and only the very drunk still lingered.

Owen Elias was slumped over a table with an empty pewter tankard in his hand. He groaned as he contemplated the ruins of his theatrical career. Westfield's Men — in the person of their moving spirit — had expelled him. The company which had been his whole life for so long had now hurled him out into the wilderness. After touching real power on a stage at last, he was reduced to complete impotence. His prospects of fresh employment were slight. A twenty-line speech had sealed his doom as an actor.

He became aware of a figure sitting down beside him and of an arm looping around his sagging shoulders. Owen Elias turned bloodshot eyes upon the newcomer but it

173

was a full minute before he recognized Giles Randolph. Jerked out of his maudlin self-pity, he sat up with a start and blinked. He knew the other actor by sight and respected him for his achievements but he had never expected to share a bench in a tavern with such a luminary.

Randolph made his offer with a persuasive smile.

'We have need of you, Owen.'

'Of *me*, sir?'

'Of you, my fine friend.'

'How so?'

'Join a company where your true mettle is appreciated.'

'Banbury's Men?'

'We have a part that only Owen Elias may play.'

'This is no jest?'

'Come with me, sir, and I will prove it.'

The Welshman needed no time at all to think it over. They left together.

Chapter Seven

Margery Firethorn was deeply bored with Cambridge. She found the town far too provincial for her taste, the university far too exclusive and the prevailing atmosphere of Puritanism far too oppressive. Most important of all, she found the company of her brother-in-law far too depressing and she was soon asking herself yet again why her sister had married such an inferior creature. Jonathan Jarrold was a studious man with the deficiencies of such a life writ large upon him. Small in stature and sparse of hair, he was anxious and preoccupied, his busy eyes imprisoned behind spectacles and his shoulders already rounded into a scholarly hunch. He spent as much time reading books as selling them and had no conversation that did not touch on the literary world. Jonathan Jarrold rightly feared his sister-in-law for her temper and her termagant bluntness. In Agnes, he had certainly married a more suitable and sweet companion for his academic ways. She was a dutiful wife with a pale beauty that was not entirely muffled by the dullness of

175

her apparel. Agnes Jarrold loved her husband with a kind of defensive resignation.

'He is a good man, Margery,' she said plaintively.

'His goodness is not in doubt,' said her sister. 'It is his manhood that I question. Can such a fool really perform the office of fatherhood?'

'You do him wrong!'

'Only because he has done you a graver injustice.'

'He is a fine husband.'

'Jonathan Jarrold is married to his books.'

'We have been happy here in Cambridge.'

'That shambling skeleton would not make me happy!'

'Margery!'

'I expect real passion in my bed!'

'Silence! He may hear you.'

Agnes Jarrold quivered with apprehension. They were sitting in the garden of her little house in Trinity street and she was finding her sister's presence a mixed blessing. While Margery undoubtedly gave her unstinting affection and assurance about the trial that lay ahead, she also brought an abrasive note into a gentle household. The quiet and ineffectual Jonathan Jarrold somehow enraged his sister-in-law who loathed him for his very inoffensiveness. There were still two weeks to go before the baby came to term and Agnes was praying that domestic calm could be sustained until the moment when motherhood would unite them all.

Her husband was prepared to make a supreme effort. As he came out into the garden, he manufactured a smile that had particles of real sincerity and pleasure in it.

'Are you ready for me, Margery?' he said politely.

'No, sir,' she grunted.

'The entertainment will soon begin.'

'Do not miss it on my account.'

'But I hope you will accompany me.'

'My wits are turned enough already.'

Agnes interceded. 'Go with him, sister. You have sat with me long enough. Jonathan offers you a diversion.'

'Yes,' he added. 'It is not only London that can delight with its theatrical presentation. We have drama of our own here in Cambridge.'

'It may ease the tedium,' said his wife.

Or make that tedium even more unbearable, thought Margery. Nevertheless, she allowed herself to be talked into witnessing the performance. Agnes herself was in no condition to attend a public event and she was pathetically grateful to her sister for taking her place. As soon as she set off with

her brother-in-law, however, Margery regretted her decision. In his usual sober attire,
he shuffled beside her through the narrow
streets and washed his blue-veined hands in
the air. Jonathan Jarrold sought desperately
to please.

'It is a tragedy about Richard the Third,'
he said.

'I have seen four such plays in London.'

'Students bring a freshness to the drama.'

'I am married to a Titan of the stage.'

'We'll win you over yet, Margery.'

'Do not build on that vain hope, sir.'

The beauty of Queen's College took some
of the jaundice from her eye and she actually
smiled when she saw the sun glancing off
the River Cam and turning the flotilla of
swans into a picture of feathered radiance.
In the cloistered tranquillity of an academic
foundation, Margery did find some objects
of interest and her attentive companion was
lulled into the belief that Cambridge might
yet surprise her with its talent. The performance of plays, revels and *scenici ludi* in the
college halls and chapels was a vital part of
university life and Jonathan Jarrold shared
joyfully in it. That joy was kept from Margery
Firethorn. When she took her seat in the
hall at Queen's College, she discovered that
the play about Richard the Third was called

Richardus Tertius because it was written entirely in Latin.

'I will not understand a word of it!' she complained.

'The acting will explain all,' said Jarrold. 'Wake me if I snore.'

It was a prophetic utterance. The play began and she sank beneath the weight of its dreariness. *Richardus Tertius* was an earnest work that drew a sort of blundering eagerness out of its undergraduate cast. They entered with spirit then stood with wooden awfulness while they tried to declaim the tortuous Latin. Those who attempted gesture and movement made so many errors that they quickly abandoned the experiment and resorted to tableau acting. Classical scholars found much to admire and there was a deal of nodding throughout but there was nothing to hold a simple playgoer. Margery's head only nodded forward on to her ample bosom. Caught up in the severe brilliance of the verse, her brother-in-law was well in Act Three before he heard the unladylike snoring beside him.

Before he could wake her, real drama intervened.

'Come, sir. Come quickly, sir.'

'What is it, Nan?'

'Your wife has need of you, sir. Come at once.'

The old servant plucked at her master's sleeve and earned a broadside of protests from the audience all around her. Jonathan Jarrold was annoyed at the interruption but immediately aware of its implications. His third child was about to make its entry into the world. A sharp nudge brought Margery back to life and an urgent whisper made her leap to her feet. Her voice rang out through the hall and brought the play to a halt.

'Take me to my sister!' she yelled imperiously. 'Her ordeal can be no worse than this one — and at least she will not have the baby in Latin!'

Lawrence Firethorn missed his wife dreadfully and was quite unable to take advantage of the fact. It rankled. Days of licence had yielded nothing more than disappointment. Nights of freedom had yet to be marked by a conquest. He writhed in torment. His life as an actor had always been one of peaks and troughs but the two had never been simultaneous before. As he scaled the very heights of his profession, he was cast down into the abyss of misery. Beatrice Capaldi had turned him down. The letter which Nicholas Bracewell delivered was an invitation to dine with him that evening but she rejected it with a disdainful shake of her head. Two hours of King Gondar had left him in a state of blissful delirium but a spectator in the lower gallery destroyed it instantly. Nor was there compensation to be found. Firethorn had summoned an old acquaintance to warm his bed but she had failed him badly. While his head lusted for her, his heart remained true to Beatrice Capaldi and his naked body voted with the latter party. For the first time in his life, a beautiful woman left his chamber unsatisfied.

His work inevitably suffered. During the performance of *The Two Maids of Milchester* on the following afternoon, he was so subdued that Barnaby Gill was able to wrest scene after scene from him. Firethorn did not even seem to notice the indignity, let alone to care. His mind was on higher things. When the play was over and a disgruntled audience had filed out of the Queen's Head, the actor turned to the one man in the company who might yet save him.

'Advise me, Nick!' he begged.

'My advice is to forget this lady,' said Nicholas.

'She *spurned* me. No woman has ever done that before. Am I not Lawrence Firethorn? Am I not King Gondar and Tarquin and Black Antonio and Pompey the Great and

181

Richard the Lionheart and all the other giants of the London stage?'

'You are indeed, sir.'

'Yet she spurns me. She spurns every one of me!'

'It may be for the best.'

'When it murders my very soul!'

Firethorn's howl shook the timbers of the private room where they conversed. Nicholas Bracewell had to balance honesty against diplomacy. He was thankful that Mistress Beatrice Capaldi had turned down the invitation from his employer but he would not dare to say that to an infatuated man of legendary temper. Besides, he had come to understand the nature of that infatuation now that he had seen the lady herself at close range. Beatrice Capaldi was a cut above the conventional beauties who idolized the famous actor and who flung themselves at his feet. They were all victims of his charm and his arrogant manliness. Beatrice Capaldi would never join their number. She liked victims of her own.

'Why does she dare to scorn me?' demanded Firethorn.

'The lady may be fast married, sir.'

'That is no barrier. I have borrowed a wife from many a husband before now and will do so again. Besides, she brought no

Master Capaldi to watch me perform. When you gave her my letter, you said she was attended by two manservants.'

'It is true, sir.'

'Then her husband is of no account,' decided Firethorn with a snap of his fingers. 'If he exists, it is my bounden duty to cuckold the rogue. If not, let's waste no more breath upon him. Beatrice came to me alone. I cling to that.'

'Consider her name,' suggested Nicholas, making one last attempt to deter his employer. 'Mistress Capaldi.'

'I consider it every minute of the day, Nick.'

'The lady is of Italian extraction.'

'It is the essence of her beauty.'

'She may also be wed to an Italian gentleman.'

'Your conclusion?'

'Beatrice Capaldi is a Roman Catholic.'

'Love is without denomination!' said Firethorn grandly. 'Were she Protestant, Jew or Presbyterian, I could worship her no less. Were she a godless child of an African heathen, it would not alter my heart. Were she got between two Druids in some pagan rite, I would not stay my hand here. I *love* her!'

'That is plain, sir.'

'Then help me, Nick!'

'I am yours to command.'

'What game does she play with me?'

Beatrice Capaldi stood bolt upright while her dressmaker made a few final adjustments to his latest creation. With an ingratiating bow, he then backed away so that she could inspect the result in the huge gilt-framed mirror that dominated one wall of her bedchamber. The dress was a work of art in white and silver. Simple and heavily-padded, it had a close-fitting bodice with a long-fronted stomacher that dipped in a deep point to the stiffened basque of the French farthingale. The basque was made of the same material as the flounced bell-shaped skirt and concealed the hard line of the wheeled farthingale. Trunk sleeves were full at the top and tapered to the wrists, giving the demi-cannon effect that was now in fashion. Beatrice Capaldi examined each detail with care until she was entirely satisfied. She then walked around the room to get the feel of her new dress and to enjoy the sensual swish of its skirt. When she had had her fill, she repaid her dressmaker with an indulgent smile. He bowed frantically then backed out with servile gratitude. Left alone in front of the mirror, she toyed with the low square *décolletage* across the front of the dress so that she could display a more generous area of her full breasts. There was a tap on the door and a manservant entered with writing materials on a tray. Beatrice Capaldi crossed to sit at the little table and the paper was put in front of her. Dipping the quill in the inkwell, she wrote a single line.

'True love requires a true sacrifice.'

The letter was sealed but not signed and the name of Master Lawrence Firethorn was added with a flourish. She handed the missive to the manservant with a curt order.

'See it delivered to the Queen's Head directly.'

Nimbus was equal to the occasion. The London début of Cornelius Gant and His Amazing Horse was a comprehensive success. It took place in the yard at the Feathers where fifty or more casual bystanders were transformed into a rapt audience. The performers showed enough of their skills to dazzle the spectators while holding back their principal tricks for use before larger gatherings at a later date. Dancing and counting were the basis of their act. While the versatile Gant played on a pipe, Nimbus went through a whole series of dances, beginning with a coranto and ending with a sprightly galliard. But it was the money trick which tricked money out of purses.

'Place your coins in this hat, sirs,' invited Gant as he held it out. 'You'll get it back with interest, I warrant.' When the spectators hesitated, Nimbus grabbed the hat in grinning teeth to take it around. Twenty or more coins were tossed laughingly into the receptacle which was then taken back to Cornelius Gant. Taking hold of the hat, he pulled out a gold coin and held it up.

'Who gave you this, Nimbus?'

The horse picked out the donor at once and nudged him. Gant indicated another man and asked how much he had contributed. Nimbus promptly tapped his foot three times and three coins were returned to their astonished owner. And so it went on. The animal was able to identify both the giver and the amount given until the hat was completely empty. The applause was vigorous and coins came back more plentifully. By way of an encore, Gant let his partner tip the takings on to the ground so that they could be added up with a tapped hoof. Nimbus was a precise accountant whose nimble work brought forth another hail of money.

It was a gratifying response to an unusual act but it was not only his full purse that pleased Gant. He took more satisfaction from the impact they had had upon the watching patrons. Those men would spread the word throughout and beyond Eastcheap. The seeds of reputation would be sown and future audiences would be primed and set up.

Cornelius Gant and Nimbus had arrived.

The influence of Lord Westfield opened doors for Nicholas Bracewell once again. He visited Andrew Carrick in the cell in the Beauchamp Tower and gave him an account both of the funeral and of his nocturnal investigations in Clerkenwell. The lawyer thanked him profusely for all that he had done but warned him against taking too many risks. Nicholas had now removed the bandaging from his head to reveal a dark bruise and an ugly scar. He insisted that he was willing to collect more wounds if they would take him closer to the murderer of Sebastian Carrick. The father was touched.

Grief pressed down upon him. Having lost a son, he was anxious to console his daughter but he was kept in the Tower because his sovereign had a fit of pique. While the Queen was ill, all hope of release had vanished. Andrew Carrick was surprisingly well-informed about the progress of events.

'Her Majesty fades quietly away,' he said, 'and her courtiers rush around to find themselves a successor who will favour them.

Several names have been mentioned and each has its party and its parasites.'

'Is the Queen's illness so serious?' asked Nicholas.

'All reports confirm it.'

'How can you know this?'

'Imprisonment sharpens a man's hearing and they talk of nothing else here. People in royal service hang upon every shift of royal power. My friend, Master Fellowes, who is Clerk of Ordnance here, keeps me abreast of all developments.'

'Does he know the nature of the Queen's malady?'

'Old age is her chiefest complaint.'

'She is but sixty and takes great care of her person.'

'That is why the rumour has grown abroad.'

'What rumour, sir?'

'The Queen has succumbed to some vile poison.'

'Poison?' said Nicholas in surprise. 'Administered by whom? Only her physicians could get close enough to her.'

'You may have identified the villain, sir.'

'Who is he?'

'Dr Lopez.'

Nicholas was sceptical about the theory but he could see how it must have arisen.

Roderigo Lopez was one of the most hated and envied members of the medical profession. A Portuguese Jew who fled the Inquisition, he came to England to practise as a doctor and serve as house physician at St Bartholomew's Hospital. His renown as a dietician and a wise counsellor spread until he included the Earl of Leicester and Sir Francis Walsingham among his patients. In 1586 he was appointed chief physician to Queen Elizabeth but Lopez was not content with a solely medical role. He used his position at court to champion the cause of Antonio Perez, the Portuguese pretender. Breaking with the latter, the doctor rashly quarrelled with the Earl of Essex who was the main English supporter of the Perez party. Dr Lopez was later arrested at the instigation of Essex who claimed that he had discovered a conspiracy in which the chief physician was to poison the Queen. Her sickness might now seem to confirm the allegations but Nicholas had severe doubts.

'Dr Lopez is under lock and key,' he said. 'He has not been near Her Majesty for months.'

Carrick shrugged. 'The poison may be slow-acting. It could have been given to her by Lopez in the guise of some medicinal remedy.'

'The Queen is watched over with too much care.'

'Some confederate may have done the deed.'

'Her physicians have not even said that poison is at all involved here,' said Nicholas. 'Dr Lopez is too hastily accused. The charges brought by the Earl of Essex have yet to be proved against him. No treason may have occurred. The doctor has been imprisoned for two other crimes.'

'What are they, Master Bracewell?'

'He is a foreigner and he is a Jew.'

Andrew Carrick nodded. 'You speak well. We show little respect to the stranger in these islands of ours. We despise what is different and see it only as a threat.' He gave a tired smile. 'But this anxiety over the Queen has brought reward to some quarters. Your rivals prosper.'

'Banbury's Men?'

'I hear tell of a play called *The Spanish Jew*. It could not be more timely. Cross out the name of Spain, insert its neighbour country and you have the villain of the piece.'

'Dr Roderigo Lopez.'

'The play draws huge audiences.'

'It feeds on hatred and prejudice,' said Nicholas.

'Banbury's Men have stolen the march on

you. Let us hope that their patron does not do the same.'

'How do you mean, sir?'

'A battle for the succession would also be a battle for supremacy on the stage,' argued Carrick. 'Lord Westfield will support the claim of King James of Scotland who has a fondness for the drama. If he is to be our next ruler, you and your fellows might be translated into the King's Men.'

'We are not yet ready to lose our Queen,' said Nicholas loyally. 'But what of the Earl of Banbury? Which party does he follow in this matter?'

'One that will serve him best,' said Carrick. 'Pray God that his candidate does not reach our throne. Banbury's Men would surely triumph then. Your company would be destroyed.'

'By the new king?'

'By the new queen.'

Hardwick Hall was an arresting sight. Even in its present unfinished state, it could stir the spirit and excite the imagination. In little over two years, industrious builders had substantially completed the main structure and they continued to swarm busily over it. Six miles to the south-east of Chesterfield, the house was the brainchild of the redoubtable

Elizabeth Hardwick, Countess of Shrewsbury. Widowed by her fourth husband, she was not only the richest woman in the kingdom but one of the most ambitious and powerful as well. The house was to be a lasting monument to her and she emphasized the fact by having her initials carved in stone on top of the four massive square towers of the west front. Restraint was unknown to Bess of Hardwick. In the imposing west front of the house were no less than fifty windows, some of huge dimensions. The quiet Derbyshire landscape had never seen such an expanse of glass.

'Our visit was worthwhile.'

'I could have been spared the tour of the house.'

'Bess is inordinately proud of it,' said the Earl of Chichester. 'We must humour the lady.'

'There is only one way to do that, Roger.'

'Is there?'

'Become her fifth husband.'

'God's wounds! That would be purgatory!'

'She is a lusty widow.'

'Let her vent her lust on Hardwick Hall.'

The Earl of Banbury laughed at his friend's discomfort. Their carriage was bumping along the drive that cut through the extensive front gardens of the estate. Bending backs could be seen all around as a team of urgent gardeners strove to provide the magnificent house with an appropriate horticultural setting. Symmetry was the keynote for hall and garden alike. The noble travellers hoped that their plans would achieve a similar neatness of line.

'The girl is ours,' decided the old soldier.

'She comes at a fearful price,' said Banbury. 'We must suffer that grandmother of hers.'

'Bess can be managed easily.'

'Four husbands would disagree with you.'

'We have our queen. What more do we need?'

'A throne on which to set her.'

'It will soon be vacant.'

'And fit to receive our nominated monarch.'

'Arabella Stuart.'

'Queen of England!'

The earls congratulated themselves on the speed with which they had moved and the diplomacy which they had shown. Arabella Stuart was an attractive young girl of seventeen with a claim to the throne at least as strong as that of James VI of Scotland. She was the fruit of a dynastic marriage arranged by the manipulative Bess between her own daughter, Elizabeth, and Charles Stuart, Earl of Lennox. When Arabella was orphaned, she came into the care of her ever-scheming grandmother who considered marrying her to the Duke of Parma's son, Rainutio Farnese, who had a tenuous link with the English crown through descent from John of Gaunt. During this period, Arabella spent some valuable time at court but the death of her elected bridegroom in 1592 saw her returned to Derbyshire. Inclined to be wayward, the girl was subjected to grandmotherly vigilance of the most intense kind. The visitors from London had been highly conscious of it.

'Poor creature!' said Banbury. 'Arabella cannot draw breath without permission from the old harridan.'

'A queen will take no orders.'

'They will still be given, Roger.'

'Bess can be silenced,' said his colleague. 'We will have Her Majesty's ear without the intervening inconvenience of a grandmother.' He slapped his thigh. 'We've done it, man! All parties are well-served here. England will have her new queen. Arabella will have her throne. We will have supreme influence. Our friends will have their due reward and our enemies will be roundly swinged.'

'And what of that meddling grandmother?'

'Bess will be too busy with Hardwick Hall.'

They turned around to take a last look at

the building. Even from that distance and even in its incomplete state, it was a superb piece of architecture. Its scope was quite stunning and its boldness of line echoed the temperament of its creator. Bess of Hardwick was well into her sixties. This latest obsession would surely occupy her remaining years to the full.

The Earl of Chichester gave a throaty laugh.

'We are the true architects here,' he boasted.

'Are we?'

'Bess only builds a house.'

'What do we create, Roger?'

'A kingdom!'

Lawrence Firethorn could not believe his drink-blurred eyes. As he held the letter close to the candle, he read the words a dozen times to be sure of their meaning and confident of their authorship. He was downing another goblet of Canary wine with Barnaby Gill when the messenger sought him out in the taproom at the Queen's Head. Fumbling fingers broke the seal and six words effected his metamorphosis.

'True love requires a true sacrifice.'

It was a message from Beatrice Capaldi and its import made him laugh with joy before banging the table impulsively with his fist. Barnaby Gill grabbed his own goblet as it danced its way across the vibrating timber.

'Hold steady!' he yelled.

'She has spoken, Barnaby!'

'Then close her mouth at once.'

'Beatrice wants me! Beatrice needs me!'

'Play this mad scene somewhere else, sir.'

'Look!' said Firethorn, thrusting the letter at him. 'What else can these words mean? She *invites* me!'

Gill gave the paper a disdainful glance before issuing one of his contemptuous snorts. 'This woman is like all others of her kind, Lawrence,' he said. 'She is the highway to damnation.'

'No, Barnaby. She is the road to Elysium.'

'Turn back while there is still time, man.'

'See what she asks for — true sacrifice?'

'You have already sacrificed your wits and your wilting codpiece to her! Do not sacrifice your company as well.'

'Beatrice calls to me!'

'Listen to your friends instead.'

'A true sacrifice! Do you not understand?'

'Only too well, sir!'

Firethorn read the letter again to extract its command. The true sacrifice was the play which had twice brought his Beatrice to him. She was now ordering a third performance as King Gondar. That was the way to win her heart. Beatrice had only refused to dine with him in order to whet his appetite. When she was given further proof of his love, he believed, she would submit herself to his wildest demands. Firethorn waved the letter above his head like the captured flag of a beaten enemy. His decision was immediate.

'We must alter our plans for The Theatre.'

'No!' Gill was horrified.

'*Love's Sacrifice* must be staged again.'

'Not in Shoreditch!' protested the other. 'Our agreed choice is *Cupid's Folly*.'

'It will be replaced.'

'This is cruelty, Lawrence!'

'Beatrice has spoken.'

'Think with your brain and not with your pizzle!'

'We play *Love's Sacrifice*.'

Gill stamped a petulant foot. '*Cupid's Folly!*'

'A ragged piece that we can well neglect.'

'I was *promised!*'

'Beatrice must not be denied.'

The rank injustice of it all made Gill shake with fury. It was not often that they performed at The Theatre and it was even rarer for his favourite play to be presented there. *Cupid's Folly* was a rumbustious comedy which allowed Gill a starring role as Rigormortis and set him above all other stage clowns. To have the play cancelled was bad enough: to see it callously replaced by a drama in which Firethorn took all the plaudits was a professional wound that would fester in perpetuity. Gill's bitter hatred of the female sex was exacerbated but his complaints went unheard.

'Would you rob me of my *Cupid's Folly?*' he cried.

'I simply ask you to give it up for me, Barnaby.'

'No, no, no!'

Firethorn slipped an avuncular arm around him.

'True love requires a true sacrifice . . .'

Owen Elias still had vestigial doubts about his move to another company. Banbury's Men gave him an important supporting role in a new play that was staged at The Curtain before an appreciative audience but the experience did not wipe away all his reservations. Employment was a boon for which he was deeply grateful even though he did not yet know how it had come about. Giles Randolph enlightened him.

'Tomorrow, we play *The Spanish Jew.*'

'It is much talked about, Master Randolph.'

'Yes,' said the other, 'and it will cause

even more conversation now. This sickness of Her Majesty has put the name of Dr Lopez on every tongue. I have but to appear on stage in his guise and they love to revile me.'

'What part will I take?' said Elias.

'The Governor of the city.' He handed the Welshman a sheaf of papers. 'Here are the sides for you to study.'

'It feels like a weighty role.'

'It is indeed, Owen.'

'How must I play it?'

'There you come to the heart of the matter.'

Giles Randolph could hardly contain his mirth as he whispered his instructions. Puzzled at first, Owen Elias soon came to see the virtues in what was being suggested to him. *The Spanish Jew* would give him more than a challenging role. It would help him to settle an old score.

The two men were soon helpless with laughter.

The long years spent in the exclusive company of actors had rubbed off on Nicholas Bracewell. A book holder had to cope with all manner of emergency and there had been a number of occasions when he had made impromptu appearances on stage himself in minor roles. He enjoyed these brief excursions enough to feel confident of his ability to deceive. If not a true actor, he had learned how to look, speak and move on a stage. These skills now had a practical application.

'Will you buy me a drink, sir?'

'Order what you wish.'

'Then I'll begin with a kiss.'

'As many as you like.'

Nicholas had returned to the Pickt-hatch in Clerkenwell that night. Dressed like a gallant, hair and beard trimmed by a barber, he was able to gain entry without being recognized. Peg, who had entertained him on his first visit, now thought she was blandishing an entirely different client. He bought wine for them both and used a slurred voice to hide his distinctive West Country burr. By hunching his shoulders, he altered the whole shape of his body. Bess Bidgood had been fooled by the disguise and Peg was equally taken in.

'Will you climb the stairs with me, sir?' she said.

'Soon, mistress. Very soon.'

'Will you let me please you?'

'In every way that you choose.'

Peg giggled. 'I'll not disappoint you, sir.'

Nicholas exchanged mild banter with her while keeping the room under careful observation. It was full of raucous noise as other gallants sported with other courtesans. There was drinking, gambling, singing and frank groping. Couples would occasionally totter off upstairs but they would soon be replaced by returning pairs. There was a limit to how long Nicholas could maintain his surveillance. His purse was not large enough to sustain endless purchase of wine and he would not be able to keep Peg at bay indefinitely. He was fast approaching the moment when he would have to feign vomiting in order to escape from the premises when he was given additional proof that he was in the right place.

There was a thunderous clatter as a young gallant came tumbling down the stairs. It brought a jeer from his fellows but no sympathy. Nicholas crossed to help the drunken youth up and found him relatively unharmed. Carrying his doublet over his arm, the gallant was wearing a white shirt above his hose. Even in the gloom, Nicholas could see the streaks of blood down the back of the shirt and his curiosity quickened at once.

'You bleed, young sir,' he said.

'In the service of love!'

'Who gave you these wounds?'

'The mistress of the bedchamber.'

'What is her name?'

'Perfection, sir . . .'

The youth gave a loud belch then staggered across to a group of friends who caught him as he pitched forward into their hands. He had taken his pleasures and was now dead to the world for a long time. Nicholas would get no more from him but the Pickt-hatch had yielded vital confirmation. He was very close to the murderer of Sebastian Carrick. She lay in a bed in one of the rooms upstairs. Peg came over to embrace him and to drag him towards the stairs so Nicholas pretended to retch violently. The girl pushed him away in disgust and strong male hands soon ejected him into the lane outside. His visit to the establishment was over but he was now completely convinced.

The mad courtesan was there.

It was a difficult labour. Agnes Jarrold struggled hard and suffered greatly. The little house in Cambridge echoed with her cries of pain for several hours. Though the child was anxious to come before its time, the mother seemed strangely reluctant to bear it. Stark memories of two previous births held her back. While it remained inside and part of her, the baby was patently alive and safe. In delivering it to the outside world, Agnes felt, she would be consigning it to the grave alongside its two predecessors. In the marital bed in Trinity Street, the battle between mind and body raged on. There was no anaesthetic to ease her torment, no medicine to take away the phantoms that haunted her. Caught up in the eternal mystery of childbirth, a fond housewife was racked by the eternal pangs. What made the crucial difference for her on this occasion was the presence of her elder sister.

'Hold me tight, Agnes.'

'I have no strength left.'

'Push hard, push hard!'

'I faint, I fail . . .'

'Now, Agnes! Be a mother and *fight* for the child!'

Margery Firethorn was there throughout, encouraging her sister, sharing her travail, stilling her fears, bossing the surgeon, bullying the midwife and keeping the anguished husband on the other side of the bedroom door with a series of abusive yells. When the exhausted mother found one last burst of energy to give birth, it was Margery who talked her through it and who told her she was now the mother of a fine son. Agnes Jarrold gave her a smile of thanks before lapsing into unconsciousness. The surgeon looked to his patient, the midwife wrapped the yowling infant in swaddling clothes and Margery was able to recall the existence of a husband.

When she went downstairs, she found Jonathan Jarrold trying to read a Greek lexicon to occupy his mind. After issuing a reprimand, Margery told him that he was a father once more and that mother and baby were in good health. The bookseller went weak at the knees with sheer relief and jabbered his gratitude in English, Latin and Greek. His sister-in-law cut through his tri-lingual hysteria.

'What will the boy be called?' she said.

'The boy?'

'Your son, you dolt! Children need names.'

'We have not settled on one as yet.'

'Then do so now, sir,' insisted Margery, determined to wrest some contribution from him. 'Your wife has risked her life to deliver a third child. This infant Jarrold should be dignified with a name. Pronounce it, sir!'

'You have done so yourself, Margery,' he said.

'Have I?'

'This is indeed a third child. Therein lies its name.'

'Stop talking in Greek.'

'I favour Latin.'

'What?'

'Richardus Tertius.'

'An innocent babe called after a tedious play!'

'No, Margery. Our son will be called Richard Jarrold.'

'Richard III.'

'Fortune favours us.'

'A third time pays for all.'

Chapter Eight

Nicholas Bracewell strolled into the yard at the Queen's Head to find that he was not, for once, the first member of the Westfield's Men to arrive. Two figures stepped out of the morning mist to waylay him. Before he could even begin to defend himself, he was belaboured by their demands.

'Stop him, Nick!'

'Prevent this lunacy!'

'Intercede on our behalf!'

'Use your influence!'

'Acquaint him with reason!'

'Insist on *Cupid's Folly!*'

'Save our reputations!'

'Save our company!'

'Save our lives!'

Edmund Hoode and Barnaby Gill seldom agreed on anything so wholeheartedly. Again, though the playwright was a trusted friend of the book holder, the comedian most assuredly was not. To get either man there so early and so articulate was a wonder in itself. For the pair of them to be acting in concert — with Gill suppressing his dislike of Nicholas in order to appeal for his help — was a mark of real desperation. He let them rehearse their grievances without interruption and learned of the fatal letter from Mistress Beatrice Capaldi. Convinced that conquest was now in the offing, Lawrence Firethorn had drawn the resident poet into his fledgling love affair.

'He orders verses for his dark Italian!' said Hoode with disgust. 'I have plays to write for Westfield's Men and he would have me charm his lady's clothes off with rhyming couplets. My love poems will not serve his lust!'

'Nor will *I* suffer for her sake!' asserted Gill. 'We chose my Rigormortis for The Theatre and that is what all London wishes to see. Are we to let some powdered female dictate our performances? I'll not bear it, sirs!'

'Lawrence must be *told*, Nick.'

'If necessary, he must be threatened.'

'He is sacrificing the whole company here.'

Nicholas was seriously disquieted. He shared their resistance to the intrusion of Beatrice Capaldi and was alarmed by the latest development. It came at a time when Westfield's Men had to look to their laurels. Their rivals were winning applause on all sides as a dynastic tussle was replicated in the competition between the theatre companies. If Lawrence Firethorn were to lead his troupe on into a new reign, he needed to concentrate all his efforts to that end. There was no place in the scheme of things for a distraction like Beatrice Capaldi.

Barnaby Gill offered one solution to the problem.

'Ride to Cambridge. Bring back Margery.'

'Yes,' said Hoode. 'She would soon dampen his ardour.'

'Wives do have their uses sometimes.'

'She would tear him to pieces for his folly.'

'Send word to her at once.'

'No,' said Nicholas. 'Mistress Firethorn journeyed to Cambridge on an important errand and may be gone for weeks. She will not be prised away from her duty.'

Hoode shrugged helplessly. 'What, then, is the answer?'

Nicholas calmed them down and agreed to tackle the actor-manager in due course. Whether she was ignoring him or tempting him, Beatrice Capaldi was having a detrimental effect on his company and it had to be pointed out to him. One more thankless task had been added to the book holder's already long list. His approach needed careful thought.

It was an hour or more before Lawrence

Firethorn came riding into the yard on his horse. He was a new man. Gone was the morose individual of the previous day who had been smarting at his rejection. In his place was a buoyant creature who overflowed with such geniality that he could even bestow a kindly smile upon Alexander Marwood, the doom-laden innkeeper of the Queen's Head. Nicholas held back while the rehearsal was on, letting Firethorn expend some of his manic energy on the makeshift stage. When the book holder finally made his move, the actor was ready for him.

'You waste your breath, Nick,' he said. 'Whatever vile arguments Edmund and Barnaby have thrust upon you, I'll not hear them. We play *Love's Sacrifice* at The Theatre. Aye, and Westfield's Men will stage the piece three times a week if that is the only way to see my beloved Beatrice.'

Nicholas quickly shifted the argument to other ground.

'King Gondar will need his funeral speech,' he said.

'So?'

'Owen Elias must be wooed back.'

'Never! The villain has been exiled.'

'He will go elsewhere for employment, sir.'

'Let the rogue!'

'Even if he joins Banbury's Men?'

'The best place for him,' said Firethorn scornfully. 'A snake will be at home in a nest of vipers. Of one thing you may be certain, Nick.' He drew himself up to his full height and spat the words out with venom. 'Owen Elias will never again share a stage with Lawrence Firethorn!'

Giles Randolph sank once more into a vat of boiling oil at The Curtain and sent the audience into a frenzy of applause. *The Spanish Jew* had been given a spurious topicality by the turn of events and the resident playwright with Banbury's Men had exploited the coincidence by adding some new scenes and speeches to the piece. Not only did the play excoriate all money-lenders and all Jews, it more clearly identified its central character with Dr Roderigo Lopez and implied a link between his knowledge of poisons and the continuing sickness of the Queen. Giles Randolph was as brilliant as ever but he now excited more hatred than amusement. The play had taken on a distinctly sinister and biting edge.

Humour was by no means expunged from *The Spanish Jew*. In the role of the Governor — chief adversary and scourge of the villain — Owen Elias managed to combine authority with comic daring. His authority flowed naturally from his stage presence but the humour arose from another source. Seasoned play-goers recognized his impersonation at once. Instead of giving a straight reading of the part, the Welshman mimicked the way that Lawrence Firethorn would have addressed it and the result was uncannily accurate. In appearance, voice and gesture, he was Firethorn to the last detail and the force of his mockery was irresistible. The packed audience at The Curtain was reduced to uncontrollable laughter. As his rival was turned into a figure of fun, Giles Randolph prospered accordingly. Everyone leaving the theatre thought him to be the greatest actor alive.

Lawrence Firethorn was mistaken. Owen Elias had shared a stage with him, after all.

Three more faultless performances in three carefully-chosen inn yards had elevated the status of Cornelius Gant and Nimbus. They offered quality entertainment that appealed to a wide spectrum of people and word continued to spread. To give his horse a well-earned rest, Gant decided to explore some of the alternative diversions in the city and he was drawn ineluctably across the river and into Paris Garden. Stairs gave access from the Thames to this notorious place of amusement which abounded in trees, bushes,

211

fish-ponds and illicit assignations. Cornelius Gant joined the crowd which converged on the wooden amphitheatre. Over a thousand spectators were crammed into the circular gamehouse for an afternoon's sport. Having paid his twopence, Gant secured a prime place in the lower gallery. He missed nothing.

The audience was in a boisterous mood before the entertainment began but it became much more vocal when the first bear was led in. The animal's legs were fastened to a stout post by thick chains, enabling it to move no more than a few yards in each direction. When the bearward stepped out of the arena, howling mastiffs were released to bait the hapless creature. They moved in swiftly to snap at its legs or lunge at its body or jump for its throat. Sharp teeth sank into thick fur and blood flowed freely. With the crowd yelling them on, the dogs increased the ferocity of their attack and the bear incurred deep wounds as it tried to fight them off. Its brute strength eventually began to tell. Flashing claws opened one dog up, snapping teeth tore the head off another and a third was crushed to death in a hug. As the carcasses were tossed to the ground, fresh mastiffs came in to take their place and renew the assault.

Cornelius Gant was appalled. Cruel and

uncaring in many ways, he had a love of dumb animals that was deeply offended by what was happening. Almost as bad as the bestiality in the ring was the baying satisfaction of the multitude. It was all a far cry from the harmless antics of a well-trained horse and a considerate master.

When the first bear was white with lather and dripping with gore, it was taken out by the bearward. Whining dogs were dragged out on leashes to lick their wounds and rue any tactical errors. The new bear that was brought in had been blinded by its owner to provide another kind of sport for the bawling spectators. Chained to the post, the animal was faced by a semi-circle of six men who were each armed with a long whip. On a given command, they began to beat the bear unmercifully, splitting open its flesh with patent relish as they piled torment on torment. All that it could do by way of defence was to lurch out at its hidden attackers and make the post shudder with its rattling chains. Cornelius Gant was even more horrified at this spectacle but he gained some consolatory pleasure when one of the men slipped, rolled in close to the bear and had his face ripped away with one savage cuff from the huge claws.

The popularity of the hideous entertainment could not be denied and it was not aimed at the vulgar taste of the lower sort. People from all classes of society were present and Gant saw shrieking ladies on the arms of their gallants as well as powdered punks being fondled by their clients. If he was shocked by the treatment of the bears, he was even more revolted by what followed. As a last sop to the blood-lust of the crowd, a pony was chased into the ring with a monkey tied to its back. The pony scurried around in a circle of pain as its rider bit, gouged and pulled at its mane but the monkey was the least of its problems. More dogs poured in to bite at the slender legs as they went faster and faster around the arena. Laughter and jeers sent the pony into an even deeper panic as it ran madly towards a vicious fate.

It was still vainly trying to shake off its pursuers as Cornelius Gant stalked out of the building in disgust.

Lord Westfield always took a keen interest in the fortunes of his theatre company but events in the royal household made that interest even more intense. Having watched a rousing performance of *Hector of Troy* at the Queen's Head that afternoon, he repaired to his private room with a small entourage to partake of refreshment and to discuss plans

214

for the future with the leading sharers. The noble gentleman might be vain and sybaritic but he was shrewd enough to discern the hand that worked so hard and so efficiently in the cause of Westfield's Men. As a result, Nicholas Bracewell was invited to join the gathering and he hovered on its fringes. Lawrence Firethorn, restored to his best form by a message of love, lapped up the compliments and flirted gently with the two young ladies in the room. Barnaby Gill preened himself in a corner and Edmund Hoode lurked silently. There was a deal of idle chatter but Lord Westfield was the only person who was saying anything of value.

'This illness of Her Majesty is inopportune,' he said.

'For whom?' asked Firethorn.

'Why, for Her Majesty, of course,' risked Gill with a wicked grin that was instantly replaced by a mask of deep loyalty. 'I respect our dear Queen as much as any man in the kingdom and I pray daily for her quick recovery.'

'That may or may not come,' said Westfield. 'And we have to take the latter possibility into account. A change of monarch will mean a change of attitude towards the theatre. I would not want my company to be jeopardized.'

'Indeed, no,' agreed Firethorn with alarm.

'What may we usefully do?' said Gill.

'We carry your name with honour,' added Hoode.

Lord Westfield nodded. 'I hope that you will continue to do so, Edmund, but dangers lie ahead. It needs cautious diplomacy on my part and some wise decisions on yours.'

'You speak of dangers,' said Firethorn.

His patron turned to the book holder to cue him in.

'Tell them, Nicholas. You will know.'

'But a little, my lord,' said Nicholas politely. 'If Her Majesty dies, there will be a disputed succession and many are now rushing forward to take part in that dispute. Each party has its own claimant from whom they expect due return on their devotion. The Earl of Banbury, for instance . . .'

'That old fool!' muttered Firethorn.

'. . . has formed an alliance with the Earl of Chichester to advance the cause of Arabella Stuart. Should that lady ever sit on the throne, our rivals are like to be known henceforth as the Queen's Men.'

The suggestion rocked the three sharers so hard that they all protested and gesticulated in unison. Their patron waved them into a troubled silence.

'You see, gentlemen?' he said. 'Your book

holder is more well-informed than his masters. He can foresee consequences to this business. That is why I have formed my own alliance. Our chosen successor is King James of Scotland and our party is led by Sir Robert Cecil.'

His listeners were duly impressed. Sir Robert Cecil was Lord Burghley's son and, despite his physical short-comings, a most intelligent and able politician. With such a man at the helm, Lord Westfield's party was indeed well-served. At the same time, everyone recognized that the outcome of a disputed succession was highly uncertain. It was Nicholas Bracewell who remembered their patron's earlier comment.

'You mentioned wise decisions, my lord . . .'

'I did,' said the other. 'Every move that you make must promote the company. Every play that you choose must endorse our party. Westfield's Men must outshine all other troupes and cast those jackals of Banbury's into outer darkness.'

'It shall be done!' announced Firethorn.

'Where is our next performance, Lawrence?'

'The Theatre in Shoreditch.'

'An excellent venue for our purposes.'

'Then let us stage *Cupid's Folly*,' urged

Gill. 'My Rigormortis will outshine the sun itself.'

Westfield shook his head. 'No, Barnaby. The play is less than suitable for the gravity of the occasion.'

'Most certainly, my lord,' said Firethorn. 'That is why we have selected *Love's Sacrifice.*'

'It lends itself to our device. Edmund . . .'

'My lord?'

'Look to your text, man. See if you cannot add a speech or two in praise of Queen Elsin. Glorify her reign. Fawn and flatter at will. Let every soul in that theatre know that you speak of our own beloved sovereign.'

'I'll do it instantly, my lord.'

'Lawrence?'

'My lord?'

'That funeral oration . . .'

'It will be cut entirely.'

'I'll not hear of it,' snapped his patron. 'It gives us our best opportunity to voice our plans. King Gondar dies. The end of one reign is the start of another. Work subtly here, my fellows. Let that closing speech feed off the sorrow of a nation but make it advertise our intent.'

Firethorn grunted. 'It shall be done, my lord.'

'You have such a fine actor to speak the lines.'

'Owen Elias has left us,' said Nicholas softly.

'Yes,' said Gill, seizing the opportunity to discomfit his colleague. 'Lawrence expelled him in spite of my earnest entreaties. I fought hard to retain the services of so talented a player.' He gave a little sigh. 'The rumour is that Owen Elias has joined Banbury's Men.'

'Can this be true!' demanded the apoplectic Westfield. 'Answer me, Lawrence! Tell me it is not so!'

'Well, my lord . . .'

'Can you be guilty of such idiocy?'

Lawrence Firethorn had to stand there while his patron openly admonished him. It was humiliating. The actor was given such a verbal roasting that he was reminded with horrible force of his absent wife.

Margery Firethorn had come into her own. A long and boring wait now gave way to frantic activity. She had a new baby to nurture, a sister to care for, a brother-in-law to scold and a house to run. The cloistered calm of Cambridge was hit by the whirlwind of her presence. She bustled through its streets, haggled in its markets, scattered its citizens and terrorized any of its students who strayed into her path. A city that was marked by its Puritan restraint now felt the full impact of her devastating maternalism.

Weak but happy, Agnes Jarrold lay in her bed and raised a pale hand in a gesture of gratitude.

'You have been very kind, Margery,' she said.

'I have done what needs to be done.'

'We could not have managed without you.'

'The child is healthy. That is my reward.'

'Jonathan joins with me in giving thanks.'

'Your bookworm of a spouse can thank me best by keeping out of my way. Men have no place at such times. Fatherhood is no more than a stupid grin on the face of the foolish.'

'Do not be so scornful,' said Agnes tolerantly. 'Your husband was welcome enough in your bedchamber when your own children were born.'

'He was far more welcome when they were conceived,' said Margery with a twinkle in her eye. 'Present a man with a child and he becomes one himself again.'

'That is true, sister. Jonathan is a boy of three.'

'I did not think him so old.'

The baby stirred in its crib and Margery leaned over to tuck it in. Tears clouded the mother's eyes as she looked at her tiny son. After losing two children to the grave, she viewed the survival of the third as a very special blessing. Her sister's help and brisk affection had been decisive.

'You must miss Lawrence greatly,' said Agnes.

'Only when I look at your husband.'

'Lawrence must pine for you as well.'

'I do not delude myself on that score.'

'His life must be hideously empty without you.'

Margery Firethorn mixed wistfulness with resentment.

'Lawrence has a way of filling empty spaces . . .'

Beatrice Capaldi reclined in a chair at the head of the table. She and her guests had dined royally off silver plate and tasted only the finest wines. The gentlemen caressed her with compliments while the ladies envied her poise and her mystery. In a small but select gathering, the hostess was supremely dominant. Beatrice Capaldi lived for display and effect. She savoured the power she could exert over others.

There was a tap on the door and a maid-servant came in to whisper something in her ear. She excused herself and got up to sail gracefully across the room and out into the hall. The man who was waiting bowed obsequiously then handed her the playbill which he had taken down from a post in Shoreditch. Dismissing him with a flick of her fingers, she studied what he had brought her and saw that it was an advertisement for a performance of *Love's Sacrifice* to be given at The Theatre. Beatrice Capaldi smiled. She had won the desired response from Lawrence Firethorn. While the spectators would be visiting a play, she would be going to a tryst. Preparations would need to be thorough.

'Summon my dressmaker!' she ordered.

'Now, mistress?' said the maidservant.

'This instant!'

The same playbill gave Giles Randolph a different message.

'We have him, Owen!' he said.

'Do we, sir?'

'He plays at The Theatre and we at The Curtain.'

'Shoreditch will host the two best actors in London.'

'No,' corrected Randolph. 'The Curtain will have that honour. We present Giles Randolph *and* Lawrence Firethorn.'

Owen Elias understood. *'The Spanish Jew?'*

'What else, man? The play is everywhere

in request. We have but to announce it to fill our theatre. The audience will come to hiss Dr Lopez and mock Firethorn. To have your old employer in Shoreditch on the same afternoon completes my joy. While he struggles to hold attention with *Love's Sacrifice*, we'll cut his reputation to shreds.' He gave his companion a token embrace. 'Repeat your ridicule of him, sir. Banbury's Men will be indebted to you for ever.'

'Then let me remind you of your promise, master.'

'To be sure, to be sure . . .'

'This role of mine was to win me a place as a sharer in your company,' said Owen Elias. 'I would wish that confirmed with all due haste.'

'And so it shall be,' agreed Randolph airily. 'When we have put Firethorn to flight, you'll be drawn in among us as a partner in the enterprise.'

'When may I see the contract?' pressed the other.

'My attorney will draw it up in due course.'

Owen Elias was content. His future was assured.

Nicholas Bracewell arrived at the Tower to find Andrew Carrick in conversation with a plump individual who stood no more than five feet in height. The newcomer was introduced to Harry Fellowes and he made the most of the fortuitous encounter with the Clerk of Ordnance.

'Master Carrick owes his sanity to you,' said Nicholas.

'Does he so?'

'You are his window on the outside world, sir.'

'Indeed, you are,' confirmed Carrick.

'You allow him to see beyond this bleak prison.'

Fellowes nodded fussily. 'He should never have been committed to the Tower. The least I can do is to offer my friendship and purvey my gossip.'

'It is much appreciated,' said Nicholas, 'and a ready source of wonder. Master Carrick tells me that you know the very nerves of state and hear the faintest stirrings at the palace. Is there news of Her Majesty?'

'None to cheer us, Master Bracewell. She fades.'

'These are grim tidings,' said Carrick.

'For some,' observed Nicholas, 'but not for all.'

'Yes,' said Fellowes. 'The court is one loud buzz of rumour. There are those who would put a new monarch on the throne before the old one has yet departed. They wonder who will rise, who fall, who will be ennobled, who disgraced. It is no time to lack friends or money to buy that friendship.'

'What of Her Majesty's favourites?' asked Nicholas.

'They are thrown into a frenzy,' said the other, warming to his theme. 'The Queen has spread her bounty far and wide. Robin Dudley may be dead and the dancing Hatton may have followed him to Heaven but there are still many others who hang by the thread of Her Majesty's indulgence.'

'Oxford, for one,' suggested Carrick.

Fellowes was dismissive. 'Edward de Vere does not merit her favour. He is too tiresome and quarrelsome a fellow. She will be well-quit of Oxford. Raleigh is another matter. He is distraught at her illness. The Earl of Essex is likewise shocked but he seeks to turn it to his advantage. Then there is Lord Mountjoy and half-a-dozen like him. Royal favourites who fear that the favours will cease . . .'

Nicholas Bracewell and Andrew Carrick were fascinated by the depth of his knowledge and by the breadth of his indiscretion. They fed him questions and got details of scandal and intrigue by reply. Harry Fellowes was a zealous collector of gossip who loved to distribute it freely among friends. It was only when Nicholas quizzed him about the Earl of Chichester that the Clerk of Ordnance backed off. He had said all he intended on the subject. Taking his leave of the two men, he rolled off to his official duties.

Carrick immediately switched his enquiries to an area that had more import for him. Nicholas explained how he had fared on his most recent foray into Clerkenwell. The lawyer was both excited and anxious.

'You get closer to the murderer each time,' he said, 'but I would not have you get too close, Master Bracewell. Remember what befell my son. Keep dear Sebastian in mind.'

'I do so at all times.'

'What is your next move?'

'It must not be rushed,' said Nicholas. 'Now that I have located the woman, she must be confronted but only when I have more evidence. It is not she who struck the murderous blow, though her wound was left on Sebastian's body. She has an accomplice, sir. My next task is to smoke him out.'

'Go armed, sir.'

'I will.'

'Take company for your further security.'

'It is arranged.'

'And *find* this damn rogue!'

'I found him once already.'

'What manner of man is he?'

226

'A frightened one,' said Nicholas levelly. 'He knows that I am looking for him.'

Frances lay half-asleep and half-naked on the bed in her little room at the Pickt-hatch. Marked by the violence of her loving, her last client of the night bumped his way down the stairs in a state of blissful discomfort. An hour in the arms of Frances had been true value for money. He carried his scratches with pride and his memories with boastful honour. She would be sought out again on his next visit to Clerkenwell. As he blundered out into the street, the client turned to glance up at the bedchamber he had just vacated and blew a chaste kiss up to it. He then tottered off down Turnmill Street with the words of some lewd refrain on his lips.

The man who lurked in the shadows watched him until he was out of sight and then stared up at the same window with sturdy patience. Frances appeared long enough to give a signal before she drew the ragged curtain across again. The man hurried into the building. He was a short, ugly creature in his thirties with a compressed power in his squat frame. He wore a simple buff jerkin, hose and cap. When he entered her room with a proprietary swagger, the candle illumined an unprepossessing face into which

227

a large nose had been thrust like a squashed tomato. Beady eyes went first to the money on the little table. Frances watched with trepidation as he counted it out but she relaxed when she saw his thin smile of approval. She was safe.

Tired but comforted, she soon lay in his brawny arms.

'It was a long night,' she murmured.

'Long nights pay.'

'They were all satisfied.'

'That left no work for me.'

'You were there.'

Frances snuggled up to him like a child in need of a parent's love and protection. Her snarling vitality had gone to sleep now and only her vulnerable youth remained awake. He squeezed her tightly with an indifferent affection. She lay in the dark and recalled other nights in another doomed bedchamber. The shivering returned. When his snoring began, she talked to herself.

'My mother was fifteen when I was born. I watched her bring man after man into her bed. Some liked her, some loved her and some even paid her. But others beat her. There was something about my mother that made men beat her for sport. I watched. They took all she had then rewarded her with their fists and their feet. She spilled much blood for her profession then one day there was no more to spill.' The shivering was at its height. 'I swore over her grave that it would never happen to me. They would pay for their pleasure or they would suffer. Those who cheated me would never get the chance to do it again. Thanks to you, sir . . .'

Frances nestled against him and his snoring deepened. She was about to doze off herself when a worry surfaced.

'What about *him*, sir?' she whispered. 'That man who came searching with a portrait of his dead friend. He will one day return. What shall we do?'

Her companion rolled over until she was subjected to the full crushing weight of his body. Her shivering stopped and she was able to sleep in peace. All was well.

Queen Elizabeth remained out of sight but not out of mind. Her prolonged absence served only to inflame speculation. When she cancelled appointments with foreign ambassadors, her sickness was established beyond all reasonable doubt. A clever linguist and a skilful diplomat, she loved to deal with emissaries in their native tongue and confound them with her grasp of the political niceties. Her Majesty revelled in all things majestic. To forego her most enjoyable duties argued the seriousness of her condition. It served to put a frenetic energy into the negotiations that were now whirring away all over London.

'Show me the letter, Roger.'

'I have it right here, sir.'

'When was it delivered?'

'It arrived post haste this morning.'

Roger Godolphin, Earl of Chichester, now held daily meetings with the inner circle of his party. The Earl of Banbury was the first to be given sight of the missive which had been sent from Hardwick Hall by its formidable owner, the Countess of Shrewsbury. Grandmother to the next Queen of England, she was doing her duty with admirable thoroughness.

My good Lord, I am much troubled to think that wicked and mischievous practices may be devised to entrap my poor Arabella and to rob her of her inheritance. Your warnings on this account have been observed to the letter. I will not have any unknown or suspected person to come to my house. Upon the least suspicion that may happen here, any way, I shall give advertisement to your lordship. Arabella walks not late; at such time as she shall take the air, it shall be near the house, and well attended on. She goes not to any other dwelling at all. I see her almost every hour of the day. She lies in my bedchamber. If I can be more precise than I have been, I will be. I am bound in nature to be careful for Arabella, and I find her loving and dutiful towards me. She understands our hopes for her future and will do all that you may ask of her through me. Doubt not that this business will have a joyous conclusion from which both we and the whole kingdom will draw benefit . . .

The Earl of Banbury returned the letter and nodded.

'This could not bring more content,' he said smugly.

'If only Bess would not harp on about herself.'

'We must give the old mare her head.'

'The filly is our concern,' said Chichester with a wry chuckle. 'Queen she may well be but virgin she will not stay. We must find a husband for her bed in good time.'

'The Duke of Parma offered his son.'

'The young man died with fear.'

'There are other dukes with other sons.'

'Italian? French?'

'Spanish even.' He pondered. 'No, not Spain.'

'Should we look to Holland or Germany?'

'There are possibilities enough on our own soil, Roger.'

'Then that is our way,' said Chichester, standing to attention with military suddenness. 'Arabella will try one and try all till she find the man most fitted for her lusty purposes. She can roll through the bedchambers of Europe.'

Banbury grinned. 'Royal business indeed!'

'Let her marry four of them like her grandmother!'

'Observe some decorum here, sir. You talk of the future Queen of England.'

'Elizabeth has her favourites — why not Arabella?'

'Would you turn our sovereign into a species of whore?'

'Why not?' said Chichester with a hint of soldierly coarseness, 'I believe that every woman should mix a little lunacy with her loving.'

Banbury was amused. 'A roving monarch in search of a mate. Bedding the noblest youth in all Europe.'

'Arabella Stuart — Queen of England!'

'A mad courtesan!'

Chapter Nine

Alexander Marwood was a self-appointed martyr. A man who was terrified of women married one of the most fearsome members of the breed. A person who hated responsibility and loathed riotous behaviour owned the largest and most volatile inn along Gracechurch Street. A creature who detested all plays and players found himself host to one of the best theatre companies in London. A natural recluse with an abiding contempt for mankind was daily surrounded by hundreds of abominable faces. A reluctant father spent much of his waking hours guarding the virginity of a nubile daughter. An already seriously balding individual presented himself with regular excuses to tear out the remaining tufts from his unlovely scalp. Marwood's life was death by crucifixion.

He felt another nail being driven through his palm.

'A prudent landlord should always look for profit.'

'I have enough manure at the Queen's Head, sir.'

233

'We offer your patrons a delight, Master Marwood.'

'Not on these premises.'

'But this yard is ideal for our purposes.'

'We have all the dancing nags we require.'

'Nimbus is a king among horses.'

'Crown him elsewhere.'

Cornelius Gant was meeting stiff opposition from the emaciated landlord. The more that Marwood was pressed, the more he retreated into a twitching hostility. Cavernous eyes glared. Lids fluttered violently like agitated butterflies. His slight, angular body arched and shuddered its refusal. Gant tempered his argument with rank flattery.

'You are highly regarded, sir,' he lied extravagantly. 'Many say that the Queen's Head is without a peer. Your ale is much praised and your hospitality commended. When people think of Mine Host, they think of Alexander Marwood.'

'Away with these jests!'

'Your inn is always full, your patrons always happy.'

'Do not spoil my trade with your low tricks.'

'Nimbus and I seek only to increase it.' Gant applied some real persuasion. 'Six hostelries have already given us licence and each one has begged us to return. We have put money in their purses, Master Marwood, and added a lustre to their name. Ask of us at the Feathers in Eastcheap. Go to the Brazen Serpent. Seek a report from the Antelope. They and three others will attest our merit.'

Marwood stole a glance at Nimbus then studied the owner again with unabated suspicion. Something told him that he would be widening the scope of his martyrdom if he acceded to this strange request. His twitch took up residence on his left ear and made it vibrate like the wing of a hummingbird.

Gant tried once more. 'Do you not stage plays here?'

'Against my better judgement.'

'And do they not put money into your coffers?'

'Not enough!' wailed Marwood. 'They will never yield enough to pay for the tortures I undergo in housing them.'

'Westfield's Men must give you a sizeable rent.'

'Only when I hound them for it.'

'Let me offer mine in advance, sir . . .'

Marwood was speechless. The uncouth old man in the garb of a long-discharged soldier was holding out a bag of coins. He was actually willing to buy the right to put his horse through its paces in the yard. Whatever happened during the performance, the landlord could not lose. He trapped the hummingbird ear with one hand then appraised Nimbus afresh. Cornelius Gant jingled the coins. The deal was struck.

There was no delay. Gant produced a trumpet and blew a wild alarum to gain the attention of all who lounged within earshot of the yard. When his musicianship expressed itself in the beating of a small drum, he drew dozens more out into the open air and sent Nimbus prancing in a circle on its hind legs. By the time that Gant had finished pounding and Nimbus had finished prancing, over two hundred people had formed a circle around them and more were drawn in from the street outside. The real performance could begin.

It was unerring. The precision of the dancing and the brilliance of the counting display astounded all present but their open-mouthed wonder was relieved at intervals by some inspired clowning. Cornelius Gant allowed himself to be nudged, tripped, butted, bitten, trodden upon and buffeted in a dozen different ways. At one point, Nimbus even rested his front hooves on its master's shoulders to draw him into a comic dance. When Gant took his bow, the same hooves struck his buttocks with such force that he was propelled forward into a double somersault.

Turning from foe to friend, the horse gripped the old man's collar to drag him upright once more. And so it went on.

The performers had their audience enthralled. Gant felt the familiar surge of power. Repelled by the animal-baiting he had witnessed at Paris Garden, he was yet ready to inflict pain on himself but not on his horse. It was the audience who felt the quiet gnash of his teeth and the gentle flick of his whip. They were his. He controlled their pleasure and dictated their response. Delaying their laughter with some elaborate comic business, he could introduce discomfort. Keeping them in awe for extended periods, he could separate them from the relief of applause. The men, women and children who watched the act might be joyfully absorbed but they were also drained by the cruel suspense, taxed by the multiple unpredictabilities and punished by a cunning sadist.

At the climax of his act, Gant shot the horse dead and put a bullet into the heart of everyone there. Nimbus expired with such realism that a hushed silence fell upon the yard, broken only by the sobbing of women and the cry of a terrified child. The horse stayed motionless long enough to gain full pity and instil full pain then it leapt to its feet again and danced a merry jig. Pande-monium ensued from the massive swirl of emotions that took place.

The hat of Cornelius Gant had never been filled so quickly and so generously. He collected five times what he had paid the landlord in rent. Marwood was dumbfounded. The performance had brought thirsty mouths into his yard and nimble servingmen had sold a large quantity of ale to the spectators. Nimbus had been a sound investment. There had been none of the dreadful risks associated with Westfield's Men. One man and a horse had been a drama in themselves.

Gant stressed the fact with a valedictory message.

'Thank you, my friends!' he shouted. 'You have seen a king at the Queen's Head today. Nimbus has taken the stage from your famous Lawrence Firethorn. I ask you this — who needs an ass of an actor when you have a horse of wonder!'

Alexander Marwood gave a disenchanted smirk.

Nicholas Bracewell had more than his usual cargo of worries at The Theatre that day. Having arranged the transfer of scenery, costumes and property from the Queen's Head then supervised a rather fraught rehearsal of *Love's Sacrifice*, he had to soothe troubled actors, castigate wayward stagekeepers and check that everything was in readiness for the afternoon performance. A hundred minor decisions had to be taken, then enforced, a thousand voices seemed to be calling his name and imploring his advice. But it was the additional anxieties which pressed most heavily upon the book holder.

Chief among these was Lawrence Firethorn who ordered the change of play to accommodate his romantic hopes. The significance of the event made him tense and capricious. He swung crazily between extremes of behaviour and Westfield's Men suffered as much from his rampant affability as from his fierce and indiscriminating rage. Nicholas worked at full stretch to stop arguments, prevent bloodshed and limit the damage to company morale. Beatrice Capaldi was exerting an influence upon the actor-manager that was highly dangerous and it had to be countered in some way. The book holder tried hard to understand why that influence was linked to this particular play.

Love's Sacrifice was a triumph underscored by much unhappiness. Behind the cheers it brought at The Rose and at the Queen's Head were some unpleasant facts. The play soured relations within the company. It led to the eviction of Owen Elias and, in turn, to his defection to Banbury's Men. It was now a duet between a lovesick actor and a mystery woman. It had also become the opening salvo in a propaganda battle that was being waged by their patron. Most unsettling of all to Nicholas, it contained a role that had been especially written for Sebastian Carrick. It was an association that haunted the book holder. Every time he worked on the play, he saw the dead body of his friend on the slab at the morgue. Every time he heard the controversial funeral speech, it was a requiem for his lost colleague.

'Nicholas! Nicholas!'

'Yes, Master Gill?'

'Rescue us from certain catastrophe.'

'What is the matter, sir?'

'Why, Lawrence,' said Barnaby Gill in terror. 'He is *smiling* at us. He is prowling the tiring-house like some grisly Priapus and grinning. That hideous smile will undo us all. That amorous grin will fright us into imbecility!'

As the performance neared, tempers became more frayed. Gill was the first of many who needed a soft word and a reassuring compliment. Edmund Hoode's concern was for the integrity of his text.

'It is no longer my play, Nick!' he complained.

'Nothing can dim its quality.'

'Lines have been cut, scenes moved, characters altered and songs inserted, all to please this creature who has ensnared Lawrence. He has made me write loving couplets which he can throw to her like bouquets of roses.' Hoode folded his arms in annoyance. 'I'll not change another word of *Love's Sacrifice*. There have been sacrifices enough.'

'The drama will still shine through, Edmund.'

'But it will not be *mine!*'

'Your talent improves everything you touch.'

'I would dearly like to improve Lawrence with a touch from a club had not this fatal lady already dashed out his brains.' He grasped his friend's arm. 'Who *is* she? What is her purpose here? We must find out more about her!'

Nicholas had reached that conclusion some time ago.

'We will,' he said.

Anne Hendrik was given a double duty that afternoon. She was to accompany Marion Carrick to the performance in Shoreditch and she was to take up a seat that enabled her to keep a certain member of the audience under surveillance. Nicholas Bracewell had

241

been accurate in his prediction. The dark and enigmatic Beatrice Capaldi swept into her favoured position in the middle of the lower gallery and stitted up a flurry of male interest. Anne had already selected a place at the same level but directly above the stage. She was thus able to look back around the circle of benches to make her own valuation of the lady.

Beatrice Capaldi was indeed striking and her beauty owed far more to nature than to any cosmetic aids. She held herself like a foreign princess, treating all the admiring glances and fulsome compliments that she gathered with autocratic contempt. As Anne Hendrik studied her, an ignoble thought flashed into her mind but she repudiated it with blushing speed and moved on to appraise the resplendent attire. As on the previous occasions, Beatrice Capaldi was there to see and be seen. She wore a dress of white silk that was bordered with tiny pearls and half-covered by a mantle of black silk shot with silver threads. Both sleeves and skirt were explosions of black and white but it was the hat which was the real focus of interest.

Marriage to Jacob Hendrik had taught Anne a great deal about hat-making and running her husband's business had widened that education considerably. She worked exclusively in the Dutch style to produce small hoods of lawn that were worn with an under-cap. Beatrice Capaldi, by contrast, opted for a hat in the Spanish fashion, tall-crowned but brimless and decorated with jewellery around the lower part. Its most startling ornamentation was a high-standing ostrich feather that was fastened in position with more precious stones. Anne Hendrik set a price on the hat and realized that it cost more than her entire wardrobe. What thrilled her was that she noticed idiosyncratic features which threw a name straight back at her.

She knew who had made the hat.

'I have never been to a playhouse before,' confessed Marion Carrick. 'It is so colourful and exciting.'

'You are brave to venture here at such a time.'

'I hope it is not unseemly, mistress.'

'Your brother would surely approve.'

The girl nodded. 'I mourn his death and it has made me want to know more about his profession. Master Bracewell, who has been so helpful, tells me that Sebastian was to play in *Love's Sacrifice*. Curiosity makes me want to see the role that he sadly abandoned.' She smiled. 'Master Bracewell also spoke most warmly of you.'

It was Anne's turn to smile. 'I am pleased.'

'He is a good man but he has taken on such a hazardous task on behalf of my family. I fear for his safety.'

'Nicholas is well able to look after himself.'

Further conversation was cut short by a blast on a trumpet and the running up of a flag that would flutter above the playhouse for the next two hours. Music sounded and the Prologue came out to garner the first small harvest of applause. *Love's Sacrifice* was in motion and Marion Carrick was instantly hypnotized. Anne Hendrik was absorbed as well but that did not prevent her from throwing regular glances in the direction of Beatrice Capaldi. Touched by what her lodger had said about her, she would now be able to reward him handsomely.

Nicholas would be delighted to hear about the hat.

At that moment in time, he was more concerned with the ever-changing series of doublets, cloaks, helmets, dresses, gowns and boots for which the play called. There was scenery to be taken on and offstage as well as countless props to be used and discarded. The commotion behind the scenes was every bit as dramatic as the action which was unfolding before the audience. Nicholas Bracewell coped with his usual imperturbability.

He had no qualms about the drama itself. Edmund Hoode might fulminate but *Love's Sacrifice* was not ruined in any way by the changes forced upon him. The play was sharper than it had been at The Rose and more assured than at the Queen's Head. Weak moments in the construction were completely obscured by the driving force of a superb leading actor.

Lawrence Firethorn out-distanced all superlatives. King Gondar reigned supreme. To the burning passion and the wonderful audacity of the earlier performances, he now added a note of supplication that was utterly moving. A peremptory monarch dared to show his vulnerability and it made the character infinitely more appealing. A wholly committed audience who sighed his sighs with him had no idea that his portrayal was aimed at a single spectator or that the faint smile she gave him in the middle of Act Five was worth more than a sustained round of applause to him.

With Queen Elsin in his arms, he slowly expired. Minor emendation by Edmund Hoode enabled the king to utter the operative line directly at the lower gallery.

Our tale of woe will yield this sage advice.
True love requires the truest sacrifice.

The final speech was spoken by Hoode himself, swaying with emotion over the stricken lovers and using a reedy tenor voice to declaim his verse. Its cadences lulled the audience, its sentiments delighted Lord Westfield and its soaring beauty finally found a way to the heart of Beatrice Capaldi. The prostrate Firethorn did not need to see her hand brush away the little tear. He sensed it immediately. At the third attempt, King Gondar had won her over.

No corpse went off to a royal grave in higher spirits.

The Earl of Banbury was equally pleased with his afternoon at a playhouse in Shoreditch. Seated beside Roger Godolphin at The Curtain, he saw *The Spanish Jew* whip the spectators up into a paroxysm of hatred that was then softened by some wicked comedy. Lopez was denounced and Lawrence Firethorn was maligned but nobody paused to question the justice of it all. Giles Randolph assassinated the former physician while Owen Elias derided his former employer. The topicality of the piece was greater than ever now and new material had been worked in to extol the virtues of rule by a queen. If Elizabeth was on the point of death, it was expedient to smooth the path of her chosen successor. Banbury's Men were skilful practitioners. While entertaining the citizenry of London, they also contrived to blacken the reputation of a foreign doctor, besmirch the name of an outstanding actor and offer a telling political argument.

As the spectators poured out of the theatre in animated discussion, they knew they had had a very special experience. *The Spanish Jew* was much more than a good play. It was a tract for the times and a symbol of the undoubted supremacy of Banbury's Men. In the dynastic struggle between rival claimants, Giles Randolph had finally emerged victorious. He was the uncrowned king of London theatre.

Unaware of his enforced abdication, Lawrence Firethorn went boldly into a private room at The Theatre for what he knew would be one of the critical encounters of his life. She was waiting for him. The invitation which Nicholas Bracewell had borne to her immediately after the performance had elicited the response for which Firethorn had prayed. He and Beatrice Capaldi at last stood face to face. The beauty which had mesmerized him from a distance was quite intoxicating at close quarters and his senses reeled. He recovered to give her a deep and respectful

247

bow. It was only then that he noticed that they were not alone. A female companion waited quietly in a corner with her face hidden discreetly behind a fan. Her presence did not inhibit Firethorn. As the gloved hand of Beatrice Capaldi was extended towards him, he took it between gentle fingers to place the softest of kisses upon it. Beaming with gratitude, he bowed again.

'You do me the greatest honour!' he said.

'The honour is mine, sir,' she replied in a voice which had the most tantalizing hint of an Italian accent. 'It was a privilege to watch your performance this afternoon.'

'It was wholly dedicated to you.'

'That is a compliment I will cherish.'

'Dear lady,' said Firethorn, dispensing with the formal niceties. 'Will you dine with me today?'

'Unhappily, I may not, sir.'

'Tomorrow, then? Or the next day after that?'

'It is not appropriate,' she said demurely.

He was crestfallen. 'May I never entertain you?'

Beatrice Capaldi gave a signal to her companion and the latter moved across to open the door. Her mistress glided over until she was framed in the daylight beyond.

'I would see you again, Master Firethorn,'

she said with studied affection. 'Let us meet on Saturday.'

'Name but the time and place.'

'I have a barge that will take us down the river to Chelsea. We may spend the whole afternoon together.'

'My cup of joy spills over . . .'

'Word will be sent of the precise arrangements.'

'I'll not sleep till it arrives.' He was about to give his third bow when hard fact intruded. 'One moment here. On Saturday next, I am contracted to play with Westfield's Men.'

'I had hoped you would prefer to dally with me, sir.'

'Of course, of course . . .'

'Then there is no more to be said.'

'But I cannot let my company down in this way.'

'Would you rather betray me, sir?'

'No, dear lady. My loyalty is adamantine proof.'

'It seems not,' she observed tartly. 'You may strut upon a stage any day of any week. My barge is not for general hire, I assure you. Let me test this devotion of which you speak. If it be sincere, float on the Thames with me this coming Saturday.'

'It would be a voyage to paradise!'

'Not if you prefer the demands of your calling.'

Firethorn was in pain. 'Westfield's Men rely on me . . .'

'I had thought to do the same, sir.'

'My presence would be sorely missed.'

'True love requires a true sacrifice.'

Beatrice Capaldi looked deep into his eyes to reinforce her meaning. With a gracious smile that took all resistance from him, she then turned on her heel and went out swiftly. Her companion followed and pulled the door shut. Lawrence Firethorn remained immobile for several minutes. He was overwhelmed by the interview. Beatrice Capaldi was the most remarkable woman he had ever met and his pursuit of her made all else in his life irrelevant. The air was still charged with her fragrance and he inhaled it with sensual nostrils. A leisurely journey to Chelsea in a private barge was a promise of earthly bliss. Westfield's Men vanished from his concerns as he called silently after the departed goddess.

'I am yours, my love . . .'

Marion Carrick was in a quandary. The conflicting emotions which she had brought to The Theatre that afternoon had been stirred up even more by a compelling drama and she now found herself in a state of complete ambivalence. Respect for a dead brother obliged her to remain at home with a grief that could only be relieved by daily visits to church but the urge to find out more about Sebastian was too strong. *Love's Sacrifice* made her weep, laugh, sigh, fear and tremble with sheer excitement. Her first visit to a playhouse taught her a great deal about her brother but even more about herself.

Nicholas Bracewell was a considerate host. Once he had dispatched his various tasks, he gave Marion and Anne Hendrik a brief tour behind the scenes and explained the technical effects he had devised for the play. Marion was then able to shower Edmund Hoode with her naive praise and redeem what had been a testing afternoon for the playwright. While congratulating him on his own performance, Marion was anxious to hear how her brother might have acquitted himself in the same role and she was touched by the esteem in which Hoode obviously held his departed colleague.

Nicholas took the opportunity of a few words alone with Anne Hendrik. Her identification of a hat-maker was a most unexpected bonus and he was duly grateful.

'You have done Westfield's Men a great service today.'

'By looking at a hat instead of watching

a play?' she said mischievously. 'If all spectators did the same, you and your fellows would quickly go out of business.'

'The threat to our livelihood comes from elsewhere,' he said, 'and you have helped us to measure its power. That hat will lead me to the house of Mistress Beatrice Capaldi where I may begin to unravel her mystery a little.'

Anne Hendrik felt the slightest twinge of jealousy.

'What do *you* think of the lady, Nick?'

'Me?'

'You have twice been close to her person.'

'Only on embassy from Master Firethorn.'

'You have eyes, you have feelings.'

Nicholas was tactful. 'They are engaged elsewhere.'

'A pretty answer but it evades my question.'

'I thought as any man would think, Anne,' he said honestly. 'Beatrice Capaldi is a woman of great beauty.'

'Did her charms not enslave you?'

'No.'

'Would you not like to be in Master Firethorn's shoes?'

'My own fit far more comfortably.'

'Will you admit *nothing* about this enchantress?'

He was serious. 'She is no friend of mine.'

Anne Hendrik relaxed and talked at length about the conduct of Beatrice Capaldi during the play itself. The latter seemed to be giving a performance that was as well-rehearsed and carefully-judged as any on the stage. The idea which had earlier flashed through Anne's mind now made a second momentary appearance.

'Nick . . .'

'Yes?'

'Did you observe anything else about the lady?'

'I was there but as a messenger.'

'It is only a feeling of mine . . .'

'I trust to your instincts, Anne.'

She hesitated then backed off quickly. 'No!' she said. 'It was an unkind thought brought on by merest envy. The lady is truly beautiful and she wore a hat that I would give anything to have sold her.'

Nicholas brushed a kiss against her forehead. Marion Carrick rejoined them to offer her thanks once more. As they left the playhouse, reality began to crowd in upon her again and she became the distressed sister of a murdered actor.

'We owe much to your kindness, Master Bracewell.'

'Sebastian was my friend.'

'We may never be able to repay you.'

'I do not seek reward.'

'It irks my father greatly,' she said. 'To be locked away at such a time and in such a condition. He feels the weight of our obligation to you. Father would love to be able to offer you recompense of some kind. He is searching desperately for a way to express our gratitude.'

Enforced idleness was a cumulative misery to a man such as Andrew Carrick. A conscientious lawyer with a substantial clientele, he was at his happiest when in the throes of some litigation. Because he found the cut and thrust of argument so bracing, the unforgiving gloom of the Tower of London was especially lowering. He brooded on. Harry Fellowes came to assume more importance in his life by the day. Not only did Carrick savour their brief conversations, he was given a subject for endless speculation. The Clerk of Ordnance was much more than a holder of Crown office. Eminent visitors came to call on him at the Office and Carrick noted their arrival with interest. It was conceivable that the Earl of Chichester came to the Tower to discharge official business with his junior and that the loan arranged between them — witnessed by the lawyer — was related in some way to the operation of the Ordnance Department but that explanation could not cover the others who came in earnest search of Harry Fellowes.

An astute observer like Carrick soon developed a theory and he waited patiently for a moment to put it to the test. His friend was too guileful to respond to direct questioning and so the lawyer chose a more subtle line of examination.

'I have a favour to ask of you, good sir,' he said.

'Ask away,' encouraged the other. 'I will do all I can except secure your release, and I would do that, too, if it were within my power.'

'You have been a sound friend.'

'I hate to see you suffer for such a trivial offence.'

'In future, I will attend no more marriages.'

They shared a laugh, then strolled across the courtyard. Bright sunshine streamed down to imprison them in a neat rectangle of light. Carrick grew confidential.

'Evidently, you are well-acquainted with the nobility.'

'And they with me,' said Fellowes.

'Then haply you may advise me.'

'On what matter?'

'I have this client, a gentleman of high rank . . .'

'How do you serve him?'

'Very ill while I am penned up here and his business is very pressing.' He lowered his voice. 'It is also a subject of some delicacy and one with which I am not altogether qualified to deal. My noble lord's problem . . .'

Fellowes guessed it. 'He requires money.'

'You are very perceptive, sir.'

'It needs no great insight to divine that,' he said. 'Poverty is the natural condition of our nobility. They build houses they cannot afford, keep retinues of servants whom they cannot pay, then give lavish hospitality that sends them even deeper into debt.'

'That is certainly the case with my client.'

'It is the case with most of them, Master Carrick. We have nineteen earls and marquesses in England and there are not half-a-dozen who can pay their own way.' He became more expansive. 'Such men are born to borrow. Look but upon the late Earl of Leicester. When he died in Armada year, he left behind debts of £85,000. Were they honoured by his heirs?'

'Tell me, sir.'

'They were not. Those debts were promptly increased. The great man's funeral alone cost £8,000. Even for such a royal favourite, it was an expensive hole in the ground.'

'These sums do much to reassure me.'

'Then your client's problem is of smaller degree.'

'He staged an entertainment at his country estate.'

'How much does he owe his creditors?'

'Some £650.'

'A mere trifle,' said Fellowes airily. 'I could lend him that amount myself.'

Carrick affected mild surprise. 'You, sir?'

'At a moderate rate of interest.'

'My client would be very willing to pay that.'

'May I know his name?'

'Let me first sound him out,' said Carrick. 'They lock me up but they allow me pen and ink. I will write to him forthwith and tell him I have found a trustworthy banker.'

'You may also mention that my credit is good among his peers.' Fellowes could not resist a boast. 'I have been of assistance to three earls and a duke.'

Andrew Carrick thanked him and moved gently away from the topic of his fictional client. Having confirmed one part of his theory, he now addressed another. The guard was being changed at the Tower and the soldiers went through their established drill.

Carrick watched approvingly.

'They have fine uniforms and good weapons,' he noted.

'Both are essential in the military world.'

'Do such items come within your remit?'

'Everything passes through me at one time or another,' asserted Fellowes. 'That is why I have so many junior clerks to help me keep the accounts. It is no sinecure that I hold. This month alone, I have drawn up estimates of naval charges affecting the Office and debts due within it. I have made costings of munitions for castles and blockhouses then receipted Exchequer warrants for the necessary sums. I have arranged transport of munitions to our army in Ireland. And I have provided the Earl of Essex with an aide memoire on a subject of military significance.'

'Your industry does you credit, Master Fellowes.'

'I serve the Crown as best I may.'

'We are lucky to have a man of such high probity in a position of such power,' said Carrick solemnly. 'There must be grave temptations for weaker souls.'

The Clerk of Ordnance gave a sharp reply. 'We have a List of Orders to govern all procedures,' he said sternly. 'They make abuse impossible. All records must be kept in duplicate, one for the Ordnance and another for the Council. All indentures are to be signed by three officers. No purchases may be made on the authority of a single officer. The chest where all our receipts and dockets are held in custody has a three-lock mechanism with separate keys for the Master, Lieutenant and Surveyor of Ordnances.' Fellowes adopted the pose he used in the pulpit. 'As you will see from these precautions, we are scrupulous in our dealings.'

Andrew Carrick nodded in agreement. He also noted that such stringent regulations would not have been drawn up in the first place if there had not already been widespread abuse and embezzlement in the Office. He flattered the other with unstinting praise before slipping in a last question. 'How long have you been Clerk of Ordnance . . . ?'

Josiah Taplow and William Merryweather trundled through the streets of Clerkenwell in a vain attempt to impose law and order upon an unruly neighbourhood. It was a dark night with a churlish breeze that carried the promise of rain. The two watchmen sauntered along in step and wondered if there was a less burdensome or unrewarding job than the office of constable. They had uniforms, lanterns and weapons of a sort but no status beyond that of buffoons. Taplow often thought nostalgically of his days as a plasterer and Merryweather longed to be back among his dead poultry. The former would have been more of a match for criminals with a trowel in his hand and the latter could have given a far better account of himself in a brawl if armed with his cleaver. They traded their customary moans then fell back into a dutiful silence. As their old legs measured out the reeking filth of Turnmill Street, they inhaled the air of sweeter memories. Josiah Taplow saw rows of inviting walls and William Merryweather viewed the necks of a hundred chickens.

The watchmen ambled past the Pickt-hatch but noticed nothing untoward. Riotous behaviour within and loitering gallants without were normal features of the establishment and the colleagues did not even throw the place a glance. Drunkenness thrived in the lower rooms and debauchery in those above. Indeed, if sin had a tonnage, then the whole building would have toppled over with its own weight. The two men walked all the way to Cow Cross by the time that the figure appeared at a window. Frances had met with another problem. Though her customer had paid her well, he had beaten her to heighten his pleasure and left her severely bruised.

She watched till the man came out of the building then gestured with her hand. The message was clearly understood.

Weary from his excesses, her violent lover dragged himself along in the darkness and cursed aloud as the first drops of rain began to bite at him. He swung into Cock Alley and found the wind punching angrily into his face. He spat his defiance and surged on with lowered head, ignoring the slime through which he was now trudging and kicking out at a stray dog that popped out from a doorway. Oblivious to the thickset man who trailed him, he struggled on through the damp night.

The watchmen were a hundred yards away when they heard the first yell of agony and they reacted at once. Showing a surprising turn of foot for their age, they sprinted off towards the roaring torment in Cock Alley, guided by each new howl of misery from the victim. They arrived in time to see the fallen man being kicked and struck by his assailant with wilful savagery. The speed of their approach put the attacker to flight and he vanished into the darkness. By the light of their lanterns, the watchmen assessed the condition of the groaning wreck on the ground. He was beaten to a pulp and bones had been broken all over his anatomy. It was the work of a seasoned ruffian. Instead of killing his prey with a single blow, he wanted to smash him slowly to pieces.

Josiah Taplow and William Merryweather came panting up the lane in utter astonishment. No other watchmen were due to patrol their area that night. Taplow raised his staff as if to strike and called out a command.

'Who goes there?'

'Have no fear, sir,' said Nicholas Bracewell, turning to him. 'We are friends that merely borrowed your attire for purposes of our own tonight.'

'This man needs a surgeon,' said Edmund Hoode.

'What are you?' croaked Merryweather.

Nicholas pulled off his cap to reveal himself then introduced Hoode. Their garb had been taken from the store of costumes that Westfield's Men kept at the Queen's Head. In the guise of constables, they had licence to search the streets of Clerkenwell.

'Who did you seek?' asked Josiah Taplow.

'A murderer,' said Nicholas.

'Did you find him?'

'This is his handiwork here.' Nicholas bent down beside the victim who had now lapsed into unconsciousness. 'I believe we shall find the mark of his accomplice as well.'

Because the man lay on his front, Nicholas

was able to lift his jerkin and his shirt to expose a broad back. Hoode angled his lantern so that they could all see the tattoo. Red lines of blood had been etched by wild fingernails. A night of passion had been a loveless embrace.

Nicholas was sorry for the victim but glad that he and Edmund Hoode had come to Clerkenwell that night. He felt that he was now one step closer to his quarry. It was only a question of time before the ruthless killer and his equally ruthless partner at the Pickt-hatch were called to account.

Sebastian Carrick could then rest in peace.

Chapter Ten

Childbirth was a source of mystery and pain. No woman could escape its random cruelties. Rank, wealth and the finest medical advice in the kingdom could not prevent recurring disasters in fraught bedchambers. Catherine of Aragon, first wife of Henry VIII, had numerous pregnancies but most ended in miscarriages, stillbirths or death on delivery. Only one of her children, Mary, survived infancy and when she herself came to the throne, her barren womb was mocked by phantom pregnancies that had been confirmed by learned physicians. The meanest beggarwoman who gave birth under a hedge could sometimes stand as much chance of rearing the child as the high-born ladies who underwent long confinements. Nothing about the miraculous process was certain except the fact that it cost the lives of large numbers of mothers and babies. Birth and death were familiar bedfellows.

Margery Firethorn understood this only too well. She and her sister were the two survivors of their mother's seven children and Margery had watched infant mortalities darken the households of many of her relatives and friends. Her bustling benevolence at the Cambridge abode masked her deep concern for Agnes who was not as robust as her elder sister. But each day brought a visible improvement in mother and child as well as a growing self-importance in the father as Jonathan Jarrold came to terms with his new status. After coming through a testing birth, the baby seemed to know that the worst was over and it guzzled happily at the breasts of the wet nurse. The infant Richard patently liked the world well enough to remain in it and his sense of purpose was the best possible physic for his mother. With Margery for ever at her side to reassure her, Agnes Jarrold came to believe that she would at last be able to raise a family.

Her thoughts turned fondly to her brother-in-law.

'I would dearly like to see Lawrence again,' she said.

'Then you must come to London and take your place in his audience.' Margery feigned irritation. 'My husband is so famous these days that even I have to pay a penny to catch sight of him and twopence to converse with his eminence.'

'Is he a good father to your children?'

'I hope he is not a good father to anyone else's.'

'Do not twist my words so, Margery.'

'Lawrence does what his profession allows him. Which means, alas, that he sees little enough of the children and subjects them to what outbursts of fatherhood he can muster when they do meet.' She set her jaw. 'They have me as their mother and that gives them two parents in one.'

Agnes Jarrold turned her head on the pillow to look across at the crib where her son slept. The tightly-bound linen strips allowed her to see only a portion of his face but it had the peace of true innocence upon it.

'You have been mother, father and aunt to dear Richard,' she said. 'As well as wife and friend to poor Jonathan.'

'Do not wed me to a bookseller!' protested Margery. 'And do not befriend me to a lover of Greek and Latin. I will tolerate the oaf for your sake, Agnes, but I could never lie beside his yapping scholarship.'

'But he adores you, sister.'

'Then must he be a devil-worshipper.'

They chuckled in unison. Living in Cambridge had given Margery an insight into a more conventional marriage and it made her long for her own more eccentric variation of holy matrimony. Lawrence Firethorn was

266

vain, irascible, devious and inclined to wander but he was never dull. She might have to suffer his woes but she also enjoyed his triumphs and these brought the kind of sustained exhilaration that was unknown in a quiet bookshop in a university town. When she went to see a play with Jonathan Jarrold, she snored beside him. When she visited a theatre with Lawrence Firethorn, he thrilled her to the core of her being from the centre of the stage. After all their years together, her husband could still make her feel like his leading lady.

'I am quite recovered today,' said Agnes bravely.

'You still need much rest, sister.'

'But I hate to impose upon you.'

'Do not worry on my account.'

'You have a house and family of your own, Margery.'

'They'll not melt away in my absence.'

'They will miss you painfully.'

'It will serve them right!'

'How long do you intend to stay in Cambridge?'

'As long as I deem it necessary.'

'We would hate to detain you if — '

'Stop it, Agnes!' scolded the other. 'I'll not be packed off before I am ready to go. That child needs my care, that nurse needs my guidance, those servants need my orders and that dreaming husband of yours needs a box on the ears. She leaned over the bed to kiss Agnes on the cheek. 'If all goes well, I may leave at the end of the week.'

'Lawrence will be surprised at your early return.'

'That is my hope.'

'Will you write to him, Margery?'

'I would rather take him unawares.'

'So you may depart at the end of the week?'

'On Saturday.'

'On Saturday! This is the basest treachery, man! Saturday!'

'Calm down, Barnaby.'

'Then do not put me to choler.'

'It is but one performance that I miss.'

'One is far too many, Lawrence.'

'Even the strongest of us must rest.'

'Yes,' said Barnaby Gill tetchily. 'And we all know where you will be resting, sir. Between the legs of some dark-haired lady with a fond smile.'

'You impugn my honour!'

'I did not know you had any left to impugn.'

Edmund Hoode stepped in smartly to prevent the argument from degenerating into an exchange of wild abuse. He, Barnaby Gill and Nicholas Bracewell were in Shoreditch at the actor-manager's house. The noise of debate was already so loud and the vituperation already so liberal that the other occupants of the dwelling thought that Margery must have returned from Cambridge. Gill was livid with outrage. The three visitors had come to discuss one crisis and Firethorn had immediately precipitated another by informing them that he would not be appearing with Westfield's Men on the following Saturday. It was an extraordinary decision for him to make, all the more so in the wake of the battering which his reputation had taken. *Love's Sacrifice* might have wooed its audience and won its leading actor a voyage down the Thames but the real interest among playgoers was centred on *The Spanish Jew*.

The brilliant impersonation by Owen Elias of his former master had caught the public imagination. Those who had seen it trumpeted its wicked accuracy and those who had not clamoured for it to be repeated. In his two performances to date, a discarded Welsh actor had done more harm to the professional renown of Lawrence Firethorn than Banbury's Men had contrived in two years. The full horror had made itself known to Westfield's Men. Through the person of their prime talent, they were being viciously ridiculed.

'We must strike back at once, Lawrence,' said Hoode.

'I will do just that,' promised the other grimly. 'I'll meet Owen Elias in a duel, cut his ungrateful Welsh head from his shoulders and send it back to Randolph with an apple in the mouth. That is the way to serve roast pig, sirs!'

'*The Spanish Jew* is a powerful weapon.'

'We have mightier artillery, Edmund.'

'Then let us fire it from the stage.'

'On Saturday!' insisted Gill. 'Saturday afternoon!'

'No, sir!' replied Firethorn with sudden vehemence. 'On Monday, Tuesday, Wednesday, Thursday and Friday but not this forthcoming Saturday.'

'Give us a reason,' said Hoode patiently.

Gill pouted. 'Ask the question of his codpiece.'

'I am engaged elsewhere on Saturday,' said Firethorn.

'But our schedule has *The Loyal Subject* listed for performance,' reminded its troubled author. 'We must trespass on your own loyalty here, Lawrence. Stand by your fellows.'

Firethorn posed. 'Have I ever let the company down?'

'Many times,' said Gill.

'That is still a deal less than you, sir!'

'My art is above reproach.'

'Would that the same could be said for your acting!'

'Barnaby Gill *is* Westfield's Men!'

'Then are we all digging our own graves.'

Hoode again jumped in to keep them apart then he turned a supplicatory face towards Nicholas Bracewell. The book holder had been listening in silence as he weighed up the situation. He had a potential solution to offer.

'Owen Elias is our hope of salvation here,' he said.

'Only if we kill him instantly!' hissed Firethorn.

'He is more use to us alive than dead, sir. And of far more value as one of us than as a member of Banbury's Men.' Nicholas spoke with quiet reason. 'If we can coax him back into the fold, we take the sting out of our rivals. If we can employ him at his true worth, we have a fine actor who will be a credit to us all. And if we move swiftly, we may still stage *The Loyal Subject* on Saturday, though Master Firethorn may have business elsewhere.'

'Yes!' agreed Hoode. 'Owen will take over his part.'

'And play it far better,' added Gill maliciously.

'No!' howled Firethorn. 'Never, never, never! I'll not yield one syllable to Owen Elias, let alone a whole part. I'd sooner hand the play to Giles Randolph so that he could fill my place. Are you mad, Nick? Do not even mention the name of that leek-eating rogue in my presence. He is gone for ever!'

'Not while *The Spanish Jew* holds the stage.'

'Nick speaks good sense!' said Hoode.

'Owen Elias had sold his black soul to Banbury's Men.'

'Buy it back,' urged Nick.

'Not for *anything!*'

Firethorn's yell of derision was so bloodcurdling that it terminated that stage of the argument. Nicholas weighed in with the alternative suggestion of postponing *The Loyal Subject* until such time as its star was available and of substituting *Cupid's Folly*. Barnaby Gill was revived at once by the thought of leading the company in his favourite play and Edmund Hoode conceded that it was a way to mitigate the awkwardness of the situation. When Firethorn gave his token acquiescence, both men excused themselves to give Nicholas a moment alone with the actor-manager.

The book holder did not mince his words.

'Lord Westfield is extremely distressed, sir.'

'I'm well aware of that, Nick.'

'This is not the time to let Banbury's Men gain the upper hand over us. It could have serious consequences.'

'Do not lecture me.'

'Our performances are in a set order.'

'I helped to choose them,' said Firethorn irritably, 'so do not tell me why *The Loyal Subject* was marked out for Saturday afternoon. It is the best day of the week for us and one when we can make most impact. *The Loyal Subject* was commissioned from Edmund when we performed at court. In view of Her Majesty's grievous condition, we could not make a more apt choice. The play celebrates the life of our revered Queen and enjoins all subjects to serve her devotedly.'

'Our patron has high admiration for the piece.'

'Quite rightly.'

'He is expecting to watch it this weekend.'

'Then he will be disappointed!' Firethorn's cry gave way to a hopeless shrug. 'I am torn in two here, Nick. I wish to lead my company on Saturday but I may not. I cannot. I simply *must* not.'

273

'Your excuse must be a very persuasive one.'

'I have . . . given my word,' mumbled Firethorn.

'Could not that promise be fulfilled on Sunday just as well as on Saturday?' ventured Nicholas. 'It is but a case of waiting twenty-four hours. Unlike our rivals with their theatres outside the city boundaries, Westfield's Men may not play on a Sunday. That is the time for dalliance, sir.'

'Do not make my guilt any worse.'

'But you give so much ground to Banbury's Men. If you desert us on Saturday, we lose our most telling play and turn some of our audience towards The Curtain where *The Spanish Jew* will be mounted once more.' Nicholas sighed. 'We are but an army fighting without our captain. Banbury's Men have both Saturday and Sunday to steal a march on our company.'

'You counsel well but my heart speaks louder.'

'May I talk to the lady in your stead?'

'No, no,' said Firethorn, fearful that a delicate state of relations might be upset. 'I must follow my own prompting here. But I do not do so lightly, believe me.'

'Your mind is quite fixed?'

'Immovably.'

Nicholas accepted defeat and walked to the door. Now that Firethorn was in a more tranquil mood, he prodded a tentative name towards him.

'Do not be too harsh on Owen Elias, sir.'

'I'll tear the lousy knave limb from stinking limb!'

The imprecations were still pouring out like molten lava as Nicholas waved a farewell and let himself out of the house. It had been a depressing visit. Lawrence Firethorn was even more seriously embroiled with Beatrice Capaldi than he had feared. An actor who rejoiced in his performances was letting a woman come between him and his company. She could not have appeared at a more inauspicious moment.

It was time to call on a hat-maker.

Old age and uncertain health were slowly taking their toll of the Earl of Chichester but the effects of both had been temporarily reversed by the mounting excitement of a dispute over the succession. Action rejuvenated him. It took years off his back and put paid to his incipient deafness, chronic dyspepsia and general fatigue. Roger Godolphin had always lived ostentatiously beyond his means and indulged his taste for rich food and fine wine with ruinous thoroughness. Now he had the perfect excuse to do both. Having raised yet another loan, he was able to entertain on a lavish scale once more and buy support for his cause. Suddenly, he was a power behind the throne and others gravitated towards him. If his nominee were indeed crowned, he would not live to draw full benefit from her reign but he was impelled by the thought that his family would reap untold advantage, his friends would gain immeasurably and he himself would find a niche in history. It was not given to many men to make their mark on one reign. He would have set his imprimatur on two.

'The future of England lies in the balance,' he said.

'We must tip it our way.'

'When the moment comes, we'll push with all our might.'

'But do we have enough weight?'

'Look around you, sir. Some of the heaviest names in the kingdom dine at my table today.'

'Some of them — but not all.'

The Earl of Banbury was getting nervous as the crucial time approached and he was grateful for his colleague's military self-discipline. Roger Godolphin did not flinch in battle. Banbury took due comfort. Both men were dining in the house on the Strand where the beaming host presided over a groaning board. At a lavish banquet, they could strengthen their position and gormandize at the same time. It was the ideal way to secure their prize. Important figures from state and church sat all around them, devouring their meat with relish, hungry vultures feeding on the carcass of a dead queen and toasting her successor with Tudor blood.

Banbury still hesitated. 'We need Burghley.'

'He will not commit himself one way or the other,' said the host. 'Besides, his time has passed. She goes, he falls. That gout will carry him off soon enough.'

'His son, Robert, is now leading Westfield's party.'

'That is of no account.'

'If Robert Cecil can get his father's approval . . .'

'Forget that whole family,' reassured Chichester. 'They belong to the old reign and have no place in the new. Robert Cecil may drag fools like Westfield in his wake but he is still too young and untried in the ways of the world.' He curled his lip. 'That scheming little hunchback is no match for a true politician like me, sir.'

'Indeed not, Roger.'

'I sit at the head of the table.'

It was an appropriate metaphor. The Earl

of Chichester was well able to eat, drink, order his servants, dominate his guests, keep five conversations going simultaneously and still be able to commune with Banbury in an undertone. In a very short time, he had given his party the clear advantage.

The Earl of Banbury rose to a wistful sigh.

'It will mean the end of the Tudor dynasty,' he said.

'What of that?' snapped the other.

'Her Majesty's reign has been long and stable.'

'Too long, sir.'

'We have all profited from that.'

'Your memory fails you,' said Chichester bitterly. 'The Tudors have never liked the nobility. When Henry Tudor was a peevish boy, there were sixty-four peers in England. When he seized the crown at Bosworth, there were but thirty-eight left and he did little enough to add to them.'

'His son created earls and marquesses.'

'Then had them executed out of spite. Henry VIII knew his father's rule. Strong kingship means a weak nobility. And our Queen has followed this dictate.' His bitterness deepened. 'The Tudors raise up in order to cast down. Show me a duke or a marquess in the last hundred years who was never attainted as a traitor.'

Banbury scratched his head. 'William Paulet?'

'The only one. Marquess of Winchester and now dead.'

'And if Arabella comes to the throne . . . ?'

'*When,* sir,' corrected his friend. 'When Queen Arabella is crowned, I look for a dukedom.'

As he was speaking, the old man's eyes never left the messenger who was admitted at the far end of the room, spoke with the steward and was then motioned towards the head of the table. The newcomer bowed and delivered his message in a whisper, confirming it with a letter. The Earl of Chichester broke the seal to read the contents as the banter around the table gradually ceased and everyone turned to watch him. A hefty bribe had finally delivered a result. The letter was from one of the Queen's own physicians.

The host did not need to call for silence. They were all anxious to hear the latest development and to be given reassurance that they had backed the right side.

'Word from the Palace, sirs,' said Chichester. 'Her Majesty is fighting for her life but sinking fast. If the fever does not break soon, she will die by Saturday.'

Communal sadness, relief and joy in one word.

Saturday!

Though there was no performance that afternoon, Nicholas Bracewell still had a full working day. After the early morning fracas at Lawrence Firethorn's house, he went back to the Queen's Head to set his staff in motion. Hugh Wegges, the tireman, was ordered to make new costumes, Nathan Curtis, the master-carpenter was commissioned to build some new scenic devices, Thomas Skillen, the stagekeeper, was told to buy fresh rushes to spread on the boards, and George Dart was sent off to the printers for some playbills. Nicholas also found time to instruct the apprentices in swordplay, listen to the latest songs written by Peter Digby, calm the still agitated Barnaby Gill and offer constructive criticism to Edmund Hoode when the playwright outlined the plot of his next play. No visit to the Queen's Head would be complete without a brush with the cadaverous landlord.

'Good day, Master Marwood,' said Nicholas.

'It has lacked goodness so far, sir.' He smirked. 'I may have to invite Nimbus back to my yard.'

'Nimbus?'

'Look to your reputation, Master Brace-well.'

'Why?'

'There is finer entertainment in town.'

'Of what nature?'

'Westfield's Men have been displaced in my favour.'

'By Nimbus?'

'Even so.'

'Who is he, sir?'

'A better actor than Master Firethorn.'

'I doubt that.'

'A more comical clown than Master Gill.'

'Can this be possible?'

'And a more profitable visitor than your company.'

'What does Nimbus do?' said Nicholas.

'Everything, sir.'

'He is a performer?'

'Even my wife was entranced.'

It was the highest accolade. Alexander Marwood's dark melancholy arose very largely out of his marriage to the stone-faced woman of implacable will. Anyone who could coax a response — let alone a smile — out of Sybil Marwood was indeed a remarkable performer. Nicholas was curious.

'What sort of man is this Nimbus?'

The landlord sniggered. 'He's a horse.'

Marwood trickled off and left the book

holder to digest the information. A chat with one of the ostlers brought more elucidation. While Westfield's Men had been performing at The Theatre, their place had been taken at the Queen's Head by Cornelius Gant and Nimbus. Like his employer, the ostler was full of praise and wonder. Nicholas was glad that his own employer was not there to hear it. Lawrence Firethorn would not endure a comparison with a dancing stallion.

Finishing his stint at the inn, Nicholas rushed off to Cheapside to visit the hat-maker whose name had been given to him by Anne Hendrik. An apprentice was closing up the shop when Nicholas arrived and it did not take long to wheedle the information out of him. Nicholas posed as a glover who had been commissioned by Beatrice Capaldi to make a pair of gloves to match her latest hat. The apprentice duly admitted him to the premises to view the new creation so that he could appraise its colour and material. In the course of their chat, Nicholas relieved him of the lady's address, then thanked him and slipped away.

Beatrice Capaldi lived in a house near the river at Blackfriars. Though it had a narrow frontage, it was a capacious building with a long garden at the rear as well as a small courtyard with stabling. Evidently, the place was kept in good repair by someone with an appreciable income. As Nicholas walked beside the garden he could hear snatches of a madrigal sung by a boy to the accompaniment of a lute. He fancied that he caught the voice of the lady herself as well but he could not be sure of this and he was soon distracted by the arrival of a visitor. Coaches were more populous in London now but few were of the size and magnificence of this one. It belonged to a person of some eminence and, although he did not see the man who flitted so swiftly into the house, Nicholas did catch a glimpse of the coat of arms on the departing vehicle. He had seen it before but could not remember exactly where. What he could remember was a remark that Anne Hendrik made about the mistress of the house. He listened to the madrigal more carefully.

Early evening took him to the Elephant in Shoreditch. It was the inn which stood closest to the Curtain and was thus frequented by members of the resident company there. Nicholas was conscious that he was venturing in among the enemy but he had no choice. It was the only way to see Owen Elias who was now one of Banbury's Men.

The Welshman was carousing with his new colleagues.

'Nick!' he welcomed. 'What brings you here?'

'A favour, Owen.'

'To ask or to give?'

'Both.'

'Call the boy and order more ale!'

'The treat will be mine.'

'No,' said Elias benevolently. 'On my ground, I pay.'

Nicholas let him buy the drink then detached him to a corner of the taproom. Owen Elias was in an expansive mood after another rousing performance with Banbury's Men in a testing part. He was still inebriated with his success and Nicholas let him talk about it at length. In a very short time, the actor had established himself at his new home and fallen in love with its novelty. At the same time, there was a whisper of guilt in his manner, a reluctance to look his old friend in the eye that was very untypical. Nicholas said little but heard all with interest.

Owen Elias suddenly became shifty and defensive.

'Are you sent here by Master Firethorn?' he said.

'No.'

'Then why did you come?'

'On my own account.'

'You spoke of a favour.'

'Yes,' said Nicholas. 'It is the best favour that I can offer, Owen. An invitation to return to us.'

'That's no favour but a vile threat!'

'It would be in your best interests.'

'I have done with Westfield's Men for ever.'

'You are needed, Owen.'

'Then why was I cast out?'

'Master Firethorn has a temper.'

'Let him use it on someone else. I'll none of it!'

'Do you hate him so much?'

'I swore revenge on the villain!'

'Yes,' said Nicholas quietly. 'And you have got that revenge, by all accounts. All of London is talking about your work in *The Spanish Jew*. You have swinged Master Firethorn soundly. How many more times will you do it?'

'More times?'

'When is your revenge complete?'

'Well . . .'

'After one performance, two, three? Or do you intend to blacken another man's character in perpetuity?'

'He expelled me, Nick!'

'Master Randolph may do the same.'

'Oh, no!'

'When you have served your purpose, he

may turn you out of Banbury's Men without a flicker of conscience.'

'He will not,' said Elias firmly, 'because I will be a sharer with the company. Engaged by contract.'

'Have you signed that contract?'

'Not yet.'

'Have you *seen* it then?'

'It is being drawn up.'

'And will that content you?'

Nicholas fixed him with a searching gaze that made him shift uneasily on his stool. Owen Elias emptied his pot of ale and wiped his mouth with the back of his hand.

'My life is here now, Nick,' he said.

'Can you be sure of that?'

'Master Randolph admires my work greatly.'

'How did he come to know its quality?'

'He watched me in *Love's Sacrifice* at The Rose.'

'Giles Randolph?'

'He was struck by my performance.'

'But what brought him there in the first place?' asked Nicholas. 'Why does he study Westfield's Men when he has a company of his own? He was at The Rose, you say?'

'Searching for talent.'

'And his eye lighted on you?'

'My similarity to Master Firethorn impressed him.'

Nicholas was mystified. He was also worried on his friend's behalf. He was angry at the way Owen Elias had used his skills against his old company but that did not stop him from fearing for the latter. The Welshman's lust for glory on stage was being cleverly exploited by Giles Randolph who was offering an irresistible inducement to a hired man. If Elias became a sharer, his livelihood was guaranteed but the very talents that were being used against Westfield's Men at the moment would in time threaten Randolph himself. The performance at The Rose kept rustling away at the back of Nicholas's mind. Owen Elias might have been the incidental beneficiary of Giles Randolph's visit but the latter did not come there specifically to see him. There had to be another reason to take him down to Southwark that afternoon.

'I must go, Nick,' said Elias uncomfortably.

'But I've not asked you to do me a favour yet.'

'What is it?'

'Pay off an old debt.'

'Debt?'

'To Sebastian Carrick. Yes, I know,' added Nicholas as the other was about to protest. 'He owed *you* money. But you owe Sebastian this. You owe him Banbury's Men.'

'How so?'

'Because you gained by his death. Sebastian was to have played in *Love's Sacrifice* while you were scrabbling about in the smaller parts.' Nicholas was blunt. 'Master Randolph would not have marked your excellence as a Second Servant. He would not have been struck by your King's Messenger. You took Sebastian's role to gain all this. You owe him your role in *The Spanish Jew* and your hope of a contract!'

The Welshman breathed heavily through his nose and searched the table for an answer to the charge. It was a full minute before he raised his head again.

'You are right, Nick. I am in Sebastian's debt.'

'Pay it off.'

'How?'

'Help me to catch his murderer.'

Interest quickened. 'You know who it is?'

'I know where to find him.'

'Where?'

'Will you help? It will take two of us.'

'I'll help,' said Elias soulfully. 'But for Sebastian, I would still be toiling in minor roles at the Queen's Head. If that is the favour, I'll do it gladly.'

'Thank you, Owen. I'll advise you when I need you.'

'I'll be waiting.' Nicholas clapped him on the shoulder then got up to leave. He glanced across at the other actors in the troupe then appraised his old friend again. Owen Elias worked with Banbury's Men but he did not seem like one of them and his arrogance was bound to have ruffled his new colleagues. There would be natural resentment from those who had served the company for a long time at the Welshman's promotion over their heads. It did not augur well for him.

The question was jabbed straight at the actor.

'On what condition would you return to us, Owen?'

'To Westfield's Men?'

'Name your price.'

'It is far too high, Nick.'

'I have a strong nerve.'

'Then I demand two things. A full apology.'

'You ask a lot of Master Firethorn.'

'And a contract that makes me a sharer.'

Nicholas thought it over then gritted his teeth.

'You will have both,' he said.

Nimbus began his conquest of London at a steady trot, moved up into a canter then went full gallop through the hearts and minds of its citizens. He and his astute master chose their venues with care, increasing the size of their audience each time and widening the scope of their performance. All classes watched and wondered. Every spectator rushed off to broadcast the news of this latest prodigy. Nimbus did not have to search for an arena any longer. Cornelius Gant was besieged by eager innkeepers and urgent landlords, offering handsome rewards in return for a performance at their respective hostelries. A city which revelled in the baiting of bears and bulls now talked about a sensational horse. No blood was spilled, no pain visited upon the animal, no cruelty practised yet the partners bewitched their public in a most profound way.

Gant used each occasion to advertise future delights.

'Thank you, kind friends!' he called. 'This evening, you may see us at the Black Bell in Candlewick Street. Tomorrow morning, you will find us at the Crossed Keys in Gayspur Lane and in the same afternoon, at the Gun in Cordwainer Street.' His face collapsed into a grin. 'Look for us soon at the Unicorn in Hosier Alley. Nimbus is as rare a creature as any unicorn, I warrant.'

Fresh applause broke out from the spectators at the Red Lion. Delighted with what they had seen, they wanted more and began to yell out hopes and expectations. Gant shouted out his boast above the tumult.

'Nimbus will dance across London Bridge and swim across the Thames at its widest point. He will do something that no horse has ever done before.' Gant stoked up the furnace of excitement. 'He will fly to the very top of St Paul's!'

News of the feat met with tumultuous approbation.

'When will Nimbus do it?' they cried.

'Let us ask,' said Gant.

He looked across at the horse and gave a signal. Nimbus shook his head slowly as if deep in contemplation then he came across to whinny in his master's ear. Gant waited for the laughter to subside then passed on the decision.

'Saturday!'

Josiah Taplow and William Merryweather began their rounds in Clerkenwell with the usual amalgam of duty and resignation. Shocked to discover that they had been impersonated, they now saw it as a happy accident which yielded direct benefit. It was they who were given credit for saving the life of the man who had been so grievously assaulted in Cock Alley and they who now gained a lurking respect from the denizens of the area. Men who might before have sneered at their passing now held their tongues and shrunk back. The two aged watchmen liked their brief status as heroes. They strolled along Turnmill Street with an air of authority they had never possessed before. It was gratifying to be taken seriously at last and they were particularly pleased with their impact on a man who loitered opposite the Pickt-hatch. As soon as he saw the officers of the law approach, he shot out of a doorway and tore off down the street. Taplow and Merryweather smiled.

They were so caught up in their minor triumph that they did not hear the cry of mingled pleasure and pain that came from a bedchamber above their heads. The Pickt-hatch was already open for business. Frances was putting her personal seal on the back of another exhausted customer.

Her delicate hands caressed his shoulders then drew small circles up and down his spine. As his kisses became deeper and his movements more frantic, she locked her fingers into his hair to pull him even closer. His body arched and thrust, his blood raced, his senses tingled. In the silken comfort of a four-poster, their separate madness became one long mutual ecstasy. At the very peak of their cascading joy, he rose up to let her sink her teeth into his chest and to bite hard with animal hunger. He winced, he laughed, he sighed, he collapsed with utter satisfaction.

Beatrice Capaldi also knew how to leave her mark.

Andrew Carrick was astonished to receive a visitor so late in the evening and duly delighted. Nicholas Bracewell was always welcome company. They sat on stools in the cell in the Beauchamp Tower and conversed by the light of a tallow candle. Carrick was keen to hear the latest report from Clerkenwell and to learn of his daughter's reaction to a performance by Westfield's Men. The lawyer's gratitude boiled over once again and his visitor took advantage of it.

'I come in search of help, sir,' said Nicholas.

'What may I do for you?'

'Draw up a contract.'

'Of what nature?'

'Articles of agreement between a theatre company and a new sharer. You have the means to do this, Master Carrick?'

'Why, yes,' said the other. 'Here are pen and parchment before me, as you see, and

I have all the authority that the office of attorney can bestow. But I have no knowledge of such a form of contract.'

'Could I dictate the terms to you?'

'They would have to be very exact.'

'I have memorized them with care.'

Andrew Carrick pulled the candle closer to illumine the parchment that he unrolled before him. Dipping his quill into the inkwell, he was poised for instruction. Nicholas spoke with slow precision.

'Articles of Agreement, made, concluded and agreed upon and which are to be kept and performed by Owen Elias of London Gent. unto and with Lawrence Firethorn Esquire in manner and form following, that is to say . . . Imprimis. The said Owen Elias doth covenant, praise and grant to and with the said Lawrence Firethorn, his executors, administrators and assigns in manner and form following, that is to say that he, the said Owen Elias, will play with Westfield's Men for and during the time and space of three years from the date hereof, for and at the rate of one whole share according to the custom of players . . .'

The lawyer wrote with a flowing hand. He was fascinated by the contractual obligations laid upon both parties and had several questions to ask. Nicholas was supremely well-informed. Before coming to the Tower, he had taken the trouble to examine Edmund Hoode's contract with the company and he had also been present during many of the frequent legal wrangles between Firethorn and the other sharers. Carrick was very complimentary.

'You should have been a lawyer yourself,' he said.

'In some sort, I am.'

'Here is your contract. I am glad to be of help.'

'Your assistance may prove invaluable.'

Nicholas took the scroll and secreted it inside his jerkin. He was about to take his leave when his host did him another important favour.

'Here is something that may be of interest to you.'

'Speak on.'

'Prison restricts movements but it sharpens ears,' said Carrick. 'I have learned to listen.'

'And what have you heard?'

'Enough to make a firm judgement.'

'About whom?'

'My friend, Harry Fellowes.'

'The Clerk of Ordnance?'

'That is but one of many aspects of his existence. He is also a priest, a soldier, a scholar and more besides. What concerns you most is that Harry is a money-lender.'

'You have hinted as much before.'

'I now have more proof of his dealings,' said Carrick. 'There never was such enthusiastic usury. Harry lends much and often to men of high rank. He has been doing so for many years and has a long list of noble debtors. One of those names is of especial interest to you, Master Bracewell.'

'Who is that?'

'The Earl of Chichester.'

'A close friend of Banbury's Men.'

'Chichester and Banbury intrigue to appoint the next monarch. Such machinations cost money. Politics is mostly buying and bribing.' He shrugged his disgust. 'But you will see what this means.'

'Harry Fellowes is aiding our enemies. If they should succeed, we will suffer. Westfield's Men will be cut down by a loan transacted within the Tower of London.'

Carrick grinned. 'Ask me a question.'

'Is the Clerk of Ordnance so well-paid that he can afford to give subsidies to all and sundry?'

'No,' said the other, delighted to pass on the fruit of his meditations. 'Crown officials are poorly paid. They get their reward from the status of royal service and from the incidental benefits of their employment.'

'Benefits?'

'I will come straight to it. Harry Fellowes is a kind and Christian man who has helped me to stave off boredom and despair in my imprisonment. However . . .'

'Go on, sir.'

'He is also a cunning malefactor who has made a private fortune from the public purse.' Carrick held up his palms. 'Do not ask me how he has done it because I can only guess at the details but this I can say with absolute certainty. Harry has used his position to falsify and defraud.'

Nicholas ran ahead of him. 'This loan to the Earl of Chichester must therefore give him great satisfaction. His lordship is Master of Ordnance.'

'Harry steals money from beneath his superior's nose then lends it back to him at a high rate of interest.'

Nicholas appreciated the irony of the situation but he also began to see the full ramifications. Banbury's Men had seized centre-stage with *The Spanish Jew,* an acerbic play which attacked a hated minority who were traditionally associated with usury. It was a work which served the cause of Roger Godolphin, Earl of Chichester, who was in alliance with Banbury himself. Their campaign was financed by a loan which had been raised not from foreigner or Jew — but from the Crown official who laboured at his accounts in the Tower of London. Shorn of his affability and shown in his true light, Harry Fellowes was every bit as villainous as the character who was portrayed by Giles Randolph.

All indications had Queen Elizabeth fading fast and unable or unwilling to name a successor. The conflict on that issue would be quickly resolved and the party led by the Earl of Chichester might well emerge victorious. If the educated guesswork of a lawyer was sound then Nicholas was in a position to strike a vital blow for Lord Westfield's faction. The prospect made him tremble with excitement.

Andrew Carrick spelled out the implications.

'Start here,' he said. 'Expose Harry Fellowes and you bring down the Earl of Chichester with him. There will be no Queen Arabella then. You understand me?'

'Very well indeed.'

'Westfield's Men will be safe.'

Chapter Eleven

Giles Randolph had the overweening vanity that afflicted so many in his profession but it was tempered by an acceptance of one grim truth. An actor needed a patron. Inspired as he believed himself to be and gifted as he certainly was, he never forgot to pay due respect to the Earl of Banbury and to acquaint him with each shift of company policy. Randolph was thus a familiar caller at the sumptuous residence near Charing Cross and he could always count on a goblet or two of Canary wine with his host as they flattered each other with token compliments. The earl glowed with optimism.

'All things proceed as I would wish,' he said.

'We strive to serve your lordship.'

'You must wipe Lawrence Firethorn from the stage and kill off Westfield's Men for good.' Common sense intervened. 'But you must feed wisely off the remnants. Edmund Hoode is a playwright to be wooed into my company and I would find a place for Barnaby Gill as well.'

'Neither is entirely to my taste,' said Randolph, 'and I feel sure that Hoode would never countenance working for Banbury's Men. Gill is another matter but I have severe reservations.'

'Overcome them, Giles. He is a supreme clown.'

'Yes, my lord.'

'When his company falls, rush in to pick him up.'

'I will offer him a helping hand . . .'

The bibulous earl sipped more wine and confided his hopes for the future. His politic alliance with the Earl of Chichester would bear royal fruit that would profit both himself and his troupe. He held out the possibility that the new Queen might elevate his company into her own and the purring Randolph stroked the fur of his own self-importance.

Banbury underlined the significance of Saturday.

'You must play *The Spanish Jew*,' he ordered.

'Playbills have already gone out to that effect.'

'Introduce some more material to favour us.'

'The company poet is working on that now.'

'And let that clever rogue cut Firethorn

to ribbons once more,' said the earl. 'What is his name?'

'Owen Elias.'

'An asset to Banbury's Men.'

'That is why I chose him, my lord.'

'How did you tempt him into our ranks?'

'By a promise that he would become a sharer.'

'And will he, Giles?'

The actor shook his head. 'Never, my lord.'

'What will happen to him?'

'When he has done what we need, he'll be discarded.'

'But he is an arresting player.'

'We have talent enough in the company,' said Randolph airily, 'and we have no room for this upstart Welshman. He is a quarrelsome fellow. Admit him to the rank of sharer and he will argue all day long about the roles he wishes to play.' He became supercilious. 'Owen Elias is without true quality. Only the finest talents are worthy of a place among Banbury's Men. We use him, we lose him. That is his station.'

The patron plucked at his goatee beard.

'Just another hired man, eh?'

'Yes, my lord. And hired men come and go.'

Unaware that his hold on fame was of

such short lease, Owen Elias went home to his lodging in the confident belief that he would soon become a sharer with his troupe. Sharers were stockholders in the company and, as such, were expected to make a financial investment in it but this aspect had been waived in his case — Giles Randolph told him — because they were very keen to ensure his services. Elias was so carried away with his sudden eminence that he did not hear the mutinous grumblings of the other sharers who had paid an average of fifty pounds for their position. There was no way that the Welshman could raise that amount. His weekly wage with Westfield's Men had been seven shillings.

Life with the new company had its definite drawbacks but he was ready to overlook them in exchange for the promised promotion and security. Once he had worked his way into Banbury's Men, he assured himself, the problems would disappear and he would be able to offer the world vivid proof of his outstanding talents. As he clambered up the stairs to his room, he began to declaim his first speech. When he flopped down on to the stool, he quoted whole segments of dialogue. While he lay on his back and studied the beams above his head, he went through an entire leading part from a play. Owen

Elias was a conscientious actor who wasted no opportunity to practise his craft. His voice was still bouncing off the walls as fatigue finally caught up with him. A rhyming couplet died uncompleted.

He dozed quietly off, then woke with a start only minutes later. Realization brought him fully awake. Nothing that he had recited with such affection had come from the repertoire of his new company. It had all been from his time with Westfield's Men. The work of Edmund Hoode had seeped into his mind so completely that he could produce it by the yard with word-perfect accuracy. *The Spanish Jew* was the piece in which he made his name but it did not provide the leading role which he had acted so fervently in his room. It was the role of King Gondar which had tripped readily off his tongue. Owen Elias was quoting *Love's Sacrifice*.

He felt pangs of self-doubt and slept fitfully.

Only a matter of pressing importance would make Nicholas Bracewell call on him at that hour of the night and so Lord Westfield had him admitted at once. Excusing himself from the dinner table, he left his guests and hurried into the small room at the rear of the house which he used as his study. Nicholas was waiting respectfully.

'Well, sir?' said the patron.

'I have information about the Earl of Chichester.'

'What has the old warrior been up to now?'

'Borrowing money.'

'Nothing amiss there. I raise loans myself.'

'Not from this source, my lord.'

Nicholas recounted what he heard at the Tower and it was received in rapt silence. Lord Westfield did not need to have the implications pointed out to him. He knew that he was being given an excellent opportunity to discredit a lifelong enemy, to hamper Chichester's claimant to the throne, to render an immense public service by exposing fraud at the Ordnance and — most appealing of all — to frustrate the ambitions of the Earl of Banbury. Everything turned on one issue.

'How certain can we be of the Clerk's guilt?'

'I accept Master Carrick's judgement,' said Nicholas.

'Then so will I,' decided the other. 'Lawyers are damnable fellows for using words that they may hide behind. If Carrick is making a formal allegation, he has reasons in plenty. What we now have to do is to find the evidence to flush this Harry Fellowes out.'

'I have been thinking about that, my lord.'

'You have a plan?'

'It requires some help from you.'

Nicholas outlined his idea and saw his listener's face tighten into a hard ball of concentration. Lord Westfield seemed to disapprove at first but his features gradually slipped into an admiring smile. By the time the book holder finished, his host was rocking with laughter.

'By all, that's wonderful, Nick!'

'It may serve.'

'Put the plan into action forthwith.'

'I shall, my lord.'

'Once again, you show your sterling worth to Westfield's Men. I hope that Lawrence appreciates your true value.'

'He has to be reminded of it from time to time.'

'Tell him that I will attend on Saturday.'

'Saturday?'

'*Love's Sacrifice* at the Queen's Head.'

'But we play *Cupid's Folly.*'

Lord Westfield gaped. 'What?'

'Master Firethorn is indisposed that afternoon.'

'Am I hearing this aright?' said the other in tones of disbelief. 'Banbury's Men assault us. Giles Randolph makes his bid to thrust Lawrence aside. *Love's Sacrifice* is vital to counter the effect of *The Spanish Jew* and

305

our leading actor tells us he is indisposed!'
Lord Westfield almost frothed at the mouth.
'This could well be the most telling Saturday
in the history of the company. We need to
be at full strength and performing the most
appropriate piece. Let Lawrence Firethorn
know that I request — nay, *demand* — that
he appears in the work of my choice.'

'I will convey that message to him.'

'With all due force.'

'Yes, my lord.'

'Acquaint him with the name of his patron.'

Lord Westfield showed Nicholas to the
door himself and rid himself of one last
exasperated question.

'What, in God's name, could be more important to Lawrence than leading his company?'

The barge skimmed its way up the Thames
to the beat of a dozen oars. Lawrence Firethorn lay beneath the canopy on a bank of
cushions, his head pillowed by the exquisite
breasts of Beatrice Capaldi, his hair and beard
stroked in time to the rhythm of the oarsmen.
was pure joy. He had nothing to do but
sten to the slap of the water against the
ide of the vessel and savour the tender ministrations of his beloved. They had set a

course to paradise and were sailing towards a glorious consummation.

Lawrence Firethorn awoke from his dream to find himself in a bed that now seemed impossibly empty without Beatrice Capaldi beside him. He was at home in Shoreditch, staining the marital couch with adulterous thoughts for which he felt no shred of shame. When his wife was with him, he was never deterred from letting his eye rove at will. With Margery safely out of the way in Cambridge, he was a free spirit who could do whatever he liked with whomsoever he chose. An actor who won new hearts every time he stepped onstage, he was surrounded by countless possibilities and he planned to while away Margery's absence by working steadily through them but Beatrice Capaldi changed all that. His dark lady banished all others from his mind. Since their tryst had been agreed, he had no desire at all to touch another woman. Firethorn was faithful in his infidelity. A creature who had given him no more than a single line on a sheet of paper had enslaved him to the notion of romantic extravagance.

The play was prophetic. *Love's Sacrifice* depicted a king who gave up his family, his kingdom and his reputation for the sake of his love. Firethorn had the chance to make

307

a grand gesture of his own, no less momentous in the world that he inhabited. To spend time with Beatrice and to wallow in love, he was ready to ignore the demands of his wife, his fellow-actors and his art. For an afternoon in her arms, he was willing to resign his private kingdom.

Love transformed him out of all recognition. He was kind to his children, considerate to his servants and jocund with the apprentices who also lived under his roof. They had never known such happy tranquillity in him and suspected either a secret potion or the onset of madness. Firethorn's benign mood took him all the way to the Queen's Head and informed the morning rehearsal. The sniping of Barnaby Gill could not sour it, nor could the plaintive protests of Edmund Hoode. He seemed impervious to the general misery. It was left to Nicholas Bracewell to shatter his benevolence.

'I gave my word!' bellowed Firethorn.

'Lord Westfield spoke a few words himself, sir.'

'I'll not jump to his command.'

'You are to be reminded that he is our patron.'

'My word is my bond!'

'Your place is here with us.'

Nicholas was ready to take the verbal shot

with which he was sprayed. He passed on the message from Lord Westfield and urged the actor-manager to reconsider his arrangements for Saturday afternoon. They were alone in the tiring-house but Firethorn's half of the conversation could be heard a hundred yards away. Inadvertently, Nicholas put even greater volume into the roar by making a faint insinuation.

'You commit yourself too soon and too hastily, sir.'

'Do you dare to lecture me!'

'Learn to know the lady better.'

'That is why we float on the Thames together.'

'No, master,' said Nicholas. 'Find out more about her before you plunge headlong into this tryst. There may be things about Mistress Capaldi which somewhat alter the character which she presents.'

Firethorn was outraged. 'What sort of things!'

'It is not for me to impugn her honour but . . .'

'Be silent, Nick! I've heard enough of this.'

'Wait but a week or two and — '

'SILENCE!'

Nicholas survived the broadside. 'Lord Westfield will take his seat here on Saturday afternoon.'

'His noble buttocks may sit where they wish.'

'He expects to watch *Love's Sacrifice*.'

'Prepare him for disappointment.'

'He insists on seeing King Gondar.'

'His Majesty will be on the river.'

As a last resort, the book holder applied full pressure.

'Fail us on Saturday and you put the company at risk.'

'What care I for that?'

'Westfield's Men are built around you, sir.'

'My mistress calls and I may not deny her.'

'Our patron will take it ill.'

'Then let him!' said Firethorn defiantly. 'Westfield's Men depend on me but I do not depend on them. There is a world elsewhere.' He crossed to the door and opened it with a dramatic gesture. 'I go to it on Saturday!'

Notwithstanding her combative nature, Margery Firethorn had a soft heart that was duly touched by the wonder of creation. The sight of a happy mother with a beautiful baby was more than ample reward for all the effort she herself had put in at the house, and she was even coming to see her brother-in-law in a less unfavourable light. Jonathan

Jarrold would never be the kind of man with whom she would choose to share a bed — let alone a marriage — but his delight in the office of fatherhood was moving and his commitment total. He was always ready to help and willing to learn. There were times when Margery actually had no need to scold him and she soon caught herself paying him gruff compliments. Whatever his shortcomings, Jonathan Jarrold, bookseller, was the head of a little family. When he cooed fondly over his son and heir, he made his sister-in-law think of her own brood. Happiness in Cambridge made her homesick.

Jonathan's shop was her only link with the capital.

'There is much anxiety over the Queen,' he said.

'She has the finest physicians about her.'

'The news is not good. A printer who has just come from London was in my shop this morning. Her Majesty is confined to her apartments and takes no part in the government of her realm. Everyone fears the worst.'

Margery was scornful. 'They should be on their knees to pray for her recovery. We must not give into fears. We must have faith, Jonathan.'

'It is difficult in the face of such reports.'

'Her Majesty is too young to die.'

'None of us may live forever.'

'She is every inch a Queen and every inch a woman. I'll wager that she defies those rumours yet.'

'The rumours have firm foundation.'

'Pah!' she snorted. 'Should I trust the word of a pox-ridden printer who seeks to impress his Cambridge friends with this idle chatter? Queen Elizabeth will outlive us all. We *need* her on the throne of England. God save the Queen!'

But Margery's certainty was fringed with apprehension. The rumours that came from London were now too numerous to discount and they contained a threat of dire consequences for the whole nation. At a more immediate level, there was a danger to Westfield's Men. A change of sovereign could bring about a change of attitude towards the theatre. She knew enough of the Earl of Banbury's love of intrigue to realize that he would seek to exploit the death of the Queen to the advantage of himself and his company. Margery bit her lip. Her husband's livelihood might well be put in hazard. It gave her even more incentive to return home at speed.

Saturday took on more significance.

Harry Fellowes was an unlikely poet but

his Latin verses had a pleasing sound and a cold intelligence. He was very proud of them but distressed by the lack of informed praise for his literary endeavours. There were no Classical scholars among his colleagues and the brutish surroundings of the Tower slowly crushed his creative instincts. He was all the more thrilled, therefore, to befriend someone with true learning and sincere interest. Andrew Carrick not only asked to see the published verses, he read them with care, made notes on their excellence and discussed them at length. The Clerk of Ordnance and the imprisoned lawyer who walked along together were strolling through Ancient Rome.

'And which poems delighted you most?' asked Fellowes.

'Those in the style of Ovid.'

'He was always my master.'

'Even when you stand before your congregation?' said Carrick with a teasing smile. 'I would not have thought that kind of love had any place in a pulpit.'

'Yet it belongs in the heart of every true man.'

'Indeed, indeed.'

'Each of us has many sides to his character.'

'You seem to have far more than most, Master Fellowes.'

The poet needed reassurance. 'And did my verses really give you joy, my friend?'

'They brought Cicero back to my mind.'

'Cicero?'

'Yes,' said Carrick. 'If I quote him aright. *Haec studentia adulescentiam alunt, senectutem oblectant.*'

'Oh, sir, you are too kind!' Harry Fellowes pounced gratefully on the translation. 'These studies nurture youth and delight old age.'

The lawyer grew serious. 'Your work has been a great solace to me in my cell. It held back the honors of my life and defeated time most wonderfully. It put a glow of hope into some very dark nights.'

'No praise could be higher than that. Thank you, sir.'

'Most of all, I liked your line from Virgil.'

'You recognized the theft?'

'It was no theft,' said Carrick. 'You borrowed and paid back with interest.' The money-lender laughed. 'Virgil spoke aloud on your final page. *Trahit sua quemque voluptas.*'

'Everyone is dragged down by his favourite pleasure.'

'It was the theme of all your verses.'

'There is such deep truth in it.'

Andrew Carrick sighed. '*Trahit sua quemque voluptas . . .*'

It was an accurate summary of his son's life. Sebastian Carrick was bursting with a talent that was marred by his excesses. In a Clerkenwell brothel, his favourite pleasure had dragged him down for good. The sad father tried to shake his head clear of such thoughts and turn a moment of close companionship to material advantage. His admiration of the verses was not feigned but the Ovidian strain did not blind him to the true character of the poet. Harry Fellowes might be a scholar but he was also a shrewd criminal who used his privileged position in the Ordnance Office to deceive and defraud. The hand which had turned such elegant Latin lines could embezzle with equal skill.

Andrew Carrick returned the calf-bound book to him.

'Your work must seem dull after this,' he said.

Fellowes was defensive. 'It has its own appeal.'

'There is not much scope for poetry in your ledgers.'

'They have a kind of rhythm at times.'

'I am sure that you keep them scrupulously exact.'

'My figures always tally,' said the other smugly. 'You could search through every book and not find a discrepancy.'

'I would welcome the chance to try.'

'The exercise would bore you, Master Carrick.'

'Anything is a relief from the tedium of my cell.'

Harry Fellowes looked at him carefully then glanced down at the slim volume in his hand. Gratified by the lawyer's warm response to his work, he was keen to express his thanks in a more tangible way. If he showed his friend how he laboured at his desk, he could inflate his own self-esteem even more. Andrew Carrick posed no problem. He was simply an unfortunate casualty of a marriage that aroused royal ire.

'Come with me,' invited Fellowes.

They left Ancient Rome and made their way towards a territory of numbers and receipts. Harry Fellowes was no bending author now. He was a keen mathematician who liked order and precision, moving large quantities of money around in the course of his occupation. Once launched on a boastful description of his work, he could not be stopped. The Clerk of Ordnance who was paid a mere £64 per annum claimed that he saved Her Majesty £2,000 a year.

'How?' asked Carrick.

'By taking the returns of such munitions as return from the seas unspent, which formerly were concealed and converted to private use.'

'You are a prudent steward, Master Fellowes.'

'Nothing escapes me, sir.'

Carrick encouraged him to talk on and Harry Fellowes did not pause throughout the entire visit. As he flicked through his account books, he became even more complacent and he lapped up the appreciative comments of his guest. Though he was a man of wide abilities, there was no doubting where his real interest lay. Money was the favourite pleasure of Harry Fellowes. It was inevitable that Virgil should again drift into Carrick's mind.

'Trahit sua quemque voluptas . . .'

Lawrence Firethorn's powers of recovery were remarkable. When the rehearsal ended that morning, he had been as angry as a wounded bear and clawed everyone who came within reach. When the performance began that afternoon, he was Hector of Troy to the life, leading his company in the tragedy of that name as if all was joy and harmony. The row with Nicholas Bracewell was forgotten, the deep divisions were ignored. Firethorn attacked his role with a verve that was his hallmark. Beatrice Capaldi was no‑

in the audience at the Queen's Head but he played Hector as if she were, throwing each line to the middle of the lower gallery and strutting about with even more than his usual arrogance. His superb portrait filled the stage with drama and did much to vindicate a reputation that was seriously under attack. He more than earned the ovation which he gained. None of the spectators would have guessed that the brilliant actor whom they had just seen at his peak was ready to forsake his art and his fellows for an afternoon with a woman. Firethorn himself reaffirmed his decision. Putting his fingers to his lips, he threw invisible kisses to the invisible Beatrice Capaldi and whispered his promise over the applause.

'True love requires true sacrifice . . .'

Offstage, he reverted to his former irascibility and those who tried to speak to him suffered accordingly. Barnaby Gill was cursed, Edmund Hoode reviled, Peter Digby abused, Hugh Wegges punched and the unlucky George Dart almost trampled to death. When Alexander Marwood made the mistake of praising the exploits of Cornelius Gant and Nimbus once again, Firethorn lifted him up by his shoulders and deposited him in a horse trough.

Nicholas Bracewell had to soothe many a

troubled brow before his work was done for the day. Gill and Hoode were particularly agitated by the threatened betrayal. Though the comedian was looking forward to *Cupid's Folly* on Saturday afternoon, he did not dare to fly in the face of their patron's wishes. The playwright, too, wanted *Love's Sacrifice* reinstated, if for different reasons. Nicholas told them that the decision had been taken right out of their hands by Lord Westfield who would accept no other work. It was Hoode's latest play that would be advertised for performance.

'*Love's Sacrifice?*' said Gill. 'Without Lawrence?'

'King Gondar will be there,' assured Nicholas.

Hoode was pessimistic. 'He has refused to appear.'

'Much can happen before Saturday.'

'Yes, Nick,' said Hoode. 'We may lose our Queen, our company and our profession. Much may indeed happen.'

Nicholas said no more. When he left the inn, he turned left into Gracechurch Street and kept walking briskly until Bishopsgate loomed up ahead. Leaving the city through one of its great portals, he maintained a steady pace all the way to Shoreditch. The crowds had dispersed from The Curtain and The

Theatre but the hostelries were still full of roistering gallants. Nicholas stopped at the sign of the Elephant and found a more pensive Owen Elias brooding alone on a bench outside the establishment. They exchanged greetings.

'What ails you?' said Nicholas.

Elias was evasive. 'It is no matter.'

'Did you play at The Curtain this afternoon?'

The Tragical History of King John.

'What role did you take?'

'A small one,' muttered the other. 'I died at the end of Act One. It was like being back with Westfield's Men.'

'There will be no more small parts for you there.'

'I will never go back to the Queen's Head.'

'You have signed the contract, then?'

'No. Not exactly . . .'

'When will Giles Randolph make you a sharer?'

'On Saturday, he says.'

'He says.'

'Why should he go back on his word?'

'Why are you so sad?'

Nicholas had touched a raw spot and his friend almost jumped up from the bench. Owen Elias had raised the question of his contract half an hour earlier in the taproom and he had been given the usual reassurances by Giles Randolph but somehow they lacked conviction this time. Whether it was guilt over his old company or disillusionment with his new one, he did not know but the Welshman suddenly felt the ground shudder slightly beneath his feet. Banbury's Men had given him a hero's welcome but he sensed that it would not last indefinitely. He was also well-placed to see that his new colleagues did not have the strength in depth of Westfield's Men. Giles Randolph liked good actors around him but they were not allowed to compete with him. Lawrence Firethorn, by contrast, employed the finest talents he could muster because he knew that he could hold his own against them. Indeed, the more competition he was given, the higher the pitch of his own performance.

Elias's preoccupation was written on his face and Nicholas read it with interest but without further comment. He had come to the Elephant for another reason.

'It is time to help Sebastian,' he said.

'Now?'

'If you are ready, Owen.'

'Where do we go?'

'Clerkenwell.'

'I am with you, Nick.'

'Are you armed?'

'My dagger will protect me against anything.'

'Not against an axe,' said Nicholas. 'Let's call at your lodging for a sword. There may be a brawl.'

Owen Elias chuckled. 'That cheers me up at once!'

They collected his weapon then proceeded on their way to Clerkenwell. It was a long walk and Nicholas had plenty of time to explain his plan in detail. The element of danger appealed to the actor whose solid frame had weathered many a tavern fight. Sebastian Carrick had died owing him money but he was still eager to avenge the murder. His rival had made possible the surge in his prospects.

Two other accessories were gathered along the way.

'What would you have with us?' asked Josiah Taplow.

'We seek no trouble,' said William Merryweather.

'You come but as witnesses,' said Nicholas.

He told them enough to draw them along but concealed the full story from them. The watchmen trailed in their wake and grumbled at the speed made by the two younger men but they managed to keep up. Nicholas stationed them at the end of Turnmill Street then went on more stealthily with Owen Elias. Light had faded now and they were simply two more shadowy figures in the half-darkness. Nicholas stopped well short of the Pickt-hatch and stepped into a doorway from which he could keep it under surveillance. Owen Elias walked on alone, warned of the perils but excited at the notion of taking the leading role for once. He knocked at the door and was admitted by Bess Bidgood. All that Nicholas could do was to watch, wait and beware of a man with an axe.

St Paul's Cathedral was the dominating feature of the night skyline. It rose like a mountain above all around it and imposed itself on every view of the city. One of the largest churches in Christendom, it never failed to draw gasps of astonishment from visitors to the capital who saw in its Gothic exuberance and its intimidating sprawl the power of God made manifest. Its massive crossing tower had twice been capped with a spire of wood and lead that reached a height of almost five hundred feet, making it the tallest steeple ever built, but lightning had destroyed it on both occasions. The second disaster, at the start of Elizabeth's reign, was more serious in that the fire spread from the steeple to the roof and even melted the bells. Though the damage had been patched up, there was no attempt to rebuild the spire and to risk a third calamity.

Seen against the clear night sky, St Paul's was still the great act of worship it had always been but the darkness shrouded the deterioration to its fabric. It was showing its age. Battered by time and beaten by inclement weather, its stonework was pitted, its tracery mouldering, its pinnacles encrusted with filth and its buttresses scored. Smoke from sea coal had blackened parts of its exterior and there was an air of neglect about it.

Yet the cathedral still had the capacity to surprise and to overawe. Anyone who chanced to look up at its roof that night would have seen an extraordinary sight. A single flickering candle suddenly appeared at the very top of the tower and worked its way slowly around the perimeter like a guiding light to holy pilgrims. It was a benign presence but it startled the nesting swifts and swallows, it alarmed the perching ravens and jackdaws, it fluttered the roosting pigeons and it spread panic among the predatory kites who used the mighty roof as the vantage point from which they could swoop down upon the offal of London. The candle went a little higher, the flame burned brighter and there was a thunderous flapping of wings as hundreds of tenants quit their lodgings and took to the sky.

Cornelius Gant was pleased to have such an impact on his feathered audience. He had climbed to the top of the cathedral to take stock of it from above and to finalize his preparations for Saturday's feat. The next time that he stood there, Nimbus would be beside him. As he surveyed the whole city from his lofty position, he felt once more that surge of power and ambition which had brought him to London.

He blew out his candle and laughed in the darkness.

Owen Elias was not a regular visitor to the stews. Like most actors, he took his pleasures where he could find them and so it was largely a succession of tavern wenches whom he numbered among his conquests. At the same time, however, he felt completely at ease in the Pickt-hatch. Its atmosphere of bawdy banter and tobacco smoke were second nature to him and he fitted into its snug sinfulness as well as any of the usual patrons. Various punks blandished him with their wiles and their wares but he bided his time until he found the one whom he sought. The slim and sensual Frances was indeed a different proposition. Her brand of carnality had a whiff of danger about it. Like Sebastian Carrick before him, Elias knew that an hour in her bed would be an experience not easily forgotten. When she fixed her eyes upon him, he felt the lick of her tongue and the scratch of her nails. He also saw the coffin of a murdered actor being lowered into the ground. This was the one.

He bought them both wine and acted the role in which Nicholas Bracewell had schooled him. Frances was supremely captivating. She knew how to interest, to tease, to excite and to heighten anticipation. When she finally led him towards the stairs, she gave him a first snarling kiss by way of a deposit on the madness that was to follow and Elias had to fight off the natural surge of his lust. This rustling courtesan was also a cold-blooded killer who would not scruple to send him on the same route to the grave on which she had dispatched his former colleague.

Alone together in her room, he got final confirmation.

'Your reputation is very high, Frances,' he said. 'You were recommended to me by a friend.'

She put her arms around him. 'I like to please.'

'My friend spoke of your fingernails.'

'They are yours tonight, sir,' she said, putting her hands under his doublet to gouge his back through his shirt. 'I'll scratch my name on your back as well.'

'First, you must give greeting to my friend once more.'

Owen Elias eased her away and took out the portrait of Sebastian Carrick which had been borrowed from the latter's sister. Holding the picture close to the candle, he grabbed Frances by the neck and thrust her head close to the flame. She recognized the features at once and turned on Elias with a screech of fury, going for his eyes with the fingernails she had just used to tempt him. The Welshman was ready for her. Catching her wrists, he twisted her arms behind her back then forced her across to the window. His foot kicked it open and he pushed her forward long enough for her struggle to be seen from the street. Pulling her back to him, he held her in a firm grip and took the squirming body out of the room and along the passageway.

Nicholas Bracewell was alert and ready. He had seen what he expected. The figures at the window had brought a man out of a doorway opposite the building. He hesitated in the middle of the street and gave Nicholas plenty of time to study his profile and identify it as that of the assailant whom he and Edmund Hoode had disturbed in an alleyway. When he saw the axe dangle from the man's hand, he knew that he stood close to the murderer of Sebastian Carrick. The book holder drew his sword and approached with care. Owen Elias may have played his role to perfection so far but he was now beyond the realms of his rehearsals. What happened from now on was pure improvisation.

Frances was struggling and biting for all she was worth but the strength of the actor took her down the stairs and off towards the front door. They came out in an explosion of noise and went off down Turnmill Street towards the quaking watchmen who had been posted there. The screaming woman was the ideal bait. Elias had hauled her no more than thirty yards before the accomplice moved in to strike. Nicholas yelled a warning that saved his friend's life. As the axe was lifted into the air, Elias spun round to hold Frances beneath it and subject her to the horror which her victims had suffered. At the same moment, Nicholas Bracewell pricked the upraised arm with the point of his sword.

The man let out a stream of curses and turned his venom on the newcomer, hurling the axe with such force that it would have split his face in two had it connected. But

Nicholas ducked just in time and the weapon thudded into the door of a house behind him like the knock of doom. Elias still held the flailing woman and the two watchmen inched closer to the action. Having lost his axe, the man drew his own sword and closed with Nicholas. It was a short and vicious encounter. Blades flashed then locked tight. Fists and forearms were used, knees and feet inflicted further bruises. The man was a practised street-fighter but he never met opponents on equal terms. In Nicholas Bracewell, he was up against someone who was bigger, stronger and more agile.

As they grappled with increasing ferocity, it was the firmer purpose of the book holder which told. Impelled by a vow to a murdered friend, he found the extra energy to twist the man's sword from his hand and sent it clattering to the ground. His adversary replied with a kick which sent him down on one knee. Pulling a dagger from his belt, the man hurled himself upon Nicholas with a manic rage that was his own undoing for he impaled himself on the sword that was held up to meet him. With a long, slow, blood-curdling howl of pain, he fell backwards and expired in the filth of Turnmill Street. The killing of Sebastian Carrick was avenged.

'NO!' shrieked Frances in despair.

She broke free from her bonds and flung herself down upon the dead man to weep tears of true remorse. Snatching up his dagger, she then leapt up to confront Nicholas, Elias and the two watchmen. She spat her hatred at them then held the weapon in both hands before sinking it into her chest. They watched in silence as she used her last brief seconds on earth to crawl across the man whom she loved so that she could die in his arms. It was a grotesque but not unmoving sight. Full revenge had now been exacted.

Josiah Taplow and William Merryweather trembled.

'They are yours now, sirs,' said Nicholas. 'You have solved a crime and brought malefactors to judgement.'

'Have we?' said Taplow nervously.

'Josiah and I but watched,' admitted Merryweather.

'No,' said Nicholas unselfishly. 'You are the real spirit of the law here. My friend and I simply helped you to bring these two wretches to account. You must take all the credit, sirs. Make a full report.'

Uncertain smiles spread over the gnarled faces.

They had tamed Clerkenwell at last.

★ ★ ★

A long night held still further surprises for both Owen Elias and Nicholas Bracewell. After making sworn statements to the authorities — and heaping agreed praise upon the two old watchmen — they went off to a tavern to celebrate their success and to drink to the memory of Sebastian Carrick. It was Elias who pointed out that the fatal brawl in Turmnill Street bore a marked resemblance to the sword fight in which Nicholas had instructed the late actor. Stage violence had anticipated its real counterpart. When his friend was at his most relaxed, Nicholas reopened a crucial debate.

'Do you still play at The Curtain on Saturday?'

'Yes,' said Owen with a scowl.

The Spanish Jew?'

'It has brought me acclamation, Nick.'

'Stolen from Lawrence Firethorn,' noted the other. 'No man is great by imitation, Owen. You have talent enough to succeed on your own account. Why ape a fellow-actor?'

'It is . . . required of me.'

'In return for the promised contract.'

'Master Randolph will have it ready by Saturday.'

'Westfield's Men have theirs ready now.' Nicholas slipped a hand inside his jerkin to pull out the contract which Andrew Carrick had drawn up with legal precision. Elias was frankly amazed. He read through the terms by the light of a candle and was touched. It was everything that he had hoped for during his long service with his old company but the contract had a defect.

'It has not been signed by Master Firethorn,' he said.

'It will be.'

'You give me food for thought here.'

'See if Banbury's Men can match those terms.'

'But if I play in *The Spanish Jew* . . . ?'

'Then this will be null and void,' said Nicholas, taking the contract and secreting it away. 'Think it over, Owen, and remember one thing. You acted for Westfield's Men tonight in Clerkenwell and your performance was without fault.'

The Welshman nodded. He was in for another disturbed night. Nicholas took his leave and headed towards the river. He made a slight detour so that his route took him towards Blackfriars. The house of Beatrice Capaldi looked smaller in the darkness and Nicholas walked around it three times as he tried to divine the secrets that lay within. He was about to continue on his way when a vague idea at the back of his mind was given real substance. The front door of the house opened and Beatrice Capaldi herself appeared, wearing a long pink robe over a shift. She stood on bare feet to plant a farewell kiss on the lips of her lover, then she waved a hand as he strode off towards the stables to get his horse. As the couple stood together in the light for those fleeting seconds, Nicholas got a look at the departing visitor.

It was Giles Randolph.

Chapter Twelve

London was burnished by bright summer sunshine but a tempest raged in the hearts of its citizens. Faint suspicions which first started in the corridors of the Palace spread quickly and developed into full-blown rumours. By the time they worked their way down to the very roots of society, they had hardened into incontrovertible fact. Queen Elizabeth was dying. Everyone knew it, from the mightiest earl in his mansion to the meanest wretch who begged outside Bedlam. The report of her slow demise was a thunderclap that destroyed the hearts of thousands. They had known no sovereign but her and had come to see her as a timeless guardian of themselves and their children after them. Conquest and expansion had distinguished a reign that was also remarkable for its peace and stability. Change had been exiled for over thirty years. Its imminent return was menacing. The capital was thrown into gusting confusion and the people who rushed so madly about were so many dry leaves whisked here and there at will by the heartless caprices of Fate.

The Earl of Chichester summed up the common experience.

'Oh, what an earthquake is the alteration of the state!'

Then he proceeded to exploit the phenomenon with bland irreverence. Others thronged to his alliance or formed new ones as the issue of the succession predominated. Church leaders met in hasty synods to decide where best to bestow their blessing. Puritans advanced their ideas, Presbyterians wanted their say in the election and Catholics looked to Rome for counsel. Every nobleman in the land was jolted out of his complacency and forced to rediscover the meaning of conspiracy and cabal. Lust for power was a giant needle which embroidered its way through the great houses of the nation with politic speed. Vaulting ambition was a thread of gold.

Hopes, fears and wild conjectures were given a sharper focus by two significant events. Lord Burghley vanished and Dr John Mordrake appeared on the scene. The old fox who had served his Queen so faithfully throughout her reign had now gone to ground. William Cecil, Baron Burghley, was the Lord High Treasurer, the senior figure in the government, a man of real political vision with a firm grasp on the complexities of state. In fading from view and affecting an attack of gout, he was giving tacit acknowledgement of the hopelessness of the situation. Dead queens need no bulwarks.

Dr John Mordrake's intervention was an even clearer signal. He was a desperate last gamble. Orthodox medicine had failed and so it was time to invoke magic. Dr John Mordrake was a scholar, sage, mathematician, alchemist and astrologer. His detractors called him a mountebank and his adherents a genius but nobody could gainsay the fact that a stream of small miracles had flowed through his eccentric career. The long, lean, bending creature in the black gown and black buckled shoes lived and worked in his laboratory in Knightrider Street. A mane of silver-grey hair gave him an almost saintly quality but it was offset by the dark power that seemed to emanate from him. Nobody could be sure whether the huge medallion which dangled from a chain around his neck was a holy relic or the badge of Satan.

The Earl of Banbury inclined to the latter view.

'Was the old devil allowed to see Her Majesty?'

'He was in her private apartments for an hour.'

'What took place, Roger?'

'Even my spies cannot peer through walls.'

'Mordrake will not save her!' said Banbury with ripe contempt. 'Though he practises the arts of necromancy, he will not raise her mouldering old body from the dead.'

Chichester smiled thinly. 'He left with a bottle.'

'What did it contain?'

'What else but the Queen's own urine?' said the other. 'Doctor Mordrake hastened back to Knightrider Street to put the royal piss to the test. My man tracked him. This time he *was* able to peer through walls?'

'How so?'

'Because walls have windows, sir. By bribing his way into the bedchamber opposite Mordrake's house, he was able to take part in the experiments as if he were standing at the shoulder of the venerable fraud.'

'Did Mordrake examine the contents of the bottle?'

'In every way.' Roger Godolphin grew lyrical. 'He touched, he tasted, he held it up to the light. He applied chemicals to change its colour and heat to change its consistency. In short, sir, he did everything but drink the draught down and sing an anthem. From that one pint of liquid history — taken, as it were, from the past life of our dear departing Majesty — he could foretell the future.' He chuckled quietly. 'And he did not like what he saw.'

'How can you be sure?'

'Because he began to shudder so much with fear and shake so much with horror that he dropped the bottle on the floor and it was smashed to pieces. The worthy doctor has given a precise diagnosis here. Queen Elizabeth fades away. All he has to remember her by is some damp floorboards.'

'Your spy deserves ten crowns for this!'

'He rendered better service yet.'

'Did he so?'

'When Mordrake recovered his wits enough to be able to hold a pen, he scribbled a letter and sent it off to the Palace by messenger.' The Earl of Chichester smirked. 'My fellow intercepted that messenger. A few gold coins gained him a glance at the letter.'

'What did it say, Roger?'

'Forty-eight hours.'

'That is all?'

'What more was necessary? Death sentence is passed.'

Banbury rubbed greedy palms. 'Forty-eight hours!'

'Two more days of the Tudor dynasty

then we move in! Dr John Mordrake has earned his fee, I warrant. That learned magician, who can read the signs of the zodiac has seen the future of the English nation in a bottle of piss.'

'I applaud his inspiration.'

'But forty-eight hours to wait.'

'How many of the Privy Council have we bought?'

'Enough.'

'How many of Westfield's supporters have we lured?'

'More than enough.'

'And Burghley?'

'We still practise on him,' said the other. 'Bess has bestirred herself in Hardwick Hall. She made her gout-ridden stepson, Gilbert Talbot, write to Burghley to advise him to make trial of oil of stag's blood for his ailment. The Earl of Shrewsbury will win over the Lord High Treasurer by means of the pains in their feet. They will soon walk as one!'

The Earl of Banbury executed a little dance of triumph then threw his arms around his host in congratulation.

'You have been a supreme general, sir!'

'Yes,' said Chichester smugly. 'I have deployed my army like a strategist. A case of money well-spent!'

* * *

Nicholas Bracewell took against Cornelius Gant the moment that he saw him. He detected a veiled hostility in Gant's manner, an ingratiating smile that was really a smirk of malice, friendly gestures that hid a deep contempt, a mock humility that cloaked a soaring arrogance. Nicholas had a job which required him to weigh men up at a glance and he found Gant severely wanting. He could sometimes enjoy the company of plausible rogues — Sebastian Carrick had been a case in point — but here was a more malevolent species. It was paradoxical that a religious purpose brought Gant to the Queen's Head so early in the morning.

'I have come for the angels' wings, sir,' he said.

'Wings?'

'Master Marwood told me of them. You staged a play in his yard that had an angel in the story. He remembers those wings very well, sir.'

'What of it?' said Nicholas warily.

'I wish to buy them from you.'

'We never sell our costumes.'

'Then let me rent the wings.'

'That is not our policy.'

'I will pay well.'

Cornelius Gant flipped back the edge of his coat and detached a large bag of coin

340

from his belt. He tossed it to Nicholas who got an immediate idea of its worth. Westfield's Men were being offered far more for the loan of their wings than it cost to make them in the first place. It would be a profitable deal but the book holder hesitated. Gant read his mind and threw in another hand-washing grin.

'You think I will fly off with your wings!' he said with a cackle. 'But I will bring them back even as I take them. To this end . . .' A second purse was untied from his belt. 'I leave this as surety. When the wings return, you give me back this purse. Is not this fair?'

'It is, sir.'

'Then the deal is settled.'

'Why do you want those wings?'

'I do not wish to be an angel, that I can tell you.'

'Is it for some kind of play?'

'Come to St Paul's on Saturday.'

Cornelius Gant would say no more but his money was real and his terms generous. The wings had been made for an early play by Edmund Hoode that had now fallen out of the repertoire and they were simply taking up space in the room at the inn where Westfield's Men stored their costumes and properties. Nicholas consented. When he showed Gant to the storeroom, the latter was delighted with what he saw. The wings were some five feet in length, covered in white feathers and joined by a leather halter which had been fitted around the shoulders of the actor playing the angel. It was this device that particularly thrilled Gant and he tried the wings on, flapping them for effect.

'Thank you, Master Bracewell. They are ideal.'

'Be careful, sir. They are partly held by wax.'

'So?'

'Remember Icarus. Do not fly near the sun.'

Gant went off into a paroxysm of reedy cackling.

Nicholas was now treated to one of the most unlikely sights he had ever witnessed at the Queen's Head. Its landlord came skipping blithely over to them. At a time of national calamity, when a dying sovereign was turning the capital into a city of sadness, Alexander Marwood might finally have come into his own. His sustained misery would at last be appropriate, his skulking despair a common mode of behaviour. Instead of this, he was sprightly and joyful. He fell on his visitor as if Gant were his oldest friend and he pressed him to free ale and victuals. Nicholas watched it in bewildered silence. When the two men went off arm in arm, he wondered if he had taken leave of his senses.

Cornelius Gant was not the only angel on the premises.

'Good morning, Master Bracewell.'

'Mistress Carrick! What brings you here at this hour?'

'I thought to catch you before your rehearsal.'

'Then must your reason be important.'

'It is.' Marion Carrick handed him the scroll. 'My father said that I was to put it into your hand without delay. It contains a report about one Master Fellowes.'

'That makes it almost as welcome as you, mistress.'

Nicholas had never seen her looking so lovely or so like her brother. With the sun slanting down to give her a halo, she really did have an angelic air. Her smile had a sweet innocence which he did not want to remove but there was no helping it. Taking her aside and sitting her down on a bench, he explained that her brother's killer had himself been killed in a Clerkenwell Street. Her ignorance of the area obscured its true character from her and he was able to give a version of the story which obscured the fact that Sebastian's visit to a prostitute had set the whole tragedy in motion. Marion Carrick was so grateful to hear the news that she burst into tears and had to be comforted.

As he soothed her with gentle patting, he looked down into the beautiful moist face and reflected how different she was from the two other women who had become entangled with Westfield's Men. Frances from the Pickt-hatch and Beatrice Capaldi from Blackfriars were sisters under the skin. One was paid for nightly promiscuity while the other was more highly selective in her clients but both were courtesans with a streak of madness in them. And neither would baulk at murder. Frances stabbed herself through the heart but Beatrice Capaldi inserted the blade through the breast of her victims. Lawrence Firethorn was being slowly bled to death and his company might perish with him.

Nicholas sighed and helped Marion Carrick up from the bench. In contrast to the other women, she was a decent and wholesome presence but she did not belong in the world of the theatre. Now that her brother's death had been properly avenged, she could return to her own life. Nicholas was sorry to see her go and she lingered at the parting to give him a soft kiss before hurrying off with the servant who escorted her out into the street. There was no flapping of wings but he felt as if an angel had departed from his life.

The missive remained and he unrolled it at once. Andrew Carrick had been diligent in his research. His letter was an absolute mine of information gleaned from Harry Fellowes and bearing upon the operation of the Ordnance Office. Facts and figures were set down in tabulated profusion. Nicholas knew that his plan could now be put into effect. The search for the man with the axe was over. He could now tackle the conspirators who were trying to chop down Westfield's Men.

Before that, another rehearsal beckoned.

'Gentlemen!' he yelled. 'About it straight!'

The studious inertia of Cambridge oppressed her more each day and she grew increasingly restless. She bulked large in a small house even when she was stationary but Margery Firethorn was positively overwhelming when she was on the move in such a confined space. Mother and child found her ubiquity rather unsettling. Jonathan Jarrold felt it was like sharing a cage with a hungry she-tiger. While giving her the daily dose of gratitude, he assured his sister-in-law that they could now cope without her. His son, Richard, had come through the real trial and was making visible progress. The bookseller and his wife had every reason to believe that they had finally produced a baby who had come to stay.

Margery agreed to his suggestion. Reasons to leave now greatly outnumbered reasons to stay. She would depart on Friday and break the journey to London at some intermediate hostelry where she could spend the night.

'That way,' she told her sister, 'I may arrive home in good time on Saturday.'

'Lawrence will be overjoyed to see you, Margery.'

'I will take my husband unawares.'

'That was ever your way.'

'Goodbye, sister.'

'Give our love to the whole family.'

'Mine remains with yours.'

'Lawrence will have missed your warming presence.'

Margery was rueful. 'That is my fear!'

'I love her! I need her! I want her! I must have her, Nick!'

'She sets a high price on her favours, sir.'

'Beatrice puts my devotion to the test.'

'Westfield's Men will suffer.'

'I will be away but one afternoon.'

'The company needs you tomorrow as never before.'

'Do not vex me so!'

Lawrence Firethorn was being ripped apart by competing claims on his loyalty. Lord Westfield had overridden his choice of *Cupid's Folly* as the play to be performed at the Queen's Head on the following afternoon and the determined patron had substituted *Love's Sacrifice*. It was an attempt to bring the actor-manager to heel but, as the first playbill was put up to advertise the event, a second letter arrived from Beatrice Capaldi to give details of the slow voyage along the Thames and to hint at the ultimate reward for her doting lover. Firethorn agonized between the demands of professional duty and private dalliance. Anger finally sent him running to the arms of Beatrice Capaldi.

'Lord Westfield insults me!' he snarled.

'No man admires you more,' said Nicholas.

'I'll not take it!'

'Our patron chose you as his manager.'

'Then why does he treat me as a hired man who must play as cast?' Firethorn worked himself up into a fury. 'I'll not be bullied, I'll not be forced, I'll not dance to the tune of Lord Westfield or any other man in London! Let him put up his playbills for *Love's Sacrifice*. It will not be staged.'

'It will, sir.'

'Without *me?*'

'With or without you, Master Firethorn.'

Nicholas Bracewell allowed an interval of silence so that his irate companion could calm down slightly. Having come out through Bishopsgate, they were now walking together in the direction of Shoreditch. Rehearsal and performance had gone well because Lawrence Firethorn had acted with Beatrice Capaldi's second missive next to his heart. It would have been unwise to tackle him at the Queen's Head where his raised voice abolished walls and made privacy quite impossible. Nicholas therefore waited until the two of them were well clear of the city walls before he touched once more on the delicate topic. Firethorn was leading his horse by the reins. The three of them passed Bedlam.

'Consider one more time,' pleaded Nicholas.

'It is too late.'

'Renounce this lady, sir.'

'I am too far gone in to turn back now, Nick,' said the other with sudden passion. 'This is no mere conquest that I pursue here. Beatrice is my own true love. I worship her with every fibre of my being. I would do *anything* to show her that I am in earnest.

I fret, I sigh, I long for her. Did I but know where she dwells, I would lie before her threshold all night and sleep in contented adoration.'

Nicholas steeled himself to disillusion his master.

'Mistress Capaldi lives beside the river,' he said.

'How do you know?'

'Because I tracked her to Blackfriars one night.'

'*Why?*' hissed Firethorn. 'What reason had you to spy on her? You followed my love without telling *me*? What kind of treachery is this?'

'It was on your account that I went.'

'Behind my back!'

'I had no other means of helping you.'

'Helping me! You have lost my friendship forever!'

'It grieves me to tell you any more . . .'

'Then let us part now.'

'No, Master Firethorn,' said Nicholas, detaining him with a hand on his shoulder. 'When I went past Mistress Capaldi's home, a visitor left. It was her shrewd stage manager.'

'I hope he was shrewder and more honest than mine.'

'It was Giles Randolph.'

'Never!'

'He has rehearsed this whole play, sir,' argued Nicholas bravely. 'He sent Mistress Capaldi to The Rose and he was there himself to witness her performance and its effect on you. That is how he came to see Owen Elias. *Love's Sacrifice* would not have brought him to the playhouse any more than the work of Banbury's Men would take you to The Curtain. Master Randolph was there with Beatrice Capaldi. They are trying to kill our company by cutting off its head.'

'ENOUGH!'

Lawrence's Firethorn's anguish echoed for a mile and sent his horse into a panic. The man he trusted most of all had betrayed him and his love in the most comprehensive way. Controlling his steed, he mounted with a leap, then glared down at Nicholas with a loathing he never suspected he could ever feel for him. No more words were necessary. In his now seething rage, Firethorn believed that Nicholas was trying to discredit Beatrice Capaldi on behalf of Westfield's Men. Partnership with his book holder was over, fidelity to his patron a thing of the past, commitment to his company a trifling irrelevance.

Sharp heels dug into the horse's flanks. It reared up on its hind legs then took its rider homewards at a gallop. Nicholas Bracewell sighed deeply at his failure then walked on swiftly. He still had business in Shoreditch.

Andrew Carrick gazed through the window of his cell with a glow of satisfaction in his soul. His daughter, Marion, had told him of the apprehension of the murderer in Clerkenwell and, though her account fell short of the full truth, the lawyer was able to shed a father's tears of contentment. Sebastian's death had been paid for in full and he could now rest in peace. Carrick longed for the moment when he could extract more details from Nicholas Bracewell whom he knew was the chief architect of events in Turnmill Street. In relating the tale to the bereaved sister, the book holder played down his own part in the affair but the acute father could see behind this show of modesty.

The lawyer was overcome with delight, therefore, when Nicholas actually appeared below in the yard but he was not alone on this visit. Five others marched with him. Lord Westfield led the way with a purposeful figure in the robes of a bishop and a black-garbed clerk who carried writing materials in his satchel. Two soldiers from the Palace guard flanked the deputation. Nicholas Bracewell excused himself to slip into the Beauchamp Tower and Carrick ran to his door to listen for the sound of his footsteps on the stone steps. It seemed like an hour before his gaoler unlocked the door to admit the visitor. Carrick embraced him, thanked him and asked for a complete account of what had transpired outside the Pickt-hatch. Nicholas first took him to the window and pointed at the five men who were now going into the building across the yard with firm footsteps.

'Did you see them, Master Carrick?' he asked.

'I recognized Lord Westfield.'

'He is prosecuting this matter.'

'Who was the noble churchman?'

Nicholas was impassive. 'John Aylmer, Bishop of London. With him was his clerk. And two soldiers to enforce the gravity of their embassy.'

The truth dawned. 'They visit Harry Fellowes?'

'The Clerk of Ordnance is being interviewed. Your information was of immense help, sir, and Lord Westfield has used his wide circle of friends to make further inquiry.'

'Harry has embezzled,' said Carrick unequivocally. 'There can be no doubt of his guilt. But proving it is quite another matter. A man who has defrauded the Crown so long and so cunningly will be able to wriggle out of any charge.'

'That is why I sought the power of the Church.'

'John Aylmer?'

'Yes,' said Nicholas. 'Fellowes is a rogue but he is also a priest. He will not be able to withstand the pressure that the Bishop of London may bring upon him.' His face was still impassive but his eyes twinkled. 'Our scheming Clerk will never have met a man quite like this John Aylmer.'

The Bishop of London glowered under bushy eyebrows and put the crackle of authority into his voice. Harry Fellowes swallowed hard and backed away slightly. He was seated at his desk when his room was invaded by the five menacing figures. The Clerk of Ordnance was caught offguard.

'Remember!' intoned John Aylmer, 'that you speak under oath. Do not perjure yourself before your Maker or He will call you to account for it on the Day of Judgement. Speak the truth before us here and we may be inclined to mercy. Lie, deceive or prevaricate and the full majesty of the law will descend upon you.' A finger of doom pointed. 'One thing more, Master Fellowes. Though you have neglected your flock this long while, you are still an ordained priest. It was my predecessor as Bishop of London, Edmund Grindal, who brought you into the clergy. That revered Churchman, who went on to become His Grace the Archbishop of Canterbury, looks down on you from Heaven at this moment and implores you to hold faith with him. Confess your sins to him, to us and to God.'

Harry Fellowes reeled from the grim warning. It was his first meeting with the Bishop of London and he knew instantly that he would not seek to renew the acquaintance. John Aylmer was a sturdy man of middle height with a challenging religiosity about him. In his distress, it never occurred to Fellowes to wonder why a man who hailed from the Norfolk gentry spoke with a Welsh lilt.

Lord Westfield read out the stern indictment.

'Henry Fellowes, Clerk of Ordnance, we charge you with fraud and embezzlement in the execution of your office and summon you to appear before Sir Walter Mildmay, Chancellor of the Exchequer. The allegations are as follows, that you did wilfully indulge in false recording in the office books, that you did sell Crown property into private lands for your own profit, that you did misappropriate government monies, that you did maliciously and unlawfully . . .'

It was all there. Harry Fellowes was hit with such a powerful blend of fact and conjecture that he did not pause to disentangle the two. Guesswork was cruelly on target. He was arraigned for sending unserviceable shot to Barbary, for shipping a consignment of unwearable boots to the army in Ireland, for selling ammunition, already paid for, to a naval depot so that he could pocket the second amount, for listing equipment in the two ledgers delivered to the Auditors of the Prest which had not been purchased as stated, but simply taken from the Ordnance store. Indeed, it was Fellowes' skill at making departments pay for things they never received or requisitions they never made that was the basis of his fraud. One consignment of muskets circulated between six different regiments without ever leaving the boxes in which they were stored. Harry Fellowes embezzled with a sense of humour.

Lord Westfield rolled on remorselessly, John Aylmer lent his ecclesiastical presence and the black-clad secretary wrote down every word. Fellowes could not have done it alone and they soon prised out of him the names of his now wealthy accomplices, Geoffrey Turville, the Purveyor of Materials and Richard Bowland, the Keeper of the Store. Collusion between the trio defeated all the administrative precautions taken and allowed Harry Fellowes, as the instigator of the various schemes, to amass a large personal fortune which he either disseminated throughout his family or used to finance a series of highly profitable loans. When Lord Westfield put the tentative figure of deceits at £10,000, Harry Fellowes admitted it at once in order to conceal the fact that it was almost twice that amount.

John Aylmer, Bishop of London came back into action.

'All that you have said has been taken down, Master Fellowes. Read what my secretary has written. If it be a fair and true account of your confession, sign it forthwith then pray to God for mercy.'

'Yes, your grace.'

Fellowes read the document, startled by the range of frauds which had been detected and relieved by the number which had escaped scrutiny. He signed with a shaking hand. Lord Westfield produced another document for perusal.

'Here is a warrant for your arrest, sir,' he said with due solemnity. 'It is signed by Sir Robert Cecil who helped me to initiate these investigations.' He turned to the guards.

'Take the villain away!'

Stripped of his office, the Clerk of Ordnance was duly delivered to the Constable of the Tower who promptly incarcerated him in a dank cell and left him there to contemplate the miseries that lay ahead. Nicholas Bracewell joined the deputation as they left by the main gate. They were some distance from the Tower before they broke into laughter. Lord Westfield was gleeful.

'I should be a member of my own company!' he said. 'But it was John Aylmer here who really put our man to flight.'

'I've always wanted to be a bishop,' admitted Owen Elias, playing with the cross on his chest. 'But I'd not waste myself on London. Make me Bishop of Wales and let me lead my wayward people back to the Lord.'

They adjourned to a nearby inn where Nicholas had already reserved a private room. The Bishop of London became Owen Elias again, his secretary emerged as Matthew Lipton, the regular scrivener to Westfield's Men, and the two soldiers were now restored to their status as hired men with the company. Impersonation on that scale rendered all four of them liable to prosecution but Nicholas felt the risk was worth taking. A fraudulent Clerk had been outwitted by a fraudulent

357

bishop. With a signed confession, Lord West-field could now hand the whole matter over to the Chancellor of the Exchequer. As he battled for his survival, Harry Fellowes would forget all about the ruse which had entrapped him.

Lord Westfield had a final word alone with Nicholas.

'The deepest pleasure of all is yet to come,' he said. 'Roger Godolphin, Earl of Chichester, will be ruined by these disclosures. Instead of making a queen of Arabella Stuart, he has simply made an arrant fool of himself!' He chuckled happily. 'This will make those lions rampant on his coat of arms lie on their backs with their feet in the air!'

Nicholas recalled the coach he had seen outside the home of Beatrice Capaldi. Its identity was now confirmed. The coat of arms had belonged to the Godolphin family. The Earl of Chichester was not using all the money he borrowed from Harry Fellowes to finance his daring bid for political power. Some of it went to subsidize his pleasures at the house in Blackfriars. It was an interesting coincidence.

Nicholas wondered if Giles Randolph knew about it.

Beatrice Capaldi reclined on her fourposter

and sipped wine from a Venetian glass goblet. Even when naked and covered with a film of perspiration, she still had natural poise and distinction. A toss of her head turned unkempt hair into a faultless coiffure once more. A lift of her black eyebrow restored full hauteur to her mien. She was an aristocrat in a profession of commoners. Beatrice Capaldi was no ordinary whore who could be bought by anyone with enough money. She was a voluptuous woman of high ambition and a discerning taste. Suitors of all manner besieged her but she rejected the vast majority and chose only the select few. Giles Randolph, actor-manager with Banbury's Men, was one of those chosen few. Indeed, he had been encouraged to believe that he was now the only one of them.

He lay beside her and fingered the new love-bite she had just implanted on his chest. Still panting from his exertions, he threw down a mouthful of wine and smiled. 'You are a woman in a thousand, Beatrice!'

'Ten thousand.'

'A hundred thousand, a million!' He kissed the porcelain skin of her shoulders. 'And you are all mine!'

'Yes, Giles. I am all yours.'

'No wonder Firethorn wants you so much!'

'Can *any* man resist me?' she said easily.

'Not if he has red blood in his veins.'

She laughed and gave him another little bite. Randolph nestled back in the pillows to marvel at her wonder afresh. Beatrice Capaldi was the child of an Italian father and an English mother, inheriting her passion from the former and her dignity from the other, then adding capacities for guile and intrigue that were all her own. Her slender body could deliver all its rich promises, her succulent mouth could draw the very soul out of a man. He was hers. Giles Randolph saw her as his conquest but he was very much her possession. A rich and successful actor, he had money enough to keep her and charms enough to amuse her. When he involved her in the capture of Lawrence Firethorn, she played a game at which she was a consummate expert. Both were ruthless and neither would stop at anything. They were kindred spirits.

'Tomorrow night we will celebrate,' he said fondly.

'All will be achieved.'

'Firethorn will be outlawed and his company disbanded.'

'Banbury's Men will be unrivalled.'

'Yes,' he said, looping an arm around her. 'One day will change both our lifetimes. A queen will die and a new king will attend his coronation in the theatre. We will stay together for ever and rule the whole city.'

Beatrice Capaldi smiled with determined pleasure.

'I expect no less . . .'

London awoke at first light to begin the fateful day. The markets were erected and filled with bustling urgency by noisy stall-holders. Butchers set out their meat, bakers their bread and fishmongers the latest catch. Farmers streamed into the city with their animals and produce to increase the pungency of the odours and swell the general pande-monium. Careful housewives were up just after dawn to find the best bargains. Children, dogs, beggars and masterless men filtered into the throng. Major streets were turned into human rivers that ebbed and flowed with tidal force. Market time was one long continuous act of collective lunacy.

Cornelius Gant was among the first visitors to the maelstrom. Though nobody knew him by sight, he heard his name on dozens of tongues as the miraculous Nimbus was dis-cussed. Bills had been posted up to advertise the attempted flight to the top of St Paul's but it was word of mouth which would bring in the bulk of the audience. Gant would be ready for them. Aided by a boy with a hand-cart, he bought up baskets of doves, pigeons and any other birds he could find. When the baskets were piled high on the cart, he and the boy pushed its cooing, cawing, fluttering cargo in the direction of the cathedral. Gant was keeping an appointment with the verger.

Further down river, another market was being held. The unintentional vendor was Queen Elizabeth herself and the commodity on sale was nothing less than her crown. Whitehall Palace was no seething mass of urgent bodies but the figures who glided about in profusion were no less intent on making a profit on their transaction. A buoyant Lord Westfield was there with his entourage and a chastened Earl of Chichester loitered with his adherents. Other alliances stood in other corners and eyed the competition with resentful enmity. It was a market where most would be turned away disappointed. There was only one item for sale and its price was rightly exorbitant.

The Earl of Banbury scurried in with high hopes that were dashed instantly by the leader of his campaign. News of the arrest of Harry Fellowes had been communicated to the Master of Ordnance. Chichester had funded his enterprise with tainted money. The consequences were too frightful to reflect upon.

His reputation would never survive the scandal and all who were associated with him would be stigmatized. The watching Lord Westfield saw the face of his rival turn puce as he received the intelligence. It was worth getting up at such an ungodly hour to observe the priceless discomfiture of the Earl of Banbury. Dreams of endless bounty from the gracious hands of Queen Arabella vanished at once.

Word arrived that an official announcement was to be made about the Queen in one of the larger chambers. Every room, corridor and staircase in the palace emptied its occupants and they converged on a moment of history. Lord Westfield looked around at the distinguished gathering. All the royal favourites were there with their retinues of hopeful supporters. Essex posed, Oxford twitched, Raleigh was pensive, Mountjoy was sad and the others composed their features into what they felt was the appropriate face for such a solemn occasion. A staff was banged once on the floor to command immediate silence then a door opened and two rather decrepit old gentlemen came in.

Their laboured gait and their sense of effort was reminiscent of Josiah Taplow and William Merryweather but these were no tired watchmen. They were trusted servants of the state who were bowed down with grief. Lord Burghley hobbled along with the aid of a walking stick and Dr John Mordrake looked in need of some similar assistance as well. They climbed awkwardly up on to the dais and turned to face the whole court. It should have fallen to the Lord Treasurer to make the grim announcement but he deferred to the old astrologer who was now bent double by the weight of his medallion. Dr John Mordrake cleared his throat.

'She is gone,' he said.

A wave of pain hit even the most cynical listeners and a loud murmur started up. Mordrake quelled it at once with a skeletal hand. Having been in at the death, he wanted the privilege of describing it.

'I was called in too late,' he continued. 'Had they let me see her earlier, I might have prolonged a life that was a joy to all who came into contact with her. I count myself lucky to have been her friend and her adviser for many a year and her memory is engraved on my old heart. When I made my examination of her, I knew the worst. She had less than forty-eight hours to live. And so it proved.' Tears welled. 'Forgive these moist eyes of mine but we shared a special bond. She was godmother to my only son. Moreover . . .'

The silence which had fallen on the chamber was charged with mild hysteria. Dr John Mordrake was not talking about Queen Elizabeth at all. As he burbled on about a dear lady with high principles and a love of duty, it was evident that the deceased was Blanche Parry. The astonishing woman who had been at Her Majesty's side for over three decades as her closest friend had finally passed away, taking with her the scholarly enthusiasm and the love for ostentation which she had shared with the Queen. In the circumstances, it was not surprising that the sovereign had retired into seclusion to watch over her beloved gentlewoman during her last days and the presence of the astrologer now made more sense. Dr John Mordrake had been introduced to the Queen by none other than Blanche Parry herself. The bottle he had borne away from the palace had contained the specimen from a blind old lady.

Muttering broke out as relieved courtiers heard that their sinecures would continue and fraught politicians realised that all their machinations had come to nothing. Lord Burghley came forward to make a crisp announcement to the effect that Her Majesty would hold court later that morning. Those closest to him caught the whisper of a smile on the face of the old fox. His gout improved.

Lord Westfield was amongst the first to recover. His own support of King James of Scotland as the next monarch had foundered but it could be revived at a later date. The campaign of the Earls of Chichester and Banbury had run aground permanently and there would be corrosive letters from Hardwick Hall to endure. Others, too, had showed their hand in a way that they now regretted and the heavy murmur was largely produced by earnest disclaimers from embarrassed nobles. Saturday at Whitehall was yielding rich rewards for Lord Westfield. Not only did he find a Queen whom he loved alive and well, not only could he watch loathed enemies wince and squirm, he could take real pleasure from the element of intrigue. It was all deliberate.

Blanche Parry was dying and the Queen wished to be with her but she turned the occasion to full political advantage. By retiring to her apartments and maintaining a steadfast silence, she knew that she would create alarm and spread false hope. The question of the succession would bring all the swirling enmities out into the open as the courtiers who had been dearest to her wooed other possible claimants with undue haste and zeal. Long days in hiding had acquainted Queen Elizabeth with the darker truths of her position. She would henceforth reign with an even firmer grip.

Lord Westfield turned to his companions.

'Can you not see it, sirs?' he said jovially. 'Blanche Parry was but the excuse to make examination of her court. Her Majesty wanted to see which way her royal favourites would scatter if she died. She was toying with them.'

'Why?' asked a crony.

'For sport and for education.'

'She took pleasure from all this?'

'Yes,' said Westfield. 'It softened the pain of Blanche Parry's death. The Queen has been playing her favourites against each other. She may be the greatest sovereign in Christendom but she is also a mad old courtesan!'

They drifted out of the chamber and along a corridor.

'Will you go to court, my lord?' said the crony.

'Most assuredly. Then on to the Gracechurch Street to watch a play. *Love's Sacrifice* is an apter choice than ever now. It will celebrate the reign of an adorable Queen. I'll have special lines written by Edmund Hoode to be worked into the speeches of King Gondar.'

'What of *The Spanish Jew?*'

'Who will wish to see that now?' said Westfield. 'Her Majesty was not poisoned by Dr

Lopez and the worst usurer in London is no Jew but that damnable Clerk of Ordnance.'

The entourage laughed appreciatively. Lord Westfield saw only one cloud on the horizon. Banbury's Men had been vanquished but his own company was haunted by a disaster.

'Lawrence Firethorn *must* be there!' he said.

'And if he is not . . . ?'

Night was an unrelieved torment. Lawrence Firethorn twisted and turned in his empty bed as ugly thoughts skewered his brain. Love for Beatrice Capaldi intensified with each passing hour but so did his respect for Nicholas Bracewell. Though he galloped away from the book holder, he was soon overtaken by the horror of the information which Nicholas imparted. Beatrice unfaithful? Her invitation a device to separate him from his company? Their whole relationship a contrivance by Giles Randolph? He could accept none of the propositions and yet he could not deny them either. It was unlike Nicholas to make false accusations but this was a special case. Anxious to secure the actor-manager's presence on Saturday afternoon, even a normally truthful man might bend the facts, especially if he were prompted by such a self-willed patron as Lord Westfield. There was salvation in sight yet. Firethorn was on the rack but only one person could release him and that was Beatrice Capaldi herself. Only if he honoured the tryst, would he learn the truth.

He left Shoreditch early to ride into the city and stable his horse near the wharf where he was due to meet her barge. Hours stretched before him and he spent them in tense meandering along the river. As a nearby clock struck the hour, his guilt was stirred by the reminder that Westfield's Men were now rehearsing *Love's Sacrifice* without him. Some balm did soothe him. The news from Whitehall Palace ran through the city to make it crackle with joy. Firethorn was not betraying his patron at a critical time in a dispute over the succession and that reduced the severity of his guilt. He tried to concentrate on Beatrice and the magic of their love but the face of Giles Randolph kept leering over her shoulder. Italian passion was blighted by a Spanish Jew.

Lurching up into the narrow streets, he found himself part of an excited crowd that converged on St Paul's. His mind might be obsessed with a dark lady but it was a black stallion which drew spectators to the cathedral. Firethorn was soon staring up at the roof with the thousands of others who had come to witness a miracle of biblical stature. The actor in him was outraged. A play with Lawrence Firethorn in it would never draw such a throng. Why had the whole city turned out? Resentment and envy made him bristle.

The choice of St Paul's for such crude entertainment was natural. As well as being the focal point of worship in the capital, the great church with its cavernous interior, its walks and its busy courtyard, had served as the nexus for spectacular performances of all kinds. Sermons and masses were on offer but so were occasional bouts of wild audacity. Many still talked of the Spaniard who descended headfirst from battlements to ground by means of a taut rope that was stretched between the two points. Those who tried to emulate him fell to their death or to hideous mutilation. Another man committed suicide by tying a rope to a pinnacle before putting the noose around his neck and diving off. There was even an acrobatic cripple who once stole the weathercock of gilt-plated copper. Countless others had given the noble edifice the status of an occasional fairground.

Nimbus had been promised for noon and Cornelius Gant did not renege on that vow. As the great bell boomed out in the clocktower, the eyes of London scanned the Heavens for the latter-day Pegasus but he was nowhere to be seen. Just as they were losing patience, their vigilance was rewarded. Cornelius Gant used a rope in a way that was every bit as ingenious as the lithe Spaniard of yesteryear. It was threaded carefully through the handles of the baskets of birds so that each would be released at a sharp flick. The noonday clock chimed its fill and left its echo hanging in the air. Gant pulled hard on the rope. The lids of twenty baskets sprang open to send up thick clouds of birds who were quickly joined by the rest of the feathered community up on the roof. The suddenness of it all was breath-taking.

Viewed from below, it was indeed a miracle. Hundreds of birds burst out of the tower to fly up to heaven and there behind them, standing on hind legs so that all could see properly, was a black horse with black wings sprouting out of its shoulders. In that extraordinary moment of revelation, it seemed to all who watched that Nimbus had flown to the top of St Paul's. Cornelius Gant stepped forward to wave his hat and to set off a veritable broadside of cheering. Nobody knew how he had done it but all accepted one thing. Nimbus was the finest horse in creation.

Lawrence Firethorn was angry with himself

for having been momentarily carried away by the spectacle. A man whose life revolved around cleverly-devised stage effects knew some deft handiwork when he saw it and he tried to work out exactly how it was all done. He was not helped by the rapturous ovation that was being accorded to his new rival for the public's adoration.

Nimbus.

Beatrice Capaldi arrived in her barge at the wharf well before the appointed time. When the vessel was moored, the four oarsmen went ashore to stretch their legs. Beatrice remained under the rich canopy which covered the raised area in the stern of the boat. Lying back on cushions, she was protected from the prying eyes of the rougher sort who hung about the waterfront. Her lutenist sat on a stool nearby and played soft airs. Beatrice was at her most elegant in a dress of black and red that exactly matched the colours of her latest hat in the Spanish fashion. A silver fan could be used to cool or conceal, a pomander kept the odours of the river away from her nostrils.

The swift approach of a horse made her sit up. She did not expect Lawrence Firethorn to appear quite so early. His impatience was testimony to the fevered love which he bore her. She heard the horse being reigned in then urgent feet ran along the planking on the wharf. Her visitor came aboard without ceremony and she looked up to greet him. But it was not the over-eager Firethorn. It was Giles Randolph.

'We must speak alone,' he said pointedly.

'As you wish.' She dismissed the lutenist with a flick of her fan then delivered a mild reproach to her visitor. 'This is most unseemly, sir.'

'You have deceived me, Beatrice.'

'That is a lie!'

'Your promises were mere nothings.'

'Have a care, Giles.'

'You entertained a visitor at your house.'

'I deny it.'

'You swore to be true to me!' he accused.

'And so I have.'

'I know the day, the time, the man.' Randolph let his pain show through. 'Beatrice, how could you consort with that disgusting old lecher?'

'Of whom do you speak?'

'Roger Godolphin, Earl of Chichester.'

The momentary pause and the flicker of her eyelids were enough to condemn her. Giles Randolph began to upbraid her in the strongest terms but was silenced by a blazing retort.

'It is my house,' she said proudly, 'and I entertain whomsoever I wish. You are not my keeper, sir. I may have my pick of any man in London. Why should I deign to favour an actor when I may choose an earl? Giles Randolph is not even an aristocrat in his own profession. Lawrence Firethorn will always outrank him.' She stabbed home her advantage. 'If I want the best — and nothing less will suffice — I should give myself to him this very afternoon.'

'No, Beatrice!' It was a howl of anguish.

She retreated into silence and let him dribble his apologies all over her. When he had humbled himself completely before her, she probed for details.

'Who told you of the Earl of Chichester?'

'Owen Elias.'

She was contemptuous. 'A hired man!'

'He quit the company this morning,' said Randolph sourly, 'and left *The Spanish Jew* without its ridicule of Firethorn. His parting shot concerned yourself. I was to ask you why the coach bearing the Godolphin coat of arms was seen outside your house on a certain night.'

'I hate all Welshmen!' she asserted.

Randolph found consolation. 'Owen Elias has cut his own throat. He has left our company and Westfield's Men have disowned him. Firethorn will never let that ugly Celtic visage anywhere near the Queen's Head!'

Owen Elias sat in the taproom at the Queen's Head and took his final instructions from Nicholas Bracewell. The morning rehearsal was uncertain but by no means calamitous. It was just conceivable that *Love's Sacrifice* could survive before an audience without Lawrence Firethorn in the leading role. Owen Elias was a more muted King Gondar but he gave a very competent reading of the part. Barnaby Gill and Edmund Hoode sat at the table to add their counsel. The four men were determined to rescue the company from the wilful absence of its actor-manager. Alexander Marwood interrupted their discussions with an uncharactersitic chuckle.

'Good day, gentlemen!' he said warmly. 'You'll have spectators enough in my yard today.'

'Why do you say that?' asked Nicholas.

'Because of the promise I have from Master Gant.'

'Cornelius Gant?'

'He and Nimbus are the wonders of London,' said the twitching landlord. 'And *you* helped them, Master Bracewell. You gave Nimbus the wings to fly!'

375

Marwood gave an excited if garbled account of what had happened at St Paul's Cathedral. Nimbus and his master were now being hailed on all sides. What thrilled the landlord was the fact that he had engaged the pair to make another appearance at the Queen's Head. They were to perform briefly on stage after *Love's Sacrifice* had run its course. The yard would be packed to the limit with thirsty patrons. It would be one of the most profitable afternoons that the inn had ever known. Alexander Marwood was inebriated at the very thought.

The four men were duly horrified. They did not wish to share their venue with a performing animal. Barnaby Gill stood on his dignity, Edmund Hoode threatened to withdraw his play and Owen Elias refused to have his first attempt at a leading role overshadowed by an actor with four legs. It was the threatened use of their makeshift stage which worried Nicholas because it might not bear the weight of a dancing horse. The argument was over as soon as it began. A figure swept into the taproom and confronted them with a demand that drove every other thought from their mind.

Margery Firethorn was at her most forceful. 'Where is my husband?' she said.

★ ★ ★

Lawrence Firethorn waited until the buzzing crowd began to disperse then he drifted slowly towards the river. Nimbus hung over him like a black cloud. It rankled. He was both hurt and jealous. Firethorn had worked at his craft for many long years to achieve a standard of excellence that nobody could match; yet it was not his name that was the touchstone of the citizenry. Cornelius Gant and his black stallion had pushed the actor aside. In the space of five minutes atop St Paul's Cathedral, they had dazzled an audience which was ten times the size of any that Firethorn had attracted. It was deeply insulting. The actor offered a dramatic experience that captivated for two hours then stayed in the memory forever. Nimbus was palmed off on an unsuspecting public by means of a clever conjuring trick and he would be forgotten when the next sensation diverted the commonalty.

Firethorn knew the secret of the flying horse. Nimbus was taken up to the top of the cathedral by means of the circular staircase then brought into view in a flurry of flapping wings. The real skill lay not in getting the animal up there to create the optical illusion but in bringing it down again. Horses could be trained to climb stairs but their gait and their co-ordination forbade any descent. To bring Nimbus down spiralling stone steps was a phenomenon in itself. Firethorn decided that the animal was either carried in some way or that it had been taught to walk backwards.

The wings also puzzled him. They looked very familiar. They were black now instead of being white but he felt certain he had seen them before. The dreadful thought formed in his mind that they had been hired from Westfield's Men and that his own company had actually aided the spectacular flight of Nimbus. His sense of betrayal was acute. Lawrence Firethorn heard the ripple of water and realized he was now standing beside the Thames. The wharf was in front of him and the barge was moored to it. Four oarsmen and a young lutenist lingered. Beatrice Capaldi was there.

Yet even as his desire was rekindled, it fell short of its former glow. The antics on the roof of St Paul's had done something which he would never have believed possible. They had focused his mind on the dignity of his profession. Nimbus had dispossessed Beatrice Capaldi. His beloved was waiting for him and the busy river lay before them but he no longer lusted after her company. Doubts crowded in. Guilt resurfaced. He was in an agony of indecision. Part of him wanted to run to the barge to embrace her while another part wished that he was at the Queen's Head to rub out the vision of a performing animal with his own brand of magic.

After all his suffering, he had to learn the truth. He strode towards the barge and caught her perfume on the air. The brief enchantment of Beatrice Capaldi returned to be shattered forever.

'Lawrence!'

He froze where he stood and turned around. The coach which came thundering towards the wharf bore the Westfield coat of arms. Margery Firethorn was leaning through the window to hail him. As the horses were reined in and the vehicle came to a squealing halt, Nicholas Bracewell opened the door and assisted Margery out. The contrite husband rushed to his wife's arms and lifted her up to kiss her. As they circled in ecstatic reunion, he glanced over her shoulder at the barge where Giles Randolph and Beatrice Capaldi had come into view. A violent argument was ending and Randolph stalked off. He and his courtesan had parted and his priority was now to get back to The Curtain in time to perform *The Spanish Jew*. At one stroke, Beatrice Capaldi lost two brilliant actors. Lawrence Firethorn felt infatuation leave him like a discarded cloak. He was free again, he was happy, he was married. After tossing Beatrice a look of disdain, he kissed his wife with ready passion.

Nicholas Bracewell took charge. They had to get to the Queen's Head at once. Firethorn's horse was tied to the back of the coach, then it set off at reckless speed with its three passengers. Margery Firethorn knew that only another woman could have led her spouse astray but this was no time to chastise him. *Love's Sacrifice* required some sacrifice on her part. After giving him the good news from Cambridge, she contented herself with nestling beside him and listening to his conversation with Nicholas.

'You rehearsed this morning?' said the surprised actor.

'The play is expected.'

'You would have staged it without me?'

'Lord Westfield would not be denied,' said Nicholas. 'We found another King Gondar to carry the piece.'

'Another?'

'Owen Elias.'

'WHAT!'

Firethorn's explosion was contained by some scolding words from his wife who had been told enough of what had happened to side with Nicholas in the matter. Quelled into silence, Firethorn heard how Owen Elias had helped to catch the murderer of Sebastian Carrick and to ensnare the devious Clerk of Ordnance. Lord Westfield's admiration of the Welshman knew no bounds and he was adamant that Owen Elias be welcomed back into his company. When Firethorn learned that the actor had left Banbury's Men in turmoil, he was partially mollified but his pride was still affronted.

'Owen tries to supplant me,' he complained. 'He either mocks me at The Curtain or strives to take my place at the Queen's Head. He wants to rule as King Gondar.'

'Not if we arrive in time,' said Nicholas.

Panic assisted performance. The uncertainty which lasted until minutes before the play was due to start keyed up the actors. When Lawrence Firethorn burst into the tiring-house in full stride, they broke into applause and tears. Owen Elias quickly handed over the robes of King Gondar and there was a moment of tension when he handed Firethorn the crown but *Love's Sacrifice* outlawed all personal differences. Westfield's Men went out on to the stage with the arrogant confidence of a conquering army. Firethorn led his troupe magnificently and made this fourth performance of the work the best yet. Nor was he deprived of inspiration from the middle of the lower gallery. Margery Firethorn had elbowed herself into a place there and he acted for her. Unlike the calculating Beatrice Capaldi, his wife would not keep him at arm's length that night. Their reconciliation would be shot through with high emotion and it was only when he lay there sated that she would ask about a barge on the Thames.

King Gondar was back where he truly belonged.

It was only after Firethorn's triumph had been cheered to the echo that Nicholas Bracewell dared to tell him what was due to follow. The whole tiring-house shook.

'I am to be followed by a horse!' he bellowed. 'King Gondar is to hand over his throne to Nimbus!'

It was Owen Elias who stepped in to calm him and to suggest a solution. Westfield's Men were all appalled that the grasping landlord was using their work as a prologue to a dancing animal and they wanted retribution. Nicholas was annoyed that the white wings he had loaned to Cornelius Gant had been painted black without permission so he had further reason to seek recompense. The book holder had discussed the matter with Owen Elias and the latter fashioned a plan.

'The horse is clever,' said Elias, 'but only when he is controlled by his master. I saw these two hold an audience at the Elephant in Shoreditch with their tricks. Gant is like a puppeteer. Every move is dictated by him.'

'How does this help us?' growled Firethorn.

'Nimbus obeys because his eye never leaves Gant.'

'So?'

'What would happen if it did?'

Owen Elias whispered to his employer and Firethorn underwent a transformation. An angry face smiled, a broad grin followed and helpless laughter shook the tiring-house.

'Bring Nimbus forth!' he called. 'We'll have him now.'

The Queen's Head was besieged and Alexander Marwood could have filled his yard five times over. Playgoers who stayed behind were joined by a huge influx of excited spectators who wanted to view the flying horse once more. Cornelius Gant had reserved some special tricks for the occasion. The stage-keepers cleared away the scenery then scattered straw upon the boards. Lawrence Firethorn and his wife joined Lord Westfield up in the gallery. Most of the company came out to watch. The two exceptions were Owen Elias and Nicholas Bracewell who lurked neaa stable in the corner. Elias held a lead-rope while Nicholas fondled a small mirror. The accessories were a vital part of the performance.

Alexander Marwood came on to the stage to announce what he saw as a triumph of management on his part. Nimbus and Cornelius Gant came out to thunderous applause. They began with a dance but it was soon interrupted. Every movement of the horse was controlled by Gant who maintained eye-contact with his animal at all times. But that contact was broken when the sun dazzled him with such force that he had to turn away. Try as he may, he was unable to gain his former control because Nicholas Bracewell used his mirror with such skill to direct the rays of the sun. Deprived of commands, Nimbus came to a halt and stood waiting before a soon dissatisfied audience. Shouts and threats replaced the earlier cheers.

Entertainment was at hand. While Gant moved around to dodge the sun's rays, Owen Elias led a chestnut mare out on stage and its seductive whinny turned the head of Nimbus ruinously away from his master. The mare was called Jenny. She had been procured by the head ostler at the instigation of Elias and she was evidently in season. Nimbus showed dramatic interest. The horse was given many rewards but denied this greatest pleasure of all and the pain of that denial was now extreme.

Jenny rubbed her nose along his flank then swung her hind quarters around to twitch her tail. It was Nimbus's turn to whinny. Here was better sport than dancing before a crowd. Here was altogether more fitting recreation for a stallion than struggling to the top of St Paul's Cathedral. Gant yelled and slapped his partner's rump but he was too late. The love affair proceeded apace. Jenny swayed to entice Nimbus and he needed no more invitation. Urged on by the roaring crowd, he mounted her as if his whole career as a performer had been a rehearsal for this moment then rapid consummation ensued.

Cornelius Gant was destroyed. He could do nothing to stop the progress of true love and earned the derision of the crowd for even trying to interfere. The control he had built up by years of living with Nimbus was fractured in a matter of minutes. After tasting glory on the top of St Paul's Cathedral, he had literally plunged down to earth. Alexander Marwood was crestfallen. His greed had led him into disaster. A theatrical company caused problems but at least it gave the performance that was advertised. Nimbus had resigned from public performance. Jenny had taught him things which had been cruelly withheld from him.

The show was over, the crowd dispersed, the casualties sneaked away. Lawrence Firethorn came bounding on to the stage to throw his arms around Owen Elias and to cover him with apologies. Nicholas stood by in readiness.

'I should never have doubted you, Owen!' said Firethorn.

'We are friends again.'

'I even forgive you that treachery at The Curtain.'

Elias was honest. 'I was but a pale shadow of you, sir.'

'All has been redeemed this afternoon. Lord Westfield insists that you stay with the company. This trick with Nimbus was as pretty a piece of theatre as I've ever seen.' Enthusiasm sent him into another embrace. 'Such a man should be a sharer with the company. If I had a contract, I would offer it to you this instant.'

Nicholas produced the document and handed it over.

'Then do so, Master Firethorn,' he said.

The actor-manager was taken aback at first then he led the laughter. Owen Elias was finally given a contract. When he went off to celebrate in the taproom, he left Firethorn alone on stage with Nicholas Bracewell. The yard was empty now but it still reverberated with the sounds of the great events it had witnessed that afternoon. Westfield's Men had vindicated themselves. Cornelius Gant and Giles Randolph had been put firmly in their places. Margery was now home from Cambridge and all was well in the world.

Lawrence Firethorn was aware that he owed a profound debt to Nicholas Bracewell and he was generous with his thanks. He was also able to rely on the discretion of his book holder. Margery would be told only a fraction of the truth in the privacy of the marriage bed but Firethorn hid nothing from his friend.

'I was a blind fool, Nick,' he confided. 'I laughed with the rest of them at Nimbus but I was only watching myself. I was a stallion led astray by a mare. You stopped me from making an exhibition of myself before the whole company.'

Nicholas was tactful. 'We are glad to have you back.'

'Sebastian and I were yoked together in lunacy.'

'Were you?'

'Both of us succumbed to mad courtesans.'

'Sebastian paid the higher price.'

'I'll not forget that.' Firethorn sighed. 'His

father and his sister have much to thank you for, Nick, and my own gratitude will be never-ending.' He put an affectionate arm around the other's shoulders. 'Look at this place. We have known such joys, such victories, such acclamation in this inn yard. Hector of Troy has fought here. And Vincentio, and King Richard, and Pompey the Great, and Black Antonio, and Julius Caesar, and Troilus, and the mighty King Gondar.'

'Do not forget Jenny, sir.'

'Jenny?'

'The chestnut mare.'

'Ah, yes! It was Jenny who conquered Nimbus.'

'She was the maddest courtesan of them all.'